TIME OUT

TIME OUT

DELACORTE PRESS / NEW YORK

DAVID ELY

Many of these stories originally appeared in
*Cosmopolitan, The Saturday Evening Post,
The Massachusetts Review, Playboy,
Ellery Queen's Mystery Magazine,
Alfred Hitchcock's Mystery Magazine*
—to the editors of which the writer extends
his cordial good wishes and thanks.

"The Academy" and "An Angel of Mercy"
originally appeared in *Playboy* magazine.

Library of Congress Catalog Card Number: 68–20108
Manufactured in the United States of America
First printing

TO
TOM BOHEN

Contents

Contents

TIME OUT

The
Academy

¶ The Academy lay in the center of a valley, its red-brick buildings arranged in a square. Beyond the surrounding athletic and drill fields were thick woods that rose gradually on all sides, forming a shield of privacy that made the Academy seem in fact to be, in the words of the school brochure, "a little world of its own."

Mr. Holston parked his car in the area marked for visitors. Before proceeding toward the administration building, he paused to watch several groups of uniformed cadets marching to and fro on one of the fields. There was an atmosphere of regularity and tradition that he found quite pleasing. The buildings were old and solid, their bricks weathered to a pale hue, and the stone steps worn down by generations of cadets. The concrete walkways were scrubbed clean and bordered by grass meticulously clipped and weeded. Even the trees of the forest stood in formation.

In front of the administration building was the statue of an elderly man in military dress, one hand resting benignly on the stone shoulder of a young cadet, the other arm extended in a pointing gesture. Mr. Holston supposed this might represent the Academy's founder, perhaps a retired Civil War general, but the legend inscribed on the base was so faded that he could not read it. The symbolism of the man and boy was conventional, of course—the firm but kindly teacher indicating the horizon of manhood to his youthful charge—although Mr. Holston noted that the figures were facing so that the stone commander was pointing toward the school, rather than in the direction of the outside world, which would have been more appropriate.

In the lobby of the administration building, Mr. Holston gave his name to the cadet at the reception desk, and was at once ushered down a hallway to the Director's office.

The office was as spare and neat as everything else Mr. Holston had observed about the Academy. It contained a filing cabinet, a single chair for visitors, and a desk, behind which the Director himself was in the process of rising.

The Director was a strongly built man whose white hair was closely cut in military fashion, and his handshake was vigorous. He wore the gray uniform of the school, with a single star on each shoulder to denote his rank.

"Well, Mr. Holston," he said, after the customary exchange of amenities, "I've studied your boy's transcript and test records, and I've discussed them with the Admissions Committee, and without beating around the bush, sir, we're prepared to look favorably on a formal application, if you care to make one."

"I see," said Mr. Holston, who had not expected such an immediate response. "That's very encouraging to hear." Feeling slightly ill at ease under the Director's gaze, he glanced around at the walls, which, however, were absolutely bare.

"So," continued the Director, "the only question that remains is whether you want your son to be enrolled here. I'm assuming there's no special financial problem involved, naturally."

"Oh, no. We have that all worked out." Mr. Holston hesitated, thinking that such an important matter should not be disposed of so simply. "I would like to ask about one thing," he said. "Your catalogue mentioned a policy of not having any home visits the first year."

The Director nodded. "Yes. Well, we've worked out our system over a long period of time, and we've found that home visits just don't fit into the picture until the cadet is thoroughly oriented to our way of doing things. We say 'a year' merely as a general guide. Sometimes it's longer than that. Parents can visit here, of course, at specified times." The Director gazed inquiringly at Mr. Holston, who tried to think of some more questions, but could not. "Actually," the Director continued, "the cadets seem to prefer it this way, once they get started. What we're looking for, Mr. Holston, is to motivate them—motivate them to achieve success, which means success in becoming a fully oriented member of this community, and you can see how home visits might cause a little disruption in the process."

"Oh, yes," said Mr. Holston.

"Well," said the Director. "You'll want to see a little more of the Academy before making up your mind, I should imagine. Classrooms, dormitories, and so forth."

"If it isn't too much trouble."

"No trouble at all." The Director rose and escorted Mr. Holston out to the hall. "Nothing special about our classrooms," the Director remarked, stopping at one of the doors. He opened it. The instructor, a gray-haired man, roared "*Attention!*" and the entire class leaped up smartly, as the instructor did a left-face and saluted the Director. "At ease, Grimes," said the Director, returning the salute. "Proceed with instruction."

"Very good, sir."

The Director closed the door again, so that Mr. Holston had only a glimpse of the class—a roomful of gray-uniformed figures, heads so closely cropped that they were almost shaven, with nothing much to distinguish one cadet from the next.

"Those were big fellows," remarked Mr. Holston, as they continued along the hallway. "I suppose they're your seniors."

"We don't go by the usual class designations, Mr. Holston. Each cadet is paced according to his needs and capacities. Our purpose is to build men, sir, and you simply can't find a formula to satisfy the requirements of every case. Now here," said the Director, pushing open a pair of swinging doors, "is our cafeteria, which is staffed by the cadets themselves. Part of our community work program."

It was the middle of the afternoon, and the cafeteria was empty, except for a few men who were mopping the floor and scrubbing the serving counters. They, too, snapped to attention when the visitors appeared, until the Director motioned for them to continue their work, as he escorted Mr. Holston on into the kitchen, where several male cooks were busy preparing food for the evening meal.

"At ease," the Director called out, for the cooks, too, had come to attention. "All modern equipment, Mr. Holston, as you can see," he said, indicating the gleaming ranges, the sinks and the neat rows of cleavers, knives, and other implements hanging on the white walls. "You will understand," he added, "that we can't run a military establishment in a sloppy fashion. We try to be thorough, sir. We have, as I say, a little world here, and it's a world that happens to be organized along military lines." He turned to an elderly cook. "Looks good, Carson."

"Thank you, sir." Carson saluted.

Mr. Holston and the Director left the kitchen by the rear door, passing into the square formed by the Academy buildings. "I suppose," said Mr. Holston, "that you find a lot of employees who like the military way. Old Army men, say."

The Director was busy returning the salute of an instructor who was marching a platoon of cadets nearby. He stood silently watching the ranks pass by. "Drill," he declared finally. "Sometimes I think it's the greatest lesson of all. When a boy knows drill, Mr. Holston, then he knows something about life, don't you think?"

"Ah, yes," said Mr. Holston, a bit uncertainly. "Of course, it's a splendid training, especially when a boy goes on to have a career in the services."

"Not only there, sir, if you'll permit me. Drill has important values in civilian pursuits as well, in my opinion. And I don't mean only physical drill," the Director added, as he and his guest walked on. "We use drill techniques in classroom work, to instill habits of mental discipline and personal courtesy. We've been given hopeless cases, Mr. Holston, but we've managed in every single one, sir, to find the right answer. And the key to it has been drill, whether on the parade ground or in the classroom. Of course," he said, ushering Mr. Holston into the next building, "in some instances it takes more time than in others, and I don't mean to imply that the Academy deals primarily with so-called problem boys. Not at all. The great majority are like your own son—good, decent young fellows from fine upstanding homes." He opened a door. "This is one of our dormitories, Mr. Holston."

The room ran the length of the building. The wall was lined with beds spaced out to accommodate lockers, chairs and desks. The few cadets who were then studying in the room sprang from their chairs.

"Maybe you'd like to chat with one of the boys," the Director said to Mr. Holston, after he had put the cadets at ease. "Here," he said, as they approached the nearest student, who was taller than either of the men, "it's Cadet Sloan, isn't it?"

"Yes, sir."

"Well, this is Mr. Holston, Sloan, and he'll have a few words with you," said the Director, who then moved off along the row of beds, inspecting the blanket corners and testing here and there for dust.

Mr. Holston, left with Cadet Sloan, did not know quite what to say.

"Well," he began, "how do you like it here?"

"I like it very well, sir."

"That's good. Um, the food and everything . . . you find it all right?"

"Everything is very good, sir."

"Ah," said Mr. Holston, rubbing his hands together, trying to think of additional questions while Cadet Sloan gazed at him with polite attention. "Well, I suppose you're planning on some college or other, aren't you?"

"My plans aren't too definite at present, sir."

"Yes, yes. Well, I can see you're a hard worker on your books, Mr. Sloan," Mr. Holston continued, glancing first at the stack of texts on the desk and then at Cadet Sloan's face, which wore a studious look that was reinforced by little wrinkles of concentration around the eyes and mouth.

"We have plenty to do, sir, that's right."

"Your parents must be proud to have such a hard-working son."

"My parents aren't living, sir."

"Oh—I'm sorry." Mr. Holston regretted his blunder. No wonder Sloan looked drawn.

"That's all right, sir. It's been quite a while."

"Ah, yes. Well." Mr. Holston could not help being struck by the manly demeanor of Cadet Sloan. He put out his hand. "Nice to talk with you, son," he said. "And good luck."

"Thank you, sir."

The Director and his guest walked back toward the administration building. On all sides, Mr. Holston was aware of organized and purposeful activity. Several groups of cadets were marching along the paths on their way from one building to another; a soccer game was in progress on a field nearby, and on the main parade ground, a full company in dress uniform was executing a complex series of drill maneuvers.

"It's all very impressive," said Mr. Holston.

The Director smiled. "We try to keep our young men busy."

"That cadet I talked to back there," Mr. Holston added. "Sloan. He seemed to be a remarkably mature person."

"We strive to build a sense of maturity, Mr. Holston."

"Yes, yes. I can certainly tell that." Mr. Holston saw that they were approaching the stone figures of teacher and student which were turned the wrong way. He gestured toward the statues. "That's quite a piece of sculpture."

"Thank you. We're very proud of it."

Mr. Holston could not repress his curiosity. "It does seem a little—well, unconventional. I mean, the positioning. You know, facing toward the Academy instead of away from it."

The Director nodded. "Yes, most visitors notice that, Mr. Holston. At first glance, it does seem to be a mistake, I agree." He paused beside the figures and gazed approvingly up at the stern features of the teacher. Mr. Holston thought he saw a resemblance between the Director and the statue, which, he reflected further, might be no mere fancy, for the operation of the Academy could very well be a family matter, with the leadership being passed on from one generation to the next.

"For us, you see," said the Director, continuing with his explanation, "the important thing is the Academy. This is our world, Mr. Holston. All that a boy needs is to be found right here. So that the symbolism of the figures, sir, is to represent a welcome to this little world—rather than the more conventional theme of farewell which would be indicated if the man were pointing away from the Academy."

"Of course," said Mr. Holston.

They returned to the Director's office, where an elderly man in green fatigues was polishing the desk. He stopped as they entered and stood stiffly near the wall.

"At ease, Morgan," said the Director. "That'll be all."

"Very good, sir." The elderly man saluted and hobbled out.

The Director seated himself behind the desk and briefly inspected its top for signs of dust. "Well, Mr. Holston," he said, "now you've seen something of the Academy, and I'm sure you've had an opportunity to consider a little further the question of whether it may be what you're looking for, to help your boy."

"Yes, yes. Of course." Mr. Holston nodded. "You have a fine institution here, I must say. Everything seems to be organized with . . . with real efficiency." He glanced toward the door beyond which he thought he could still hear the shuffling steps of the elderly man in fatigues. "It's a real example of what the military method can achieve," he added, feeling that perhaps he had not sufficiently expressed his admiration for all that the Director had shown him.

The Director took a folder from a drawer and placed it on the desk.

"As for my son," said Mr. Holston, "that's the important question, of course. Whether this would be the right place for him. Or rather," he amended, "whether he would be right for you. I'm sure there are many instances where boys simply don't fit in."

The Director smiled. "We don't believe in failure here, Mr. Holston. When we agree to admit a boy, sir, that means we are laying our reputation on the line." He opened the folder and took out a letter. "And without intending to boast, Mr. Holston, I think I can truthfully say that we have yet to concede defeat." He pushed the letter across the desk. Mr. Holston saw that it was an official notice of acceptance, complete except for his own signature as parent. He felt in his pocket for his fountain pen.

"In some cases, naturally," the Director continued, "we need to have more patience than in others. But patience is built into our system."

"Patience, yes," said Mr. Holston. He laid his pen beside the letter of acceptance. "Boys need patience. You're right there, of course. Some boys need a lot of that, I agree." He moved the letter slightly, so that it was squared off with the edge of the desk. "He's not a bad boy, though. Not at all," he added.

"Mr. Holston, in my experience there is no such thing as a bad boy."

"I mean, he's gotten into a couple of little scrapes—that's in the records, of course—but nothing really . . ." Mr. Holston cleared his throat.

"Boys will be boys, sir. Lack of proper motivation leads to trouble, even in the best of families. You have nothing to be ashamed of, sir."

"Oh, we're not ashamed. We just feel—my wife and I—we feel that he would be better off in the kind of atmosphere you provide here, especially during the, um, difficult years."

"That's what we're here for, Mr. Holston," said the Director.

"I mean, it's not as though we were trying to avoid our own responsibilities as parents—"

"Far from it, sir," agreed the Director.

"—but in certain situations it seems advisable to, um . . ."

"To place a boy in congenial surroundings under the proper form of supervision," said the Director, helpfully completing Mr. Holston's thought. "You're absolutely right, sir. Believe me, I deal with parents every day of the year, and I know all of the things that pass through their minds." He clasped his hands together and smiled at his visitor.

"Some people think it's a kind of rejection of the child. I mean, getting rid of him—"

"Oh, I've heard plenty of that, Mr. Holston. It's all this modern psychiatric stuff. Guilt feelings!" The Director gave a short laugh and shook his head. "I tell you, when a father and mother are prepared to undergo heavy financial sacrifice in order to see their boy receive a decent chance in life—well, if that's getting rid of him, then it's a pretty conscientious way of doing it!"

"Yes, yes," said Mr. Holston quickly. They smiled at each other. In the brief pause that followed, Mr. Holston heard the commands of the drill instructors faintly in the distance, and the muffled beat of the marching cadets. There was marching in the hallway, too, and he supposed that it was a class, moving in formation from one room to another.

"Perhaps you have some further questions," the Director remarked.

Mr. Holston picked up his pen. "Oh, not at all. No, I think you've covered everything." He tested the point of the pen against his thumb, to be sure it was working.

"This is the time for questions, Mr. Holston," the Director continued. "It's better to ask them now, I mean to say, while the Academy is fresh in your mind. Sometimes it's hard for a parent to remember later on the things he wanted to ask."

"Oh, yes, I can understand that," said Mr. Holston, studying the letter before him.

"For example, you might like to know more about our cooperative work program for the cadets. The cafeteria was an instance of that."

"It was a very fine cafeteria," said Mr. Holston. "No, I don't really have any questions about it."

"Then there's the academic program. Perhaps you feel insufficiently informed on that aspect."

"No, the catalogue was quite complete. I really can't think of anything it didn't cover."

"We are great believers in the value of learning by teaching. Let me explain that. The cadets take turns, you see, in the instruction program—"

"Quite so," said Mr. Holston. "I'm sure it's a remarkably effective feature of your system."

"Oh, it is indeed. That classroom that you saw, for example—"

"Really, I have no questions," said Mr. Holston. He signed his name in the proper place, put his pen in his pocket, and pushed the letter back across the desk.

"Thank you," said the Director, placing the letter carefully in the folder. "Actually, few parents do have questions." He smiled at Mr. Holston, who, however, was glancing at his watch and pushing back his chair. "They seem to sense right away whether the Academy is what they really want for their boys. Like yourself, sir, if I am not mistaken."

"Absolutely," said Mr. Holston. He stood up and touched his face with his handkerchief, for the air in the room seemed close.

The Director rose and shook his hand. "Of course, the very best guarantee of satisfaction for the parent is to see the experienced cadet and have a chance to chat with him. As you did with Sloan, I believe."

"Yes, Sloan." Mr. Holston went to the door. "I can find my way out, sir. Don't you bother."

"No bother at all, Mr. Holston," said the Director, accompanying his visitor along the hallway. "Sloan—yes, a fine cadet, Sloan. He's been with us for quite a while now. Let's see—"

"Goodbye, sir," said Mr. Holston, as they reached the front entrance.

"—it must be nearly . . ."

But Mr. Holston did not stay to hear. He went quickly down the worn stone steps, passed by the statues of the man and boy without looking up at them, and hastened to his car. On his way out, he drove by a group of cadets in sweat shirts resting by the road after a session of calisthenics. They got quickly to their feet at the command of their instructor, but Mr. Holston concentrated on his driving, and although it seemed to him that several of the cadets were bald and that others were quite gray, he gave them only a glance, and thought no more about it.

Creatures of
the Sea

¶ "Give me a little kiss."

With his eyes closed, Gregory turned his head lazily toward her, feeling the sand trickle from his neck. Their heads were so close he could feel her breath on his face.

"A little kiss," Louisa repeated.

He touched her lips with the tip of his tongue. Then, he pretended to bite her lips—watching her preparing dreamily to submit to that tiny outrage—but instead, kissed her quickly and rolled over again on his back in the hot sand.

She would not leave him alone. With one finger, she traced teasingly on his chest and then, propped on one elbow and studying his face with affectionate curiosity, traced over his arms and legs, too, with an electric swiftness. In retaliation, Gregory told her deliberately and precisely how he intended to possess her—there on the beach, at that moment, with a dozen bathers and plodding shell collectors as witnesses. Louisa pretended to be shocked, but he knew she secretly relished his voice, his words and the image of a forbidden ecstasy.

Thus, together, they teased and excited one another until Gregory could stand it no longer and broke away in a sand-scattering rush for the surf. The water restored his equilibrium, but as he plowed back out, smoothing his hair and kicking off the anklets of seaweed, he was still left with the aftertaste: Louisa again had been the one who had begun their little game of love, and once more, she had worsted him. She was always ready to arouse him in circumstances that led only to frustration. In fact, she seemed to delight in it, as though to prove to them both, over and over, that she was in control. Although they were as good as engaged, she refused what she delicately referred to as "completion." He padded across the sand. She sat on her folded legs, brushing her black hair, smiling mockingly at him, her breasts moving in concert with her busy, upraised arms; Gregory sat down several yards away, sardonic and chastened. For a moment, he watched her; then, as her movements became deliberately insolent, he glanced away, to forestall a further proof of her capabilities.

"Your mother's coming," he said.

All along the beach, middle-aged women wearing kerchiefs or straw hats browsed at the water's edge with baskets, looking for shells. Whenever they spied some likely treasure, they would bend over with little cries, presenting broad posteriors to each other. Overhead, the gulls soared, turned, wheeled, dived. The birds sought the meat, the women the hard bright husks. Between them, they scoured the beach.

Mrs. Wainwright scudded across the sand in blood-red slippers, holding up something, smiling with joy.

"Darlings—a lion's paw!" She swept up like an eager, knowing bird, fluttering and studiously gay. Gregory was aware of perfume, salt, suntan lotion and a suggestion of sweat.

"It's very good," he said politely.

Mrs. Wainwright flourished the shell in triumph, then delved into her basket. "Look at this!"

It was a giant conch, alive and dripping. She handed it to Gregory, then opened the basket. Inside were two more. She displayed them with smugness.

"How will you get the creatures out?"

"Get them out?" Mrs. Wainwright cocked her handsome head roguishly and placed a smooth hand on his arm. "If they're gentlemen, why, then," she said, "they'll just *walk* out."

Gregory felt her fingernails tapping gently on his skin. "And if they refuse?"

"Then I shall simply have to boil them out," Mrs. Wainwright said.

"Boil them?" Gregory examined the conch. The creature inside the shell had extruded an inch of its slimy self, cautiously. He touched it and it withdrew.

Louisa explained, in a matter-of-fact voice: "You put them in boiling water for a while and that kills them. Then you sort of dig them out."

"It sounds gruesome."

She shrugged. "No, the worst part is later. They always leave a piece of themselves inside, so you have to put them outside in the sun."

"Why?"

"To let the ants finish them off. But they stink to high heaven."

"A small price to pay," Mrs. Wainwright said, taking the conch from Gregory with an exaggerated tenderness. "If you had the true shelling spirit, my dears, you would be out with the rest of us—" She laughed and swung her hips, a merry widow. "But perhaps you find each other—more interesting!" Then she whirled, in a display of careless high spirits, and actually scampered off, calling out after she had reached the waterline: "Remember—we drink at five!"

Louisa and Gregory ran into the water for a final swim. He dived into one breaker; a second, close behind, knocked him over. Farther out, Louisa managed the onrushing waves with practiced timing, challenging the gathering crests, then eluding their power with swift plunges. She laughed and beckoned, but Gregory had turned toward the beach. Near his feet something yellow flashed and tumbled in the last reaches of the surf. He backed away with the Northerner's instinctive distrust of the treacherous life of Southern seas, until he saw that it was merely a shell and picked it up. It was cone-shaped and dappled with black. If Louisa had not come splashing in behind him with the next breaker, he would have tossed it back, for it was still a living thing.

"What's that?"

"Just a yellow shell."

Louisa snatched it from his hand. "My God," she said in honest awe. "A junonia!"

"Will it bite?"

Louisa did not smile. She cradled the shell in her palms and stared at it solemnly. "It's perfect—perfect! Oh"—she gave him a wide-eyed child's glance—"Mother will have a fit, a regular fit!"

"Why? Is it rare?"

She looked at him, again with the seriousness of a child. He almost expected her to say something, in the summing-up fashion of childhood, like: "You found a junonia!" but instead she remarked: "It *is* rare. Especially a perfect one. Mother's been shelling for fifteen years, and she's never found even a broken one." They toweled dry and prepared to leave. "She'll love you for this."

"In what way?" he asked in mock eagerness.

Louisa became a mischievous nineteen-year-old again and leaned against him as they passed beneath the first rank of palms. "I could devour you," she said in a husky Garbo voice, "utterly and forever." Her fingers scraped his arm, clawlike. Gregory laughed pleasantly, but felt the itch of desire, too, and at the same time was again uneasily impressed by the strength of her control. He was, at least now in the period of their informal engagement, her toy.

The late-afternoon sun cast palm shadows across the porch of the beach cottage which Mrs. Wainwright called her cabana. Gregory rocked in a wicker chair, a drink in his hand, gazing dreamily out across the Gulf, only half-listening.

"Sanibel," said Mrs. Wainwright, who had changed from her beach pants into a sleeveless cotton frock that displayed her unwrinkled tan arms and back. She smiled prettily at Gregory. "Shells!" In the kitchen, the conchs and the junonia were boiling in a pot on the stove, their fingerlike and defenseless bodies driven half out of their shells. In the bathroom beyond, Louisa was taking a hot shower. Wisps of steam floated through the screened porch door.

". . . one of the finest shelling beaches in the world!" Mrs.

Wainwright was saying. "The Great Barrier Reef is best, of course. Poor Henry, he always promised to take me there—but then there was the war—and then, eight years ago . . ."

Her voice trailed off; Gregory cleared his throat in sympathy. She let him know by her lapse into unaccustomed silence that she still mourned; even so, she chose this moment to prop her sandaled feet on the railing, which caused her frock to hike up above her knees. Gregory admired the legs briefly, then studiously followed a pelican's headlong dive for fish. When the pelican reappeared, ruffled, Gregory turned his head slightly. Mrs. Wainwright was watching him with a little smile, with moist eyes—but the frock was even higher. *God in heaven,* he thought, *am I being teased by the mother as well?*

"Sanibel is a lovely island," he said finally.

Mrs. Wainwright crossed her legs and sipped at her drink. "Henry and I spent our honeymoon here, you know. . . ." She rolled her eyes at Gregory, as if expecting him to have immediate and vivid images of Henry's joy. "Seeing you here with my darling girl—ah! Memories!" She laughed a twittering laugh. "And now, all I have are my shells. My lovely shells!"

Thus was Gregory reminded of the underlying reason for his visit, which was tacitly understood by them all. To "speak" to the mother, in the unavoidable absence of the father, to bow ever so slightly in the direction of the formalism of a vanished age.

"Henry was a lawyer, too, you know," she was saying. "That's why it seems so—so right, somehow. Yes. Right."

Gregory quickly took a swallow. This was cutting pretty close, he thought resentfully. Did this woman really believe that he was the kind of man who could be tugged and nudged and jostled into a declaration? After all, he was several years older than Louisa and was almost established professionally—was a man of the world, an experienced lover, even. He was tempted, for a moment, to speak to Mrs. Wainwright the way he had spoken to her daughter on the beach, to inform her precisely of the ways in which he could make her forget Henry completely. Afterward, he told himself, he would take the conchs and the junonia down to the beach and throw them far out into the water. The poor bastards.

"Tomorrow, they'll start to stink."

Louisa had come through the door in white slacks that looked thin, like pajamas. Her mother put her feet down and covered her legs with what seemed a regretful sigh.

"I've got some lovely ones inside, Gregory—you don't mind if I call you Gregory, do you? You seem almost like—like a son, already."

"Mother!" Louisa said sharply.

Gregory made a polite remark, speaking quickly to mask his annoyance. That "Mother!" had really been unnecessary. Then Louisa gently brushed the back of his neck with her fingertips and he noticed, as he followed her into the house, that the slacks were even thinner than he had at first believed.

"Chinese alphabets . . . lion's paws . . . pectens!" Inside, Mrs. Wainwright was displaying her treasures. They gleamed under their coats of varnish in cotton-lined boxes, the prizes of fifteen seasons. Gregory wondered how many pots of boiling water, how many legions of ants, had been required to dispose of the occupants. "Have you ever seen such a lovely olive shade?" On the couch Louisa lay with her shoulders back, gazing innocently through the window. "Look at the points on that one," cried Mrs. Wainwright, holding up a desiccated starfish. Gregory nodded.

When Mrs. Wainwright had stepped into the kitchen to prepare the salad, Louisa came up to him softly. Gregory found himself tensing to deal with another assault, but she spoke instead: "Do you want to see Father?"

It was merely a photograph. It showed a bald man with large eyes, a handsome nose, a full-lipped, irresolute mouth. Gregory glanced automatically into the mirror above the table where the shells were displayed. No resemblance, of course; except, perhaps, a wry expression of male watchfulness.

That night, on the lonely beach, Louisa surprised him by not only permitting "completion" but actually demanding it. Gregory was by that time so uneasily attuned to the pattern of arousal and frustration that he was caught off guard—was even, it seemed, himself abruptly taken by her, suddenly possessed by thirsty, searching, impatient innocence. Rhythmically the sea broke on the sand, rushed silently up near their bare feet, with a sigh to sink away. . . . From the indeterminate rank growth behind the palms, a bird cried out wildly and on their blanket as they lay quietly watching the turning stars, they stirred and touched each other. Louisa waited serenely now, followed his lead with almost wifely obedience, until in her mounting fierceness she tore at his back with her strong fingers. Inexhaustibly the breakers charged at them, fell short, foamed in again, strewing bits of life along the sands for the birds to find at dawn. They watched the subtle play of phosphorescence among the waves that seemed to mirror the stars. She pressed his hand; time to go. They walked back, not touching; she kept a half-pace ahead. In the cottage, he caught a glimpse of Mrs. Wainwright in her robe, fondling her shells. The two women exchanged glances—that was enough. The story was told, understood, commented on. Louisa swept calmly out of sight to her room. Gregory skulked guiltily to his, the eyes of his hostess burning on his back. His afternoon jauntiness was gone—he had been raped by the daughter, was threatened by the mother. . . .

Tossing on his cot, he waited nervously for Mrs. Wainwright to plunge on him from the darkness. Or perhaps Louisa, returning— or even, which seemed to him a quite reasonable prospect, the two of them, insatiable and terrifying. He cursed his weakness. After all, he was a man; he had just performed with credit in the possession of his fiancée. Did not the mother have a right to a vicarious sexual experience, after eight Henryless years? He twisted to one side. There, in the doorway, stood Mrs. Wainwright.

"I forgot to tell you. I'm going out shelling at dawn." She paused meaningfully. "I imagine you and Louisa will want to sleep late." She seemed to chuckle—and was gone. Gregory found himself sitting upright in bed, the sheet clutched at his chest, like a maiden aunt listening for burglars. Would Louisa come to him, then, with the sun? He promised himself that if she did, he would be the complete master this time. He flopped back, realizing, in chagrin, that he should have thought first of going to her; for if she came, it would still be on her initiative. His reaction had again been defensive.

This was his last night on Sanibel. Tomorrow, he would take a ferry to the mainland, then a taxi to Fort Myers, a helicopter to Tampa, a plane to New York. If he was to "speak" to Mrs. Wainwright, it would have to be during the day. Had Louisa sought to force the issue? That was ridiculous. In the first place, there was no need for him to speak to anyone except Louisa. They would not marry for a year or two anyway. In the second place . . .

He was awakened by Louisa, kissing him. He sought to draw her down to him, but she tickled him unbearably under the arms and slipped away, laughing; he accepted the fact that there would be no lovemaking that morning. The sun had risen hot and sharp. As they ate breakfast on the porch, they could see the women grazing along the beach. On a flat rock at the end of the porch, the remains of the conchs and the junonia were already putrefying.

"Why do you love me?"

Gregory considered the question seriously. They lay again on the beach, their toes touching, their hands locked and perspiring in the sun.

"You don't know!" Louisa bit his earlobe. "I'll tell you why I love you, then." She withdrew her hand and looked seriously up into the sky. "I love you because—you're so manly, so intelligent, so—all the things I'm not. I'm curious about you. . . ." She turned to him, her eyes unwavering and intense. "All these things—things I'll never know, except through you. Do you understand? Half of the world—in you! The male half. I'll find out . . . by living in you, by absorbing you." She bit him again.

"I'm not afraid," he said gallantly.

"Yes you are!"

She slapped his stomach sharply and ran off into the water, expecting his pursuit. But he lay there, wondering. Why *did* he love her? He did honestly and truly believe that they were bound to each other, yet, with him, it was chiefly a subconscious recognition—baffling, for he was unable to formulate it intelligibly in his mind. It was a yearning, not simply sexual, that tipped his every sense. She felt it, too, but in an easy, animal way. Before this visit, he had been relieved that there would be no father to face; but now, he wished he could have known old Henry, talked with him. There, he suspected, would have been an ally.

The moment arrived. His suitcase was packed, his bed was stripped. They sat on the edge of the porch eating grapefruit, watching some far-off children playing with a beach ball. Inside,

Mrs. Wainwright was working on her shells. The odor of the decaying corpses on the rock was penetrating. Gregory wished she had placed her victims somewhere behind the cottage.

He could, of course, say nothing. He would write faithfully. So would she. In three months, the women would be in New York, shopping; then, at the end of the summer, Louisa would be back at Bryn Mawr and there would be weekends together. But his failure to speak would be contrary to all expectations; there was a heaviness in the air that seemed to cry out for the lightning stroke of clearly voiced intentions. "Madam, I have the honor to ask for the hand . . ." That would be foolish, naturally. Still, a touch of whimsicality would not be out of place: a slightly amused nod in the direction of the Victorian image, to set off the seriousness of his lawyerlike statements. "Mrs. Wainwright, I can hardly help feeling that you have observed something a bit beyond ordinary friendship developing. . . ." Something like that.

Or—the hell with it. Was he to be rushed into a declaration by Louisa's surrender last night? Surrender! He smiled at the idea. Even now—look at her eat that grapefruit! She dug into it expertly with a tiny spoon, ripping the pink flesh neatly from the rind, greedy and sure of herself, chewing rapidly, avidly, a drop of juice on her chin. Now she had finished. But no, she had simply laid the spoon aside. She was crushing the fruit between her strong young hands, squirting the last drops of liquid into her mouth. Gregory glanced down at his own grapefruit. He had botched half of the sections and would not bother squeezing out the rest. Louisa winked at him from behind the crumpled rind, as if guessing his thoughts.

"You're finished? Nonsense. You left the best part. Let me have it, then."

And she took his and began consuming it, scraping its sides raw, working it vigorously with her fingers into a funnel so that all the juice would trickle into her hungry mouth and not a drop be lost. Gregory felt a weakness in his stomach. Was it dismay at the prospect of speaking to Mrs. Wainwright? He did not know.

Leaning against the steps, turned sideways to watch Louisa's enjoyment of the grapefruit, he was aware of other natural processes as well: on the rock, the noisome remains of the conchs, of his junonia, over which the ants were busily clustered; inside the cottage, her lips set, her fingers competent and quick, Mrs. Wainwright herself, arranging her shells, straightening the giant conchs under the dead, wary eyes of poor Henry. . . .

Gregory rose suddenly to his feet. Louisa looked up at him with fond possessiveness, her mouth wet with juice, her hands still kneading the submissive rind. He took one last look at his junonia, the lovely yellow skeleton, the mottled shred of corpse.

"Gregory, dear boy."

Mrs. Wainwright smiled. In the shadow of the room, she looked younger. Looked like Louisa. Gregory thought: *They are both ravishing.* His voice strong, his manner alert and gay, he stepped forward confidently and began to speak, deliciously stung by the salt tide of his destiny, feeling a tremor of apprehension and desire, as a force much stronger than he reached down for him with tender certainty.

The
Sailing Club

¶ Of all the important social clubs in the city, the most exclusive was also the most casual and the least known to outsiders. This was a small group of venerable origin but without formal organization. Indeed, it was without a name, although it was generally referred to as the Sailing Club, for its sole apparent activity was a short sailing cruise each summer. There were no meetings, no banquets, no other functions—in fact, no club building existed, so that it was difficult even to classify it as a club.

Nevertheless, the Sailing Club represented the zenith of a successful businessman's social ambitions, for its handful of members included the most influential men in the city, and many a top executive would have traded all of his other hard-won attainments for an opportunity to join. Even those who had no interest in sailing would willingly have sweated through long practice hours to learn, if the Club had beckoned. Few were invited, however. The

Club held its membership to the minimum necessary for the operation of its schooner, and not until death or debility created a vacancy was a new man admitted.

Who were the members of this select group? It was almost impossible to be absolutely certain. For one thing, since the Club had no legal existence, the members did not list it in their *Who's Who* paragraphs or in any other catalogue of their honors. Furthermore, they appeared reluctant to discuss it in public. At luncheons or parties, for example, the Club might be mentioned, but those who brought up the name did not seem to be members, and as for those distinguished gentlemen who carefully refrained at such times from commenting on the subject—who could tell? They might be members, or they might deliberately be assuming an air of significant detachment in the hope of being mistaken for members.

Naturally, the hint of secrecy which was thus attached to the Sailing Club made it all the more desirable in the eyes of the rising business leaders who yearned for the day when they might be tapped for membership. They realized that the goal was remote and their chances not too likely, but each still treasured in his heart the hope that in time this greatest of all distinctions would reward a lifetime of struggle and success.

One of these executives, a man named John Goforth, could without immodesty consider himself unusually eligible for the Club. He was, first of all, a brilliant success in the business world. Although he was not yet fifty, he was president of a dynamic corporation which had become preeminent in several fields through a series of mergers he himself had expertly negotiated. Each year, under his ambitious direction, the corporation expanded into new areas, snapping up less nimble competitors and spurring the others into furious battles for survival.

Early in his career Goforth had been cautious, even anxious, but year by year his confidence had increased, so that now he welcomed new responsibilities, just as he welcomed the recurrent business crises where one serious mistake in judgment might cause a large enterprise to founder and to sink. His quick rise had not dulled this sense of excitement, but rather had sharpened it. More and more, he put routine matters into the hands of subordinates, while he zestfully attacked those special problems that forced from him the full measure of daring and skill. He found himself not merely successful, but powerful, a man whose passage through the halls of a club left a wake of murmurs, admiring and envious.

This was the life he loved, and his mastery of it was his chief claim to recognition by the most influential social group of all, the Sailing Club. There was another factor which he thought might count in his favor: his lifelong attachment to the sea and to sailing.

As a boy, he had stood in fascination at the ocean's edge, staring out beyond the breakers to the distant sails, sometimes imagining himself to be the captain of a great ship; at those times, the toy bucket in his hand had become a long spyglass, or a pirate's cutlass, and the strip of reed that fluttered from his fingers had been transformed into a gallant pennant, or a black and wicked skull-and-bones. At the age of ten, he had been taught to sail at his family's summer place on the shore; later, he was allowed to take his father's boat out alone—and later still, when he was almost of college age, he was chosen for the crew of one of the yacht-club entries in the big regatta. By that time, he had come to regard the sea as a resourceful antagonist in a struggle all the more absorbing because of the danger, and a danger that was far from theoretical, for every summer at least one venturesome sailor would be lost forever, far from land, and even a sizable boat might fail to return from some holiday excursion.

Now, in his middle years, John Goforth knew the sea as something more than an invigorating physical challenge. It was that still, but he recognized that it was also an inexhaustible source of renewal for him. The harsh sting of blown spray was a climate in which he thrived, and the erratic thrusts of strength that swayed his little boat evoked a passionate response of answering strength within himself. In those moments—like the supreme moments of business crisis—he felt almost godlike, limitless, as he shared the ocean's solitude, its fierce and fitful communion with the wind, the sun and the sky.

As time passed, membership in the Sailing Club became the single remaining honor which Goforth coveted but did not have. He told himself: not a member—no, not yet! But of course he realized that this prize would not necessarily fall to him at all, despite his most strenuous efforts to seize it. He sought to put the matter out of his mind; then, failing that, he decided to learn more about the Club, to satisfy his curiosity, at least.

It was no easy task. But he was a resourceful and determined man, and before long he had obtained a fairly accurate idea of the real membership of the Sailing Club. All of these men were prominent in business or financial circles, but Goforth found it strange that they seemed to lack any other common characteristic of background or attainments. Most were university men, but a few were not. There was, similarly, a variety of ethnic strains represented among them. Some were foreign-born, even, and one or two were still foreign citizens. Moreover, while some members had a long association with sailing, others seemed to have no interest whatever in the sea.

Yet just as Goforth was prepared to shrug away the matter and conclude that there was no unifying element among the members of the Sailing Club, he became aware of some subtle element that resisted analysis. Did it actually exist, or did he merely imagine it? He studied the features of the supposed Club members more closely. They were casual, yes, and somewhat aloof—even bored, it seemed. And yet there was something else, something buried: a kind of suppressed exhilaration that winked out briefly, at odd moments, as though they shared some monumental private joke.

As his perplexing survey of the Club members continued, Goforth became conscious of a quite different sensation. He could not be sure, but he began to suspect that while he was quietly inspecting them, they in turn were examining him.

The most suggestive indication was his recent friendship with an older man named Marshall, who was almost certainly a Club member. Marshall, the chairman of a giant corporation, had taken the lead in their acquaintanceship, which had developed to the point where they lunched together at least once a week. Their conversation was ordinary enough—of business matters, usually, and sometimes of sailing, for both were ardent seamen—but each time, Goforth had a stronger impression that he was undergoing some delicate kind of interrogation which was connected with the Sailing Club.

He sought to subdue his excitement. But he often found that his palms were moist and, as he wiped them, he disciplined his nervousness, telling himself angrily that he was reacting like a college freshman being examined by the president of some desirable fraternity.

At first he tried to moderate his personality, as well. He sensed that his aggressive attitude toward his work, for example, was not in harmony with the blasé manner of the Club members. He attempted a show of nonchalance, of indifference—and all at once he became annoyed. He had nothing to be ashamed of. Why should he try to imitate what was false to his nature? He was *not* bored or indifferent, he was *not* disengaged from the competitive battle of life, and he would not pretend otherwise. The Club could elect him or not, as it chose.

At his next session with Marshall, he went out of his way to make clear how fully he enjoyed the daily combat of business. He spoke, in fact, more emphatically than he had intended to, for he was irritated by what seemed to be the other man's ironic amusement.

Once Marshall broke in, wryly: "So you really find the press of business life to be thoroughly satisfying and exciting?"

"Yes, I do," said Goforth. He repressed the desire to add: "And don't you, too?" He decided that if the Sailing Club was nothing but a refuge for burned-out men, bored by life and by themselves, then he wanted no part of it.

At the same time, he was disturbed by the thought that he had failed. The Sailing Club might be a worthless objective for a man of his temperament—still he did not like to feel that it might be beyond his grasp.

After he had parted none too cordially from Marshall, he paced along the narrow streets toward the harbor, hoping that the ocean winds would blow away his discontent. As he reached the water's edge, he saw a customs launch bounce by across the widening wake of a huge liner. A veil of spray blew softly toward him. Greedily he awaited the familiar reassurance of its bitter scent. But when it came, it was not quite what he had expected. He frowned out at the water. No, it was not at all the same.

That winter, Goforth became ill for the first time in years. It was influenza, and not a serious case, but the convalescent period stretched on and on, and before he was well enough to do any work, it was spring.

His troubles dated from that illness, he decided; not business troubles, for he had a fine executive staff, and the company did not suffer. The troubles were within himself. First, he went through a mild depression (the doctors had of course cautioned him of this as an after-effect), and then an uncharacteristic lassitude, broken by intermittent self-doubts. He noted, for example, that his executive vice-president was doing a good job of filling in the presidency—and then subsequently realized that this fact had no particular meaning for him. He became uneasy. He should have felt impatient to get back in harness, to show them that old Goforth still was on top.

But he had felt no emotion. It was this that disturbed him. Was it simply a delayed result of illness, or was it some inevitable process of aging which the illness had accelerated? He tested himself grimly. He made an analysis of a stock program proposal worked out by one of the economists. He did a masterly job; he knew it himself, with a rush of familiar pride. In its way, his study was as good as anything he had ever done. No, he was not growing feeble—not yet. The malaise that possessed him was something else, undoubtedly not permanent.

That summer he spent with his family at their place on the shore. He did not feel up to sailing; he watched others sail as he lay on the beach, and was again mildly surprised by his reaction. He did not envy them at all.

In the fall he was back at his desk, in full charge once more. But he was careful to follow the advice of the doctors and the urgings of his wife, and kept his schedule light. He avoided the rush-hour trains by going to work late and leaving early, and two or three times a month he remained at home, resting. He knew that he once would have chafed impatiently at such a regimen, but now he thought it sensible and had no sensation of loss. As always, he passed the routine problems down to his staff; but now, it seemed, so many things appeared routine that there was not much left on his desk. The shock came late in winter, when he realized that he had actually turned over to his staff a question of vital importance. It had been well-handled, true enough, and he had kept in touch with its progress, but he should have attended to it personally. Why hadn't he? Was he going through some kind of metamorphosis that would end by his becoming a semiactive chairman of the board? Perhaps he should consider early retirement. . . .

It was in his new condition of uncertainty that he had another encounter with Marshall, this time at a private university club to which they both belonged. Marshall offered to stand him a drink, and commented that he seemed to have recovered splendidly from his illness.

Goforth glanced at him, suspecting irony. He felt fully Marshall's age now, and looked, he thought, even older. But he accepted the drink, and they began to talk.

As they chatted, it occurred to him that he had nothing to lose by speaking frankly of his present perplexities. Marshall *was* older, in point of fact; possibly the man could offer some advice.

And so Goforth spoke of his illness, his slow convalescence, his disinclination to resume his old working pace, even his unthinkable transfer of responsibility to his staff—and strangest of all, his own feeling that it did not really matter, none of it.

Marshall listened attentively, nodding his head in quiet understanding, as if he had heard scores of similar accounts.

At length, Goforth's voice trailed off. He glanced at Marshall in mild embarrassment.

"So," said Marshall calmly, "you don't find business life so exciting any more?"

Goforth stirred in irritation at this echo of their previous conversation. "No," he replied, shortly.

Marshall gave him a sharp, amused look. He seemed almost triumphant, and Goforth was sorry he had spoken at all. Then Marshall leaned forward and said:

"What would you say to an invitation to join the Sailing Club?"

Goforth stared at him. "Are you serious?"

"Quite so."

It was Goforth's turn to be amused. "You know, if you'd suggested this two years ago, I'd have jumped at the chance. But now—"

"Yes?" Marshall seemed not at all taken aback.

"But now, it seems of little importance. No offense, mind you."

"I completely understand."

"To put it with absolute frankness, I don't honestly care."

Marshall smiled. "Excellent!" he declared. "That's precisely what makes you eligible!" He winked at Goforth in a conspiratorial way. "We're all of that frame of mind, my friend. We're all suffering from that same disease—"

"But I'm well now."

Marshall chuckled. "So the doctors may say. But you know otherwise, eh?" He laughed. "The only cure, my friend, is to cast your lot with fellow sufferers—the Sailing Club!"

He continued with the same heartiness to speak of the Club. Most of it Goforth already had heard. There were sixteen members, enough to provide the entire crew for the Club's schooner during its annual summer cruise. One of the sixteen had recently died, and Goforth would be nominated immediately to fill the vacancy; one word of assent from him would be enough to assure his election.

Goforth listened politely; but he had reservations. Marshall did not say exactly what the Club did on its cruises, and Goforth moodily assumed it was not worth mentioning. Probably the members simply drank too much and sang old college songs— hardly an enviable prospect.

Marshall interrupted his musing. "I promise you one thing," he said, more seriously. "You won't be bored."

There was a peculiar intensity in the way he spoke; Goforth wondered at it, then gave up and shrugged his shoulders. Why not? He sighed and smiled: "All right. Of course. I'm honored, Marshall."

The cruise was scheduled to begin on the last day of July. The evening before, Goforth was driven by Marshall far out along the shore to the estate of another member, who kept the schooner at his private dock. By the time they arrived, all of the others were there, and Goforth was duly introduced as the new crewman.

He knew them already, either as acquaintances or by reputation. They included men so eminent that they were better known than the companies or banking houses they headed. There were a few less prominent, but none below Goforth's own rank, and certainly none was in any sense obscure. He was glad to note that all of them had fought their way through the hard competitive years, just as he had done, and then in the course of the evening he slowly came to realize a further fact—that not one of these men had achieved any major triumph in recent years. He took some comfort from this. If he had fallen into a strange lassitude, then so perhaps had they. Marshall had evidently been right. He was among "fellow sufferers." This thought cheered him, and he moved more easily from group to group, chatting with as much self-possession as if he had been a member of the Club for years.

He had already been told that the ship was in full readiness and that the group was to sail before dawn, and so he was not surprised when the host, a gigantic old man named Teacher, suggested at nine o'clock that they all retire.

"Has the new member signed on?" someone inquired.

"Not yet," said Teacher. He beckoned to Goforth with one huge hairless hand. "This way, my friend," he said. He led Goforth into an adjoining room, with several of the others following and, after unlocking a wall safe, withdrew a large black volume so worn with age that bits of the binding flaked off in his fingers.

He laid it on a table, thumbed through its pages and at length called Goforth over and handed him a pen. Goforth noticed that the old man had covered the top portion of the page with a blank sheet of paper; all that showed beneath were signatures, those of the other members.

"Sign the articles, seaman," said Teacher gruffly, in imitation of an old-time sea captain.

Goforth grinned and bent over the page, although at the same time he felt a constitutional reluctance to sign something he could not first examine. He glanced at the faces surrounding him. Someone chuckled, and a voice in the background said: "You can read the whole thing, if you like—after the cruise."

There was nothing to do but sign, so he signed boldly, with a flourish, and then turned to shake the hands thrust out to him. "Well done!" someone exclaimed. They all crowded around then to initial his signature as witnesses, and Teacher insisted that they toast the new member with brandy, which they did cheerfully enough, and then went off to bed. Goforth told himself that the ceremony had been a juvenile bit of foolishness, but somehow it had warmed him with the feeling of fellowship.

His sense of well-being persisted the next morning, when in the predawn darkness he was awakened and hurriedly got dressed to join the others for breakfast.

It was still dark when they went down to the ship, each man carrying his seabag. As he climbed aboard, Goforth was just able to make out the name painted in white letters on the bow: *Freedom IV*.

Since he was experienced, he was assigned a deckhand's job, and as he worked alongside the others to ready the sails for hoisting, he sensed a marked change in the attitude of the men.

The Club had its reputation for being casual, and certainly the night before the members had seemed relaxed to the point of indolence, but there was a difference now. Each man carried out his tasks swiftly, in dead seriousness and without wasted motion, so that in a short time, the *Freedom IV* was skimming eastward along the Sound toward the heart of the red rising sun. Goforth was surprised and pleased. There was seamanship and discipline and sober purpose on this ship, and he gladly discarded his earlier notion that they would wallow about with no program beyond liquor and cards.

With satisfaction, he made a leisurely tour of the ship. Everything was smart and sharp, on deck and below, in the sleeping quarters and galley. Teacher, who seemed to be the captain, had a small cabin forward and it, too, was a model of neatness. Goforth poked his head inside to admire it further. Teacher was not there, but in a moment the old man stepped through a narrow door on the opposite bulkhead, leading to some compartment beneath the bow, followed by two other members. They greeted Goforth pleasantly, but closed and locked the door behind them, and did not offer to show him the compartment. He, for his part, refrained from asking, but later in the day he inspected the deck above it and saw that what had seemed earlier to be merely a somewhat

unorthodox arrangement of crisscross deck planking was actually a
hatchway, cleverly concealed. He crouched and ran his fingers
along the hidden edges of the hatch, then glanced up guiltily to
meet Marshall's eyes. Marshall seemed amused, but all he said
was: "Ready for chow?"

In the next few days, Goforth occasionally wondered what the
forward compartment contained. Then he all but forgot about it,
for his enjoyment of the voyage was too deep-felt to permit even
the smallest question to trouble him. He was more content now
than he had been in many months. It was not because he was
sailing again, but rather, he believed, because he was actively
sharing with others like himself a vigorous and demanding experience. It seemed, indeed, that they formed a little corporation there
on the *Freedom IV*—and what a corporation! Goforth's com-
panion on the dogwatch, who wore a huge red bandanna around
his head, was an international banker who treated with the chiefs
of foreign governments on a basis of equality, and even the
member who occupied the lowly post of cook's helper was a man
accustomed to deal in terms of millions.

Yes, what a crew it was! Now Goforth began to understand the
suppressed excitement he had long ago detected as a subtle mark
identifying members of the Sailing Club. Theirs was no ordinary
cruise, but a grand exercise of seamanship, as if they had decided
to pit their collective will against the force and cunning of the
ocean, to retrieve through a challenge to that most brutal of
antagonists the sense of daring which they once had found in their
work.

They were searching for something. For a week they had sailed
a zigzag course, always out of sight of land, but Goforth had not
the faintest notion of their whereabouts, nor did he judge that
it would be proper for him to inquire. Were they pursuing a
storm to provide them with some ultimate test with the sea? He
could not be sure. And yet he was quite willing to wait, for there
was happiness enough in each waking moment aboard the *Freedom IV*.

On the eighth day, he perceived an abrupt change. There was
an almost tangible mood of expectancy among the members, a

quickening of pace and movement, a tightening of smiles and
laughter that reminded him oddly of the atmosphere in a corporation board room, when the final crisis of some serious negotiation
approaches. He guessed that some word had been passed among
the crew, save for himself, the neophyte.

The men were tense, but it was the invigorating tensity of
trained athletes waiting in confidence for a test worthy of their
skills. The mood was infectious; without having any idea of what
lay ahead, Goforth began to share the exhilaration of his ship-
mates and to scan the horizon eagerly.

For what? He did not care now. Whatever it might be, he felt
an elemental stirring of pride and strength and knew that he
would meet whatever ultimate trial impended with all the nerve
and daring that his life had stamped into his being.

The *Freedom IV* changed course and plunged due east toward a
haze that lay beneath heavier clouds. Goforth thought perhaps the
storm lay that way and keenly watched for its signs. There was
none, but he took some heart at the sight of another yacht coming
toward them, and hopefully imagined that it was retreating from
the combat which the *Freedom IV* seemed so ardently to seek.

He studied the sky. The clouds drifted aimlessly, then broke
apart for a moment to disclose a regular expanse of blue. He
sighed as he saw it, and glanced around at the other crewmen to
share his feeling of frustration.

But there was no disappointment on those faces. Instead, the
mood of tension seemed heightened to an almost unbearable
degree. The men stood strained and stiff, their features set rigidly,
their eyes quick and piercing as they stared across the water. He
searched their faces desperately for comprehension, and as it
slowly came to him—when at last he *knew*—he felt the revelation
grip him physically with a wild penetrating excitement.

He *knew*, and so he watched with fierce absorption but without
surprise as the forward hatch swung open to permit what was
beneath to rise to the surface of the deck, and watched still more
intently as the crew leaped smartly forward to prepare it with the
speed born of long hours of practice. He stood aside then, for he
knew he would need training, too, before he could learn his part,
but after the first shot from the sleek little cannon had smashed a

great hole in the side of the other yacht, he sprang forward as readily as the others to seize the rifles which were being passed around; and as the *Freedom IV* swooped swiftly in toward the floundering survivors, his cries of delight were mixed with those of his comrades, and their weapons cracked out sharply, gaily, across the wild echoing sea.

An Angel of Mercy

¶ The blonde was on the train again, the third or fourth Monday in a row. Jacobs saw her at once as he entered the car. She sat alone in an aisle seat, bold and bright and watchful. A widow, maybe, with little lines of independence at the corners of her eyes. The commuters in their gray suits glanced at her in morning weariness, like spent, inadequate lovers.

Earth mother. Red-hot momma. Jacobs went to an empty seat across from her. Her perfume was too strong for morning; maybe it was protective, a commuter repellent. Suppose you got served a chocolate éclair for breakfast, would you touch it? She watched him as he sat. He kept his hat on, to hide his thinning hair.

He opened his attaché case, snapping both catches at once. Across the aisle, the blonde lighted a cigarette and took a big puff, almost audible. The cigarette end came out of her mouth red.

Memos in the attaché case, charts and graphs, neat and clean. (She was forty-five under that hair dye, with varicose veins and a

spare tire, probably, but you could bet that was an authentic
shirtful.) A nice little corporation budget, with contingency allow-
ances cleverly tucked away here and there . . . but what about his
own domestic budget? Full of holes. Untidy, haphazard. Mort-
gage, dentist, kids' clothes . . . where did it all go? No matter.
(She crossed her legs and tapped the cigarette. Bits of ash drifted
intimately onto his shoe tops.)

They were passing the Newark dump, steaming in the haze of
the swamps and exhaust fumes from turnpike traffic. (On her
cheek, a mole, a chorus girl's beauty spot, implying mesh stockings
and lewd little stars.) Dirty newspapers on the floor, toilet door
loose and banging, commuters sneezing on each other, yawning
and gaping in their car cage, getting ready to move to other
cages . . . subways, elevators, office cubicles.

The train went hurtling into the tunnel. Lights flickered. In the
attaché case with the budget was yesterday's puzzle, half-finished
but confidently done in ink. Six-letter word meaning condition of
loveliness. "B-e-a-u-t-y." (She let the cigarette drop, had trouble
finding it with her spiked heel, so he gallantly squashed it with his
shoe.)

"Oh—thanks."

" 'S okay."

Condition of loveliness! Above them the river boiled with
sewage and industrial wastes, the tunnel dripped with the exhala-
tions of ten thousand trains; commuters rose with bitter eagerness
and lurched into the aisle, swaying against each other in a dance of
hate.

Penn Station came sliding along in the gloom and stopped. The
blonde was somewhere up ahead, pushing along with the rest of
them, but when Jacobs got outside she was standing on the
platform, waiting.

She caught his eye. She beckoned to him. And she said to him
there amid the trains, trains, trains: "Okay. You'll do."

"I'm sorry, what—"

"Come on."

"I don't quite—"

She looked up at him, very slightly amused. "Let's go to a hotel.
You know."

A *hotel*.

He looked, illogically, at his watch. Crowds from another train were pushing all around them.

"Let's go," she said.

"I've got—a meeting at ten."

"Ten. Well, it's only eight-thirty now." She turned, pushing at his elbow. "Come on." He stared at her. "Well," she said, "what's the trouble? Look, I'm not a chippy." She pushed some more, and they began to move with the crowd toward the escalator. "I don't take a nickel. The hotel room, I got it reserved, see? It's mine. I pay for it." They stood on the escalator, rising in a forest of pale dull faces, blind eyes, stopped ears. "Just for kicks, mister." Motherly, she led him off at the top. His legs felt weak. "Ah," she said, "you want a cup of coffee first?"

First.

Hundreds of gray suits, briefcases, gray hats, gray jaws fresh-shaven . . . why him, why Jacobs?

"I don't underst—"

"I said just for kicks. Kicks. You know what kicks are." She was patient, persistent, pulling him along in the great echoing chamber.

"But I nev—"

"You religious or something?"

"No, no, it's—"

"So you're married. Listen—" They were part of the street crowd, a morning riot almost. She shouted: "It's good for marriage. Believe me, mister, I know. I had a husband once, he—"

Taxis honking, drivers cursing. Garment racks, messengers on motor bikes, cop on a horse, trucks like elephant behinds blocking side streets.

"—kept it all inside himself, see? Then finally he couldn't stand it and broke loose, run off, the weak bastard—"

Around a corner, heading straight for the side entrance to a hotel, one of those big convention palaces with small rooms and cheap towels. "If he'd sneaked a piece or two on the side, see," she said, lecturing him before an audience of two fat men, truckers in caps, chewing cigars, bored, "then he'd of stayed—worse luck for me, though. My third husband was well-to-do."

Third? Who was first, second? Where were they all now . . . waiting in the hotel room? *A con game.* Watch out, Jacobs. But

she was ahead of him, already past the doorman and inside. He
hurried after her, but stopped in the lobby when he saw she had
made it to the desk. The place was nearly deserted; a few bellboys,
shaggy rubber plants, some men reading newspapers . . . house
detectives? A ridiculous situation. He looked angrily at his watch.
Twenty to nine, and his IN box would be piled high with memos
and letters.

"Come on!" She was bellowing at him across the lobby, waving
her pocketbook. Good God, if it was a con game, the whole hotel
was in on it. Not one of those house detectives so much as batted
an eye. Jacobs hurried over to the elevator to shut her up. Was he
a dog on a leash or what?

"Now just a—"

But a middle-aged bellboy had shuffled up with the key. The
doors opened, the three of them were inside, rising silently together, partners in a sordid fate. Automatically, Jacobs removed his
hat and felt in his pocket for a tip.

The room had two double beds, a window, a television set, and
in a bureau drawer, hidden but handy, a Bible.

"Want some ice, sir?" said the bellboy. (Her brother? Husband
number two?)

"No." Jacobs gave him a dollar bill, wet from a sweating hand,
and he went out. The door snapped shut.

"Don't throw your hat on the bed," she said. He put it back on
his head. She was looking out the window. "New York always gets
me, you know?"

"Look, there's one thing I—"

"Ha. I know. You think it's some kind of racket. You're waiting
for the vice squad or something to come busting in. You guys are
all alike." She laughed.

"I've got to call the office," he said, reaching for the phone.

"Suspicions, suspicions. It's weird. A free piece comes along just
for kicks and no questions asked and everybody seems to want to
have their lawyer check it over." She took off her jacket and hung
it carefully in the closet.

Jacobs gave his office number to the hotel operator. He stood
between the beds, facing the wall. Behind him came a snap;
involuntarily he glanced over his shoulder. She had turned on the

TV set. Its noise came up quickly, cartoons for the kiddies. He
told the office switchboard girl to tell three other people he'd be
late. Behind him were waltzing Popeye and Olive, circa 1935 . . .
and his own kids, preschool, watching the same thing at home,
maybe. He hung up. She switched to another channel, news, and
left it on for him as she went into the bathroom, swinging her
pocketbook.

Jacobs sat on one of the beds, watching the news, still holding
his attaché case, listening to the water running in the bathroom.
The blonde was singing "My Blue Heaven." Riots in Malaysia. Ski
disaster in Austria. Mrs. Jacobs at home, five feet two, eyes of blue,
stripping the beds, dusting the mantel, brushing the dog. At the
office, Miss Waggoner shoveling more paper into his IN box, and
Godchaux, the accountant, looking for him. ("Where's Jacobs,
Miss W.? Shacked up in a hotel room with some blonde, hey?
Ha.") Yankees win, 5–4. Mets win, 8–5. Rain in the late afternoon . . .

"Say, you still got your *hat* on."

The blonde had come back, wearing two towels. She was broad-
shouldered and short without her shoes.

Jacobs put his attaché case in a chair and his hat on top of it.

Shades down. Bedspread whipped back.

"Well, what's the matter, mister? You're not a pansy, are
you? . . . Ha, I thought that'd shake you up. Don't get sore.
Nine guys out of ten fidget around and watch the door like
you. . . . Put the chain on it, why don't you?"

(Chain on the door, suit coat in the closet, blonde on the bed
with plump shaven legs and painted toenails.)

"Light me a cigarette, huh?"

That did it. That broke the spell. One little touch of banality—
and it was midnight for Cinderella. Fairy coach became pumpkin,
and this chesty Lilith, myth-woman of sexy daydreams, became
just a big middle-aged blonde beside him on a hotel bed. He
wanted to hear her say it again, and he asked: "What?"

"Light me a cigarette."

Yes, yes. Epitaph to magic lust, that phrase from the silver
screen. It was the first predictable thing that had happened. It
made all the rest jump into a pattern. He grinned away from her.

"Sorry, but I quit smoking last year." He lighted the cigarette anyway and, faithful to the tradition she had quoted, put it to her lips. A tobacco kiss, phallic, hinting of death.

Would she reach up and loosen his tie? Yes, she would—she did, squinting in the cigarette smoke. Jean Harlow and George Raft. Sexuality, real and synthetic, sang in his veins, drummed the blood up, leaving his hands and feet cold. . . . Predictable! A situation, a life experience!

"There's a pants hanger in the closet," she said. "Oh, say, leave the TV on, will you? I like it on."

An extra dimension, the TV. Made it seem like a public ceremony. The world must be represented, through its brainless eye. Outside in the morning streets, gray everybody was flickering in the sunlight, and there at the foot of the rumpled bed, a quiz program.

("Colombo is the capital of what?")

"Ceylon," he said, putting his tie on the hanger. Was he trembling with excitement? To be sure . . . but why was he so carefully straightening the creases of his trousers on the hanger and adjusting the upside-down pockets so his change and keys wouldn't spill out? Why hadn't he torn off the suit, flung it on the floor, ripped his tie in wild haste, pulled the towels from that acre of blonde, that thrice-married, varicose widow?

("Colum*bia* is the capital of what?")

"South Carolina."

The anticipation of passion throbbed, beat, swelled . . . and yet, there was this detachment, too. Adulterous guilt? Fear of Jove's bolt?

("Colum*bus* . . .")

"Ohio."

He hung his shirt on the closet doorknob. No guilt, no fear. The blonde would have no reason to regret her choice. He would be equal to the occasion, just as, in an hour, he would be capably handling the budget in the board room. She was, even, like the budget—a matter which had come to his attention, requiring action. A big blonde memo marked "Urgent."

It was a little sad. He took her hands. "Do you know," he said, "if I were five years younger I'd be crying now?"

"Huh?"

She didn't understand. Yes, then he would have been crying and trembling like a boy, possessed by the idea that this wild impossible Monday-morning surprise was a turning point of fate.

"I don't like 'em too young," she said, sitting up, beginning to do things.

But now . . . just an episode.

"Real young guys, they can't handle themselves right, you know? They get ideas, this and that." She was perspiring a little, one eye still on the TV.

Maybe a turning point after all, to be old enough to see no turning point. To see nothing.

"And I don't like these hot-pants types who always give me the eye. It's not so much the age, see, it's a certain look a man has when you know it's, well, okay . . ." (Breathing harder, shedding towels, but serious.)

A certain look . . . a certain time, too, when life stops being personal and becomes anybody's life, everybody's life . . . mass life, indifferent life, life as a set of problems presented, solutions offered.

"But I mean, I get a real charge out of you guys. There you are, fresh off the train, headed for the office same as usual—then wham, you wind up inside four walls with a woman. Something different, huh?"

"I'll say." No, not different. Not much different. If different, then not better. But he would not say that to her. When Florence Nightingale came through the battlefield with bandages, what soldier could tell her he hadn't noticed his wound until then?

"Any man needs a little pickup, a little satisfaction once in a while."

Her gift to the gray men. A hundred hotel beds moaning under her Samaritan flesh, a hundred men roused by potency to see the impotence of their lives.

"When it's unexpected, it's kind of special, see?"

Special . . . unexpected. Ah, poor banal Lilith, bumbling angel of sexual mercy, sagging Valkyrie, blonde destroyer of men who flung open the window of routine to let the dream-killers spring inside. How many of the gray men had broken the image of their

youth on that hopeful foolish body? How many had risen drained
of dreams to meet their anonymity and age?

She was weeping.

"Why? What's wrong?"

"Nothing. I don't know. It's okay. I mean, I always cry some."

They lay beneath the sheet. He held her in his arms, stroking
her with a lover's tenderness. Poor old nymph. Her body told her
what his mind told him. She knew there was trouble, always
trouble, even in the bright beat of desire and fulfillment . . .
something wrong that her gift could not make right but only
worse, and yet she could not help what she did and was.

"It happens," he said, softly.

She closed her eyes and smiled. "You understand. You guys do
understand."

Guys. Not just one guy. *Guys.* He laughed and held her closer.

The
Interview

¶ The personnel agent was not quite what George had expected. In the first place, he was young; his round, smooth face
fairly radiated inexperience. Then, too, the fellow was not only
unpolished but downright graceless. He had none of that brisk,
deferential manner which George had come to look for in the
company's younger staff.

At first, George was annoyed at the fact that they had sent such
a stripling to obtain the information necessary for the processing
of his promotion. However, this irritation was soon succeeded by a
tolerant amusement at the agent himself, for, while not painfully
shy, the young man was obviously aware of his own awkwardness,
and as a matter of fact seemed resigned to its tyranny. He
proceeded along the hallway with a reluctant and foreboding air,
as if he fully expected to lurch against a vase or to slip disastrously
on the edge of a rug, and when he had in fact managed to reach

the living room without mishap, he sank down on the sofa with a sigh of evident relief. George could not help but smile.

"Well," the agent announced cheerfully, "I guess we'd better start, if you're ready, sir." He dug with both hands into his briefcase and came up with a thick stack of mimeographed sheets through which he thumbed hastily to see if they were arranged in proper order. Evidently they were, for the agent gave a little nod of satisfaction, patted the sheaf of papers into a more orderly shape, drew a pen from his pocket and tested it on his forefinger to be sure it was working, and then cleared his throat portentously.

"Okay, sir. I guess I'm all set." In a slow, singsong voice, the young man began to ask questions concerning George's chronological record of employment—positions held, titles of immediate supervisors, descriptions of principal duties, and so forth.

George was mildly surprised. Surely the company had all this routine data in his file already. It was not as though he were seeking a position with some new firm; he was simply being processed for promotion to the parent concern, which had full access to the records of its subsidiary. But he contented himself with a shrug, assuming that Personnel had its own system to follow, with which it would be pointless to quarrel.

The interviewer completed the top set of questions and carefully put it aside. George eyed the remaining pile of sheets uneasily and glanced at his watch. It was a quarter to six. He could hear his wife in the kitchen. The children would eat early anyway, he thought, but Vera might not like it if their own dinner were delayed.

"Are you going to use all that material in the interview?" he asked.

"I think so, yes, sir," the young man answered rather doubtfully. "Except for maybe one or two—although in your case, I think, possibly not—"

"Well, it doesn't matter," George put in quickly, not wanting to risk confusing his visitor. "Go right ahead." He took comfort in the thought that the promotion would be worth any reasonable inconvenience. "Say," he added, "it's after work. How about a little drink?"

"Not for me, sir," the interviewer replied, with a short laugh that sounded embarrassed, as though George had made an improper suggestion. "*I'm* still working, I mean." He laughed again. "But you go ahead, sir," he said, in sudden earnestness. "Don't let me stop you."

"Well, perhaps I will, if you don't mind," said George, getting to his feet. "I don't usually drink alone, you know, but it's been a tough day. . . ."

He poured himself a stiff drink in the kitchen and warned Vera that the interview might last another hour or more. Before he returned to the living room, he took a big swallow of the whisky; immediately, he wondered why, and then realized that he had not wanted to walk back into the room with a brimming glass, for the clumsy young man did represent his employers, after all, and might make a secretive little marginal note: "Drinks to excess"!

But as soon as George had seated himself again, he thought how ridiculous such fancies were, for the agent was having a hard time handling the simple materials they had given him, and obviously was incapable of adding observations of his own.

The next two lists also dealt with ordinary matters already recorded in George's file: his educational background (schools, college) and basic family data (number and ages of his children, his wife's maiden name, etc.). George hesitated over the year of his graduation from high school. Had it been '37 or '38? The agent waited anxiously for the answer, as if the date were all-important.

"Make it '37," George said finally. "You can double-check it with my file at the company, if you like. As a matter of fact," he added, "all the rest of the information is there, too."

"Oh, really? Well, yes, of course," the young man mumbled, noting down George's answer. He appeared to be disconcerted at the thought that much more reliable answers to all the questions already reposed in a file which perhaps his superiors had not remembered to tell him about. George was annoyed at the needless duplication of effort, but he felt a kind of pity for the awkward young man, who undoubtedly was the butt of a thousand little jokes in his office.

"There's probably a good reason for getting this information a second time," George remarked soothingly. He tried to think of such a reason, and the agent waited hopefully for him to supply one. "For one thing, it's a way of cross-checking," George said. But he realized this was nonsensical; he would hardly need to be checked on the names of his children, and as for such facts as graduation years, the data in his file had been based on original records. He frowned into his drink, aware of the interviewer's disappointment. "Maybe it's this," he continued. "They may want to compare my recollection of these facts with the file itself, you see, for psychological reasons. The differences—if there are any—may be quite significant to someone who's trained to analyze these things." The agent nodded solemnly, evidently impressed by George's idea. "A man may repress or alter certain data subconsciously," George added, "and for all we know, this may provide valuable insights into his character, which the company would need to know."

"That makes sense to me," the agent declared admiringly.

Encouraged by the young man's confidence in him, George thought of yet another explanation. "It also occurs to me," he said, indicating the considerable stack of papers that remained in the agent's lap, "that the reason may be psychological in a different way." The agent blinked at him, waiting for a further revelation. "You have a lot of materials there," George explained, "and some of them are bound to deal with fairly personal matters. Possibly the routine questions you've asked me up to now are simply to prepare me—to relax me, in a sense—so that I won't be alarmed when you begin asking what they really want to know."

"Well, sir, that certainly may be true," the agent said. He shook his head wonderingly and fingered the stack of papers. "Some of these are quite personal, it's a fact," he added, "but I'm not sure—in your case, sir—if all of them—which of them, I mean . . ." He laughed, apparently in embarrassment, and shuffled the papers.

George sighed. It was odd that the company would have sent an interviewer who did not seem quite sure of what to ask and, on top of that, had no idea of the purposes underlying the interview. But of course the company undoubtedly had a good reason for it, no matter how mystifying it might seem to an outsider.

"Here we are, sir," the agent declared, having picked up the next questionnaire. He scanned the top page and pursed his lips. "You may be right, sir. This one is a bit personal. It deals with religion. May I ask your religion, sir?"

"No religion," George replied. Then, with a smile, he corrected himself, using the common phrase: "No religious preference."

"Are you sure of that?" the agent asked; but he was writing down George's answer anyway.

"Oh, yes. Of course."

The agent smiled shyly. "I didn't mean to suggest you weren't, sir. That was only the next question on the sheet. 'Are you sure of that?' I mean, it's not my question, it's theirs."

"Well, my answer's the same," George said politely. For some reason, he felt impelled to explain further. "I said 'no religion' at first, but then I decided 'no religious preference' would be better, because 'no religion' implies atheism, you see, whereas the other could well mean that I go to several different churches."

"Yes, I see," said the agent. He made a note and glanced inquiringly at George. "Well, sir, if you're sure you don't want to add anything to that . . ."

"That's all there is to say."

"No, I mean if you're Jewish or anything, you can say so. I'm Jewish, too."

"Are you really?" asked George.

The agent seemed baffled by the question. Then he ducked his head bashfully and grinned. "No, I'm not, actually," he admitted. "I'm just supposed to say so, because it makes people anxious to show that it's all right."

"To show that what's all right?"

"Anything. You see, they're sorry for me and want to make it up."

"I don't understand," said George. "Are they sorry you're a Jew?"

"Oh, no. It's just that they feel they forced me to say I'm a Jew."

"But then, you're *not* a Jew," George persisted.

The agent blushed slightly in his boyish way. "Well, I made a mistake," he conceded frankly. "I wasn't supposed to admit that I'm not a Jew. But the rest of it makes sense, doesn't it?"

His manner was so earnest that George did not want to weaken his faith in the company's peculiar psychology. "Oh, it makes good sense, I guess," George said quickly. He was puzzled by it, however, and not a little annoyed; still, he suspected that the company's tactic was probably justified, and that it merely had seemed foolish because the young agent had handled it badly. At the same time, he felt an almost paternal desire to help the young man along through the intricacies of the interview, no matter how long it might take. He glanced at the window and noticed that it had grown dark. Perhaps Vera had already put the children to bed and had eaten her meal alone. But George knew she would not really be angry, for she, too, was anxious that all the various stages leading to the promotion be carried through smoothly.

"There's certainly a lot of personal information to get," the agent remarked apologetically, after he had completed the religious questionnaire.

"That's quite all right," said George, trying to hearten his guest. "The company needs information about its senior staff. They certainly have a right to know and I'm anxious to help all I can."

"I appreciate that, sir," the agent responded formally. He eyed the next questionnaire doubtfully, as if he thought it might have slipped into his satchel by error. "This one's political, I think," he said. Then he read the first question: "Are you loyal to our form of government?"

George smiled and answered facetiously: "Oh, yes. I've only tried to overthrow it a couple of times." The agent solemnly wrote this down, and George exclaimed: "I was only kidding about that, of course."

"I understand that, sir, but we're supposed to note down everything anyway."

"Look," George said firmly, "that might cause a real misunderstanding."

"Don't worry, sir," the agent told him. "I've noted that you were merely joking." He smiled at George in a reassuring way, but George made a private resolve to keep any further pleasantries to himself.

"Next question," said the young man. "Do you feel loyal toward the company?"

"Yes, I do."

"That seems like a strange question," the agent remarked. "I mean, you would hardly admit that you *didn't* feel loyal, would you?"

"No," said George, "I suppose not."

The agent quickly jotted down his response. "I'm sorry," he said, "but that was a trick question. You see, you just admitted you might have lied."

"But I *do* feel loyal to the company," George protested.

"It isn't fair to trick you like that," the agent agreed, "but it's part of the process, you see." He put down the pen and shook his head moodily. "I can't say I like to ask trick questions, though."

The agent appeared so worried by the dubious morality of the company's questionnaire that George again sought to ease his mind. "They're really not so bad," said George. "Of course," he added, anxious on the other hand not to weaken the agent's repugnance toward what was certainly a suspect practice, "I wouldn't like to be in your shoes, having to ask questions like that."

"You think it's unprincipled?" the agent asked, with a sad expression.

"Well, yes, in a way, I think possibly so," replied George cautiously.

Once more the agent made swift notes. "I'm terribly sorry, sir," he stammered, not looking up from the papers, "but that was another of those tricks."

George was astonished. "What did you write down?"

"Well, I wrote that you felt the questions were probably unprincipled." The agent stared at his shoe tops in embarrassment. "I had to do it, sir. I hope it won't have any bad effect for you."

"Don't worry about me," said George, although he was in truth somewhat disturbed. "I'm sure I can explain everything in case the higher-ups don't like my answers."

"I sincerely hope so, sir," said the young man. He sighed and continued with the questions, which dealt with a wide range of subjects, including capital punishment, labor unions, civil rights, and foreign relations. George framed his replies with circumspection, but the trick questions that had been inserted here and there were so artfully concealed that time and again he said things which sounded absolutely foolish or dangerously subversive when the agent regretfully read them back to him. "I've got to be careful," George told himself angrily, but he was not so confident now; his hands were trembling and he kept wiping his forehead with his handkerchief, for his perspiration flowed freely.

The young man was, if anything, even more distressed than George by the turn things had taken. "Sir," he said once, "I wonder if it would be all right for me to sort of tip you off when I'm asking a trick question, by winking my eye or scratching my nose in a certain way?"

"Oh, no, that wouldn't be fair to the company," George responded firmly. Then he caught his breath. "Was that another trick?"

"Not at all, sir," the agent assured him. He pondered the matter for a few moments. "I guess you're right, sir. I couldn't very well tip you off. After all, the company is paying me to do the job the way they want it done."

George nodded. "I appreciate the thought, though," he said.

"Maybe we could start all over again," the young man said suddenly, but he quickly realized the impossibility of this suggestion, too. "No, I guess that wouldn't be fair, either."

"That's all right," George told him, with a heartiness that was more assumed than natural. "Just go ahead and don't worry about me." He forced a smile. "I've been with the company for a good many years now, and I'm sure they won't misunderstand anything I say. My feeling is, if you're fair to the company, the company will be fair to you."

"Do you really think so, sir?" The agent looked as though he would very much like to share George's opinion on the subject.

"Absolutely."

The agent gazed at George's face for a moment. "But some of these answers are going to look bad for you, sir," he insisted. "And the questions—why, they're not fair at all!" He flung his pen aside and bit his lip. "It's just not fair. It's a trick, and it's an unfair trick besides!"

Again George tried to reassure him, but the young man was bitterly indignant. "I don't see what these questions have to do with your job, sir. The company has no business to inquire into your beliefs in the first place, let alone to trick you in this way."

The agent's attitude presented a delicate problem. George felt it was absolutely necessary to answer all the questions, tricks in-

cluded, in order to obtain his promotion, but he did not want to
dilute the young man's apparently honest outrage at the company's knavish practices (although George remained convinced
that the reasons, if he could know them, would prove to be
sufficient). He sighed. It seemed almost too much trouble. He
glanced at his wrist, but discovered that his watch was missing. He
assumed he had left it in the kitchen. The darkness was broken
only by the slanting ray of the tiny adjustable ceiling lamp which
the agent had lowered so that he could read his materials more
readily.

The young man was pondering the stack of questionnaires that
remained in his lap. The pile seemed not to have diminished, but
rather to have increased, which George found disheartening, for
the interview had already taken several hours. The agent appeared
downcast, too, not so much at the amount of material yet untouched as at the character of the job he had been forced to
undertake. "I definitely don't like it, sir," he muttered.

George knew that he had the responsibility for finding some
solution to this dilemma. He thought that perhaps he could read
the questionnaires himself and write down his answers, thus reliev-
ing the agent of his unpleasant duty; but he reflected that this
would probably be in violation of personnel rules, and besides, it
would not really take care of the basic problem, which was essentially a question of reconciling this honest young man to the
bewildering and often underhanded methods of the company.

He noticed that his visitor's face, previously so fresh and
smooth, already seemed to be touched with cynicism, and he
realized that he must act quickly.

"Look here, my young friend," he said with a steady smile,
"we've got to keep our minds on the business at hand. The
company requires certain information concerning my background
and intellectual makeup, in order to assemble all the various data
necessary in the matter of my promotion. Now, it's not our job to
criticize the company; after all, they're the ones to decide what
they need to know. The questions may seem strange to us, some of
them may seem unethical, even, but this is a free country, and I
have a perfect right not to answer if I don't want to. Now,"
George went on, feeling that he was arguing with unusual clarity,

Even as he spoke, his intuition carried his understanding forward by yet another step, and he could not repress a quick chuckle of delight. "But we can't waste our time!" he exclaimed. "We've got a long way to go! No more doubts, young man! No more soul-searchings! Just ask those questions—I'll have the answers for you!"

He found that he was on his feet, flexing his knees springily, like an athlete preparing for some contest. "Let's go!" he declared exuberantly, and the agent bent obediently over his papers, reading off more questions in a voice that George could barely understand, for it was low and trembling.

George began to pace around the room, tossing off his answers in phrases that seemed to echo resonantly from wall to wall. The agent meanwhile perspired over his papers, uttering the questions automatically, then scribbling frantically in an effort to keep up with George's rapid answers.

"You're going too fast, sir!" cried the agent, but George loftily dismissed his complaint with a quick motion of his hand. "On the contrary, my boy, not fast enough!" He laughed, but shortly, for he was determined not to waste a moment. There were too many questions left unasked, and although he felt confident of his ability to answer every one without an instant's pause, he was impatient to rush ahead. He hastened his step, as if the swifter rhythm of his marching would spur the agent to greater efforts; he snapped his fingers, too, in time with the quickening tempo of their voices.

"Faster!" he cried out eagerly, dizzied by his growing comprehension. He seemed to hear the questions almost before the agent stammered them out, and his answers came so rapidly that question and answer often overlapped. "Faster!" The agent was on the verge of exhaustion, but George pressed on at an ever-increasing rate, striding energetically to and fro, so intent on his task that he even knocked down chairs and tables in his path. The agent began to gasp with shortness of breath, and his fingers tightened painfully with cramp, requiring him to shift the pen to his other hand, but still George forced the momentum of the interview, rattling off his answers with such velocity that the agent began to lag behind in his transcription, despite desperate attempts to keep up;

still George continued to accelerate his flow of words, faster and faster, so that soon their voices absolutely merged, question and answer becoming a continuous babble, punctuated by George's swiftly moving footsteps that reverberated like a lightning drum roll in all parts of the room at once.

Finally, the agent screamed out, "I can't do it!" and, with a sob, flung down the pen and slumped on the sofa, letting the stack of questionnaires cascade from his lap to the floor.

"It doesn't matter!" George shouted. He did not slacken his pace, but actually increased it, bounding now, almost floating, so quickly did he move. "You don't need to ask any more questions —I know what the company wants!" He clapped his hands together sharply and laughed. "My promotion—that's going to put me right up there with the top men, my boy, and in a position like that, it's not just services that are needed—not by a long shot!" He spread his arms wide, as if to encompass the very walls, which themselves seemed to quiver in response. "No, if I'm to become a part of the company, then they've got the right—they've got the duty—to know everything about me! And so they've got to ask *all* questions—*all!*" Then he thundered a prideful acknowledgment of the unique obligation the company had placed on him. "And I will answer all!"

He continued, calling out both questions and answers, and then dispensed with questions entirely, since the answers alone were enough. He continued even when the agent crept away and left, for he realized that his answers now were of a self-sufficient permanence that needed no recording.

On and on his voice rolled forth, his eloquence swelling ever greater. His words became song, prayer, offering. He was on his knees among the thousand sheets of paper, his arms extended toward the single feeble light. He sang aloud his dreams, his doubts, his follies, triumphs and disorders, his weaknesses and strengths.

All, all he poured forth freely, eagerly, for he knew that at last they wanted him in totality—not just his skills, as before, but his very heart and soul. Already he felt himself drawn by a new happiness toward the center of the great instrument for which he had labored faithfully for so long. Already he felt a yielding, boundless love responsive to the company's insatiable desire to know him, to possess him utterly. He cried out in his joy, for he realized, too, that he was at but the beginning of this total happiness, this total submission. The process would go on, perhaps without end. And so, even as the tiny light dulled and then darkened, and as the room grew chill in the coldness of the deepening night, he knelt happily among the mass of papers on the floor. The interview continued.

Countdown

¶ The meteorologists had correctly forecast fine weather; every-thing seemed made to order that day. The offshore winds had swept away the clouds, the sky was a clear and trackless field of blue, and the sun ranged well off toward the northern horizon, as if deliberately posted where it could not interfere with the great event taking shape on the earth below.

People had come by the thousands, in cars and buses and taxis, and the sandy waste outside the high wire fence was jammed. Here and there among the vast throng were refreshment stands, and strolling salesmen hawked souvenirs, balloons and straw hats. At the very edge of the fence a few tents had been pitched by those who had arrived days in advance to be certain of getting a first-rate location. State troopers were moving among the crowd, but their primary concern was to keep the traffic lanes free, for the people were in a quiet and expectant mood. There was no dis-order. Everyone was waiting patiently to see the climax of the International Space Year, a man rocketed up toward the planet Mars.

Within the fenced area, the atmosphere also was calm. Among the cluster of long low buildings were gathered the press and dignitaries, each group occupying its designated location. The television and newsreel cameras were set on a large wooden platform in the center of the asphalt square that separated the Commissary from the Project Headquarters building. In rows of chairs on one side sat the scores of newsmen and magazine writers who had come from virtually every country in Europe and the Americas; on the other were seated more than two hundred guests, mostly scientists and political figures. For the more important spectators, a shaded pavilion had been constructed north of the Commissary; these privileged visitors included three Chiefs of State, a dozen statesmen of ministerial rank, and a few members of royal families. Everyone remained quietly in place, anxious not to disturb the scientists and technologists who moved with sober deliberation on their final tasks.

"ZERO PLUS ONE HOUR!"

The loudspeaker system cracked out the phrase like a rifle shot. Instantly, the crowds on both sides of the wire fence were hushed, and all heads turned east toward the giant rocket that towered on its pad, across the protective belt of sand. In the deceptive haze of reflected sunlight, the slender cone seemed to quiver, as if the initial combustive thrust were already urging it heavenward.

Security Officer Farquhar leaned against the east wall of the Commissary, his thoughts uneasily revolving around the thousand possibilities for trouble. He had been assigned to the security end of a dozen manned space shots before, yet this one was the most nerve-wracking, for not only was it of top importance, but also it was an international undertaking, involving scientists from a score of nations, who had turned the area into a babel of languages, suggestive of confusion—even sabotage.

Officer Farquhar frowned, attempting to dismiss his fears. He had done everything possible to guard against sabotage. For many months, everyone connected with the Project, from the Director down to the restaurant busboys, had been rigorously investigated and kept under observation, and in the security files there was a thick dossier on each person, packed with the most intimate and revealing details. Nowhere was there the slightest hint of trouble. Farquhar's mind gradually lightened. At any rate, no one could accuse him of a lack of diligence.

"Look, sir," came the amused voice of his jeep driver nearby, "the women are starting to bawl!" The driver grinned and pointed the antenna of his walkie-talkie toward an area twenty yards north, where chairs had been set up for the convenience of Project staff. Since the scientists were at work at the pad or in the buildings, these chairs were occupied principally by wives, children and the few service personnel not on duty.

The driver was right. Several of the women were furtively dabbing at their eyes with handkerchiefs. Farquhar smiled tolerantly; the tension of so many months was nearing its climax. Why not tears? It might be better if the men could weep, too, for some relief.

He noticed one of the women in particular, partly because of her unusual beauty, partly because she remained standing, despite the liberal provision of chairs. He squinted against the sun to see more clearly. No, she was not actually crying. Something odd about her, he thought. She stood stiffly, with her hands clenched at her sides, staring fixedly out across the sands toward the rocket.

Officer Farquhar recognized her then as the wife of one of the scientists, a physicist named Whitby. To look at the woman, one would think that Whitby himself were about to climb into the rocket, instead of Captain Randazzo. Farquhar shrugged. Tension had varying effects on people. Still, he wondered a little . . .

In the main control room of the Project Headquarters building, Captain Miguel Randazzo sat calmly munching a chicken-salad sandwich and sipping a glass of milk, as if he were not in the least interested in what the immediate future held in store for him. Occasionally he would glance with mild amusement at the grave countenances of the top scientific staff members who were busily involved with charts and telephones and the banks of intricate machinery that covered the walls.

In any other man, Captain Randazzo's air of nonchalance would have been properly ascribed to a despairing bravado or to drugs. But Randazzo was neither desperate nor drugged. His handsome face displayed a quiet smile; the strong and shapely hands that held the sandwich and the glass did not tremble in the slightest, and his slim but powerful legs were crossed with an elegant casualness. One would have thought that he was merely going to travel to New York, or to Rio, instead of to Mars and back again.

If he had evidenced any unease, the fact would have been instantly noted by the two renowned men of medicine who sat respectfully beside him, watching his every move. An eminent psychiatrist stood nearby, but he had nothing to note on his scratch pad but his own nervous reactions.

Randazzo had been chosen from among some fifty volunteers with previous space-flight experience, and had subsequently confirmed the wisdom of his selection by rapidly mastering the technical skills required for the operation (and repair, if need be) of the complicated equipment in the spaceship cabin. The harsh physical trials which had eliminated so many hopefuls had not bothered him in the least, for he was well-rested from the Olympic Games, where he had won four gold medals for his proud little nation. In his spare time, Captain Randazzo pursued his hobbies —hunting Kodiak bears alone and unarmed, raising prize orchids, and writing Latin verse plays. On top of these accomplishments, the Captain had an international reputation for romantic gallantry, a reputation which he had not been able to embellish during his recent weeks of semi-seclusion at the Project.

"ZERO PLUS FIFTY!" boomed the loudspeaker system. Every man in the room—save the astronaut—started in automatic alarm.

Randazzo simply smiled, and as the Project Director walked by, he hailed him jokingly in colloquial German: "Don't forget to put plenty of steak on board for me, eh?"

The Project Director smiled quietly but passed on without response. The food supply necessary for the three-month round trip consisted solely of processed concentrates, hardly more than capsules. But even this compressed nourishment occupied more space than he would have preferred, what with the necessary protective packing and cooling mechanisms.

But the Director was more concerned with another matter at present. The cabin temperature regulating system had indicated a faint tendency to deviate from its rigid automatic control. It was the single piece of equipment that had not performed to absolute perfection during the months of testing. True, Randazzo could make adjustments by means of the manual controls, but nevertheless—

"Get me Whitby at the pad," the Director ordered his communications chief.

As he waited, he gazed through the window at the assembled dignitaries and at the sleek conical shape beyond, on which their hopes and fears were centered.

"ZERO PLUS FORTY-FIVE!"

Too many mechanical intricacies, thought the Director, touching his moist brow with a handkerchief. Too many thousands of tiny interlocking parts—something was bound to go wrong. . . .

"Whitby speaking."

The Director responded more sharply than he had intended. "How's the Temp-Reg doing, eh?"

"Seems in perfect order now," Whitby replied.

"Seems!" the Director snapped. "Do you realize that if—" He caught himself. Of course Professor Whitby knew. If Temp-Reg slipped by the tiniest fraction of a degree—and if the manual failed as well—Captain Randazzo would gradually become either parboiled or frozen.

"If you have any doubts, Whitby, now's the time," the Director said, more quietly.

"In my best judgment, Temp-Reg is in proper working condition," came the thin, pedantic voice.

"Good enough," said the Director. "Every expendable in place now?"

"All except food. Wait a minute—here comes Dr. Anders with it now. That's definitely all. We'll have everything fixed tight in two minutes."

"Good," said the Director, and handing the receiver to the communications man, he turned thoughtfully around to survey the room. Too many parts and pieces, he thought, but as his eye fell on Randazzo he felt a heartening optimism. At least the human factor in this gigantic venture was flawless. No wonder the press referred to the fellow as "The Perfect Human."

At the launching pad, Professor Whitby ran his pencil rapidly over his final checklist.

"You're a bit late, you know, Max," he said in mild reproof to a tall, gaunt chemist who was helping two technicians load several long metal cases into the gantry elevator.

"Only eighteen seconds," Dr. Anders replied with cool precision. He frowned in a preoccupied way at the cases, then gave the nearest one a pat of satisfaction. "All right," he told the elevator crew, "take them up."

He turned to Whitby. "That's everything, I suppose?" It was a purely rhetorical question, for both men knew to the last detail exactly what went inside the cabin and in what order.

Whitby looked up from his checklist. "Of course," he muttered. His eyes were darkly circled. "Well, we're all through now," he added. "Let's go."

The two men climbed into a waiting jeep and, with a final salute to the technicians who would remain at the pad until Zero Plus Ten, they drove across the hot sands toward the group of buildings and the crowd of watchers.

"Everything perfect for the Perfect Human, eh?" Dr. Anders said quietly.

Whitby gave him a quick glance. "Perfect!" He wrinkled his face in distaste. "He's perfect physically, perhaps—and superior intellectually, I suppose, but . . ." His voice trailed off.

Dr. Anders raised his eyebrows inquiringly, but Whitby said no more.

"ZERO PLUS THIRTY!"

Captain Randazzo yawned and stretched. "Time to dress for dinner," he remarked, noting the approach of two Nobel prize-winners from M.I.T. who were bringing him the space suit they had themselves designed. "Correct that error in the third lining, gentlemen?" the space traveler inquired, with a wink.

The M.I.T. luminaries smiled back, but the hovering psychiatrist leaned forward with some interest. "If I may ask, Captain, what error?"

Randazzo feigned a look of surprise. "Why, they didn't leave enough room, that's all."

"Not enough room?"

"Room for a spacewoman," declared the astronaut, in English that betrayed no trace of an accent. "Three months is a long, long time, eh?"

The M.I.T. men chuckled, but the psychiatrist made a careful note and remarked: "I suppose you will miss the companionship of women, Captain." To which the hero replied with equal gravity: "Correctly stated, sir, and if I may be allowed to abuse the convention of modesty, the reverse will also be true."

"ZERO PLUS TWENTY!"

Security Officer Farquhar winced from the loudspeaker blast as he walked along the corridor of Project Headquarters. His pace was steady but his mind was troubled by two small facts which might or might not be connected—and even if they were, might be meaningless.

First, there had been Professor Whitby's expression as the scientist left the control room, after making his final report to the Director. Farquhar had caught only a glimpse of that face, but he would not soon forget its tortured look.

The Security Officer would have dismissed it as evidence of intolerable anxiety about the success of the Project, except—

Except that he still vividly recalled the beautiful young woman who had stood rigid with grief and tension in the Staff area, staring desperately at the distant rocket. Whitby's wife.

There was a third fact, too, or rather, a rumor. Captain Randazzo was said to have indulged his romantic inclinations even in the relative isolation of the Project, although this was hard to credit, for he had been so closely watched in these recent weeks.

Farquhar shivered as he heard the crowd outside break into a sudden rising babble of excitement. He glanced at his watch. Yes, by now Randazzo would have left the building and climbed into the jeep—

He felt weak under the weight of his responsibility. It would be unthinkable to approach the Project Director at this time, solely because of the facial expressions of a husband and wife. And yet he was distinctly uncomfortable about it. Already he had slipped into the security room to check the Whitbys' dossiers. No hint of discord had been inscribed there, but Farquhar had noted down the names of the couple listed under the heading, "best friends at Project," Max and Olga Anders. He needed more information— quickly, if at all. Dr. and Mrs. Anders might know something, assuming there was something to be known.

But thus far he had been balked, for he had searched through the Staff area for Mrs. Anders without success, and her husband, too, was nowhere to be found outside.

Now, reaching the end of the corridor, Farquhar came to a door marked "Nutritional Chemistry" and stepped into a laboratory lined with huge sinks and tables and cupboards. The laboratory was empty, but Farquhar called out Dr. Anders' name anyway.

"Yes?" Dr. Anders emerged from a refrigerated room at one end of the laboratory, wiping his hands on a towel. "Oh, were you looking for me, Mr. Farquhar?" He carefully shut the cold-room door behind him. "Just cleaning up," he explained. "If you let a mess stand for a while, it's a dozen times harder—"

Farquhar interrupted him impatiently. "I'm going to ask a personal question, Dr. Anders. I hope you don't mind answering. I assure you, I have my reasons."

Dr. Anders shrugged without answering. From the corridor the loudspeaker echoed a fresh warning: ". . . PLUS TEN!"

Farquhar found he was perspiring freely. Now the astronaut would have been strapped inside the cabin . . . the hatch would be closing, the final-check crew climbing into their jeeps—and in five more minutes, the automatic controls would take charge. If there was anything to his doubts, he had better waste no time on circumlocution.

"I'm going to speak bluntly," the Officer said. "You and your wife know the Whitbys better than anyone else here. Tell me frankly—do you have any reason to believe that Mrs. Whitby has been guilty of any improper relationship with Captain Randazzo?"

Dr. Anders rubbed his lean jaw reflectively, then turned toward the window and clasped his hands behind his back. "To the best of my knowledge," he said slowly, "yes."

Farquhar did not hesitate, but reached for a telephone. "One more question," he said, as he dialed. "Does Whitby know this, too?"

"I'm fairly certain that he does, yes."

Farquhar muttered an oath, then barked an order into the telephone: "Farquhar speaking. Find Professor Whitby at once. Bring him to the nutritional lab—immediately."

He slammed down the phone and mopped his brow. Dr. Anders was regarding him with a curious look.

"I can't believe it," Farquhar said, hoarsely. "We kept him under close surveillance. We had him watched, guarded—almost every minute—"

Dr. Anders seemed amused. "Are you really surprised, Mr. Farquhar? Don't you think the Perfect Human could have devised means of evading your vigilance if he wanted something badly enough?" He laughed shortly. "That probably added to the fun of the thing, don't you think? Having not only to woo and win another man's wife—but also to outwit the security men assigned to protect him! What a challenge for a man who strangles bears as a diversion!"

"I can't believe it," Farquhar repeated, but his words were lost as the cavernous voice of the loudspeaker cut in: ". . . PLUS FIVE!" Now the automatic controls were operating. The whole system had passed into the shadowy realm of electronics, where cold mechanical intelligences whispered millions of messages at lightning speed, causing levers to drop, gauges to quiver, and microscopic doors to slam tightly shut. . . .

Even so, it could be stopped. Farquhar knew that in the control room the Director now stood tensely watching, his hand near a button marked "KILL."

It could be stopped, but at a fantastic cost. Once the myriad fine-tooled parts began to move—and they were moving now—a stoppage might ruin half of the delicate equipment, would certainly delay the shot for many months, would cost millions. No, he could not ask the Director to wreck everything on a sheer hunch. He stared down furiously at his clenched fists and only slowly became aware of Dr. Anders' voice.

". . . you can't believe that a faithful wife could be seduced, is that it, then?" Dr. Anders asked, twisting his lips ironically. "Don't be ridiculous, Farquhar! This Randazzo is no ordinary mortal—he is perfect! And beyond that—yes, far beyond that—he is a man soon to vanish on a hero's mission into the sky, perhaps never to return!" Dr. Anders folded his long arms and cocked his head to one side. "What woman could resist the appeal of such a man, a man who comes to her in secret, a man who is already a legendary figure—"

The door swung open. Whitby strode in, his blond hair disheveled. Behind him were two security agents.

Farquhar stood up. His whole body was trembling; he found it almost impossible to control his voice as he rasped out the brutal question.

Whitby's face colored, then paled. He glanced in bewilderment at Dr. Anders, but Anders had turned toward the window again.

"Yes or no!" snapped Farquhar.

Whitby stretched his hands apart in a despairing gesture. "Yes, it's true—she told me herself last night—but I don't see that it's any of your—"

He was choked off as Farquhar seized his shirt front roughly with both hands.

"Tell me, Whitby—have you done anything to—to—" The Security Officer was himself almost beyond coherence.

Dr. Anders cut in dryly: "To sabotage the rocket—"

Whitby pulled loose from the hands that clutched his shirt. He staggered back. "I? Sabotage the rocket?" He sank back against a counter and his head tipped weakly against the cupboard above it.

"Sabotage it—*did you sabotage it?*" Farquhar's voice rose to a shout.

Whitby closed his eyes and feebly waved his hands. "Are you insane? You think I would destroy—" He began to laugh, his body stiffening, his head still pressed against the cupboard. "Me?" He gasped the words out through his painful hilarity. "No—no—I knew his reputation, yes—I suspected him—but with other women, other men's wives!" He laughed again. "I never thought it would be with mine!"

Dr. Anders stepped swiftly over to Farquhar. "Look here," he said softly, "the man isn't lying. The only item of importance under his direct control is the Temp-Reg system, and—"

His voice was drowned out by the sudden roar of the loudspeaker system, beginning the final sixty seconds of the countdown: ". . . FIFTY-NINE, FIFTY-EIGHT, FIFTY-SEVEN . . ."

Dr. Anders had to yell to make himself heard. "It's automatically monitored, Farquhar! If anything is wrong with it, the Director will know at once!"

". . . FIFTY, FORTY-NINE, FORTY-EIGHT . . ."

"There's a monitor dial for everything!" Dr. Anders shouted. "You must know that yourself! Call him and check!"

Farquhar seized the telephone and dialed with shaking fingers.

Dr. Anders turned abruptly away and stared at the window's square of sky and sunlight.

". . . THIRTY-ONE, THIRTY, TWENTY-NINE . . ."

Farquhar cursed the loudspeaker's enormous voice. Suppose Whitby were lying—suppose Anders were lying, too. They might be in it together . . . perhaps Anders had a similar motive—

". . . NINETEEN, EIGHTEEN . . ."

His call was answered. But the communications officer refused to disturb the Director.

Farquhar swore at the man, begged him, ordered him—

"TEN . . . NINE . . ."

At last the Project Director's voice barked at him savagely from the receiver.

Farquhar screamed the words: "Do you have the Temp-Reg system under monitor?"

"Of course!"

"And is it working properly?"

There was a brief pause.

". . . FIVE, FOUR . . ."

The Director's voice cracked back: "Of course!"

Farquhar dropped the receiver as though its weight had suddenly become intolerable, and as it clattered on the desk, the building trembled slightly and the crowd outside burst into a prolonged roar that seemed to grow enormously in volume, and to roll in upon the men like surf, like vast gray thunderbanks—

"It's off! It's up!"

The two security agents rushed to the window to see the slowly rising column of steel and fire and smoke.

But the other three remained where they stood; Farquhar at the desk, Anders five feet behind him, and Whitby at the counter near the wall.

"You see," said Dr. Anders, slowly, "it was all right."

Whitby's body was still stretched in painful tensity against the counter. "I thought of it, Farquhar," he whispered, "Lord knows I thought of it. But I couldn't do it—no, not even for *that*."

Then his tension broke. His body relaxed so quickly that he almost fell, and as his head flopped forward, the cupboard door against which it had been pressed swung open.

By the dozens, tiny pellets came cascading out. They rained down on Whitby's head and shoulders, and spun and rolled upon the floor. The entire room seemed covered with them, and still more rolled to the cupboard's edge and dropped down.

Wonderingly, Farquhar stooped and picked one up. It was pliable in his fingers, reminding him of a yeast tablet.

He glanced at Whitby. The man's face had gone milk-white and he was staring wide-eyed, not at Farquhar, but beyond him.

"Good Lord, Max!" he hissed.

Farquhar turned around, conscious as he did so of the increasing and triumphant cheering of the crowd, and of the loudspeaker voice that crackled now above the roar with a piercing excitement: "STAGE ONE SUCCESSFUL, STAGE ONE SUCCESS-FUL . . ."

He looked at the yeasty pellet in his hand, and then at Dr. Anders. The chemist's lean face was oddly contorted; he was smiling in a quiet way, as if anticipating some subtle witticism he was about to utter.

"Was this"—Farquhar waved his hand to include the thousand pellets that lay scattered throughout the room—"was this supposed to have been in the ship?"

Dr. Anders folded his arms and inclined his head almost imperceptibly.

"You mean—you deliberately loaded empty food containers in that cabin? You mean he's off in space to starve to death?"

"Oh, no," said Dr. Anders. "He needn't starve."

Farquhar stared at the man. "But if the containers were loaded empty—"

Whitby broke in. "No! They weren't empty! They were weighed at the pad! They were fully loaded!"

Farquhar shook his head and drew his hand across his face, as if to erase some incredible idea. "Loaded? Loaded—with what?"

But Dr. Anders merely repeated, in his calm and even tones, the phrase he had just used: "*He needn't starve.*"

Whitby shuffled forward with the uncertain step of a much older man until he bumped blindly into a heavy counter and could go no farther. When he spoke, his voice was but a whisper, yet the words seemed to take shape almost palpably in the air, like smoke:

"Where's Olga, Max? Where is she? Where's your wife?"

Dr. Anders made no reply. His pale eyes were fixed on the window, on the patch of blue beyond, the great skyway that opened ever wider to where the silent planets circled in the infinite and peaceful harmony of space.

Time Out

Professor Gull had never been to England. He had always wanted to go; several times he had planned to go, and once he had even been in the process of going, but each time he had been frustrated. World War II had blocked his graduate scholarship at London University. Later, the expense of marriage had forced him to decline a modest fellowship at Cambridge (and the cost of a subsequent divorce had kept him from joining a jolly bachelor tour). Finally, he had arranged to spend a sabbatical year in London. He had boarded the ocean liner and said farewell to two colleagues who had come to see him off—but as luck would have it, this was the very day of the nuclear accident in the Arctic. Air forces were alerted and missile bases sealed, as terrifying rumors swept the world. All ships were ordered from the seas, all aircraft from the skies. Professor Gull's liner reached Sandy Hook, turned around and steamed back. He spent a gloomy and expensive week in a New York hotel; then, when the United States and Russia jointly announced that they were enforcing a moratorium on international trade and travel until tension abated, he paid his bill and took a train back to the university.

There he remained for the succeeding two years just as he had been for the preceding twenty—an uninspired but conscientious professor of history, plodding toward retirement. He was portly and bald. When he ate hot food, he perspired. His feet were subject to corns. He once bought a puppy for companionship; it swallowed a pair of his socks and died. His professional specialty, too, was a disappointment. He had embraced the modern British Liberal Party at a time when he was young and a Liberal revival seemed imminent, but it withered, so to speak, at his touch.

And yet Professor Gull was not unhappy. He was by nature hopeful and outspoken. He scorned the modern world while accepting its comforts, and he revered England, where he had never been. He wore tweeds and dark-rimmed spectacles, and on Sundays, when he trudged for exercise through the cornfields that surrounded the campus, he was topped by a billed cap, and carried a knobby cane.

Britain was still isolated by the Moratorium (as were the Americas, Europe, Africa, and Asia) but it lived as always in Professor Gull's heart. Apart from his necessary concentration on the hapless Liberals, he had no favorite historical period. He read in them all, and when he did not read, he dreamed. He became the sum of his studies and his yearnings: he was Druid, Celt, Norman; he rode with Cavaliers and Roundheads; he sat with Dr. Johnson's circle and with the Pre-Raphaelites; he went to Canterbury with Chaucer and strolled in London streets with Pepys and Boswell; he was in the crowds that witnessed the burning of witches, hanging of highwaymen, beheading of monarchs, and the cricket Test Matches. He was English in all respects but passport.

When the government unexpectedly announced a program of grants in the humanities for research in Britain, Professor Gull duly applied. He did not suppose he would be awarded one. It was the first break in the Moratorium; everyone was eager to go, and naturally the more brilliant scholars and men with government connections would be chosen. But to his great surprise, he was among those selected. "Why me?" he asked himself—and could find no answer. Presumably it had been because of the Liberal Party, on which he was perhaps the leading American authority. But that was hardly sufficient distinction. Was it possible that under the stress of the Moratorium, the British electorate had eccentrically returned the Liberals to power? Highly unlikely, thought Professor Gull. Still, with communications totally sundered—radio waves jammed, newspapers and magazines cut off, no returned tourists to quiz—anything might have happened. Who knew?

However, as he sat in his seat on the plane with forty other American professors, he was in a contented frame of mind. He was on his way at last. Through the tiny cabin window he could see banks of clouds, suitably fleecy. Thousands of feet below was the Atlantic. New York lay far behind. On his lap rested his briefcase, stuffed with the travel literature he had collected during all the years of waiting. He withdrew a map of London, spread it out and examined it greedily. Hyde Park . . . the Tower . . . the British Museum! His forefinger traced a route through the crooked streets of Soho, leaped down to the old East India docks, skipped back to Whitehall, rushed along Fleet Street and paused reverently at St. Paul's. He pulled out brochures and pamphlets, and began poring over moats and towers, altar rails and mossy turrets. He closed his eyes, overcome by an attack of Anglophilia—visions of village greens, of manor houses, of Lord Mayors with chains and maces, yeomen bearing halberds, City men with derby hats and rolled umbrellas!

Up front, a Harvard economist began jovially to sing "Rule, Britannia." Several others joined in. That was the spirit, thought Professor Gull. He began humming the tune softly and from his briefcase took more travel pamphlets: York . . . the Lake Country . . . Canterbury . . . Devonshire. He could hardly wait for the plane to touch down on English soil.

The clouds were heavy as they approached. Professor Gull peered impatiently out for his first glimpse of England. Green—it would be a sweep of springtime green, sprinkled with villages and towns crowding east to London.

The plane sank beneath the clouds. Professor Gull's ears crackled and sang. England was rushing up at him. But it was not green. It was brown. And where were the villages?

They were bumping across a vast brown plain, spotted here and there with muddy pools from a recent rain. Not a blade of grass could be seen, not a single tree or bush. The professors strained against their seat belts, muttering to one another. Obviously this was not London Airport. They had been forced by engine trouble or weather to make an unscheduled landing—but where?

"How irritating," grumbled Professor Gull.

A few moments after the plane stopped, the door was wrenched open and a man in overalls and a construction worker's helmet scrambled up a ladder and stepped inside. "Good afternoon, gentlemen," he said, wiping dust from his spectacles. "I hope you had a pleasant trip."

"Where the devil are we?" asked one of the professors.

"This is the orientation center," replied the man in the helmet. "Don't worry. Everything will be explained in short order." He put his glasses back on and motioned to the passengers. "If you'll be kind enough to leave your seats, the truck is waiting outside to take you to the briefing hall." He turned and went down the ladder.

The professors followed him, still complaining. "If it's Greenland, why doesn't the idiot say so?" one of them snapped.

As they climbed out of the plane, they could see a group of Quonset huts and tents a hundred yards away, and what appeared to be heavy-construction machines stirring up clouds of dust.

"It *is* Greenland," said Professor Gull, pulling himself up into the rear of the truck. "They've gotten us confused with a load of missile experts and they've sent us to a rocket base."

"It could be Yorkshire," said one of his neighbors. "Or somewhere in the Highlands."

"Greenland," insisted Professor Gull.

"Do they have castles in Greenland?" asked his neighbor. "Look at those ruins." Through the wooden slats on the side of the truck they could see what appeared to be the lower portion of a medieval fortress near one group of tents. The heavy gray stonework of one low tower was fenced by scaffolding and workmen were swarming over it.

"A rocket pad," said Professor Gull.

"With a crenelated tower?"

"Camouflage," said Professor Gull.

The truck stopped in front of one of the Quonset huts. The professors were ushered inside and seated in rows of metal chairs that faced a blackboard. Over the blackboard was hung a large map of the British Isles, and in front of that stood a young man with thinning hair and a solemn expression. He was wearing a black mourning armband on one sleeve of his coat. In his hands he held a wooden pointer. When he spoke, it was obvious that he was not English, but American.

"My name is Wychcote, gentlemen," he said. "I am assistant to the Under Secretary of Defense for Public Affairs." He paused, gently flexing the pointer. "Welcome to England."

"Nonsense," someone muttered.

Mr. Wychcote gravely studied his audience. "This is the first stage in your orientation, and I will make it short." He coughed into his hand. "First of all, let me mention the nuclear accident. We had known all along that something like this was possible. We knew it could happen, and we took every precaution against it. So, on their side, did the Russians. At the same time, realizing that such an accident *might* happen despite all our efforts, we had worked out various programs to deal with the hypothetical situations which might present themselves in the event of limited disaster."

"What has this got to do with us?" asked a testy voice from the audience. "We're not defense experts; we're college professors."

"Please bear with me, gentlemen." Mr. Wychcote touched his forehead with a handkerchief. "As I was saying, the possibility of accident was very much in our minds. We had also conferred privately with the Soviet Union on the subject. We had, in fact, established a working relationship with the Russians more than a year before the accident occurred. We had an informal joint executive body in constant session, producing plans and programs for consideration by the National Security Council and its Russian counterpart. We were not unprepared when what we had feared might happen, did happen."

Professor Gull was studying, at long range, the map of the British Isles and wondering whether Yorkshire or the Highlands were really as bare and desolate as the treeless plain outside the briefing hut. The land was too flat to be the Highlands, surely, and Yorkshire was covered with grassy moorlands, was it not?

He was surprised to hear his own voice ask the question:

"But it happened in the Arctic, didn't it?" A dozen heads turned his way.

"According to the public announcement, yes," Mr. Wychcote replied. He hesitated. "You've eaten your lunch on the plane, gentlemen, and so I assume you've all had your tranquilizers—to prepare you for what I'm about to say." He turned to the map. "It did not happen in the Arctic. Unfortunately. As far as the Soviet-American investigating commission has been able to determine, the nuclear explosion took place just about here." The wooden pointer came to rest on the city of Edinburgh.

The scholars stirred uneasily in their seats. Professor Gull tapped the side of his head, trying to clear the air pressure from his ears.

There was a thumbtack in the map at Edinburgh from which a length of string dangled. Mr. Wychcote took the end of the string between his thumb and forefinger and slowly revolved it in a circle, which roughly encompassed all of Britain and Ireland. "This was the area of fire storm," he said.

There was not a sound in the room. Professor Gull examined the map with continued interest. In outline, Great Britain looked very much like a seated rooster.

Mr. Wychcote released the string and faced his audience again. "It was all over in a fraction of a second," he said. "Sixty million people, gentlemen, were vaporized."

Impossible, thought Professor Gull. The map still showed towns and cities, railroads and highways, ports and airfields. It was covered with them. All that could not possibly be wiped clean. The map would not lie.

"I don't wonder at your silence, gentlemen," Mr. Wychcote was saying. "The idea is unbearable. Even those of us who have lived with the terrible reality for two years find it hard to believe. And yet it is the truth. The sedatives do help. They are powerful ones, and you will need more from time to time, until you are able to adjust . . ."

Professor Gull yawned. He felt a remote resentment at having been tranquilized, like a steer en route to the slaughterhouse. Others were yawning, too, and glancing about surreptitiously, ashamed that their reaction to the news of catastrophe should be one of languor.

Mr. Wychcote continued, speaking more briskly, as if he had delivered this part of his briefing dozens of times and knew it by heart. "From the vantage point of history," he said, "there is some small solace. Take the medieval plagues. They regularly wiped out one third or one half of the population, with horrible suffering. And then there were the religious and political wars, not to mention the torturing and beheading and whatnot of various times, and the Great Fire of 1666." He cleared his throat. "And what about World War II, gentlemen? The blitz of 1940 and later, the V-1 and the V-2? Buildings demolished. Whole blocks of them. Ancient monuments pulverized. The streets filled with the dying and the wounded. Well, the most tolerable way to look at what happened two years ago, you see, is to imagine that all these various past disasters were, so to speak, rolled into one gigantic cataclysm." Mr. Wychcote pursed his lips and surveyed his audience solemnly. "An accident, of course. A horrible accident. But at least, when compared to the previous visitations of violence and destruction throughout British history, a *humane* accident. Everything was finished in the twinkling of an eye, you might say." He lowered his head. "There was, gentlemen, no suffering."

The silence continued. Then someone sneezed.

"What about fallout?" a voice asked, timidly.

"Another humane circumstance," replied Mr. Wychcote. "The missile warhead was what we call 'clean.'"

Professor Gull stood up. The tranquilizer had done its work, for he was not shaken or faint; he did, however, feel annoyed. They had had no right to vaporize England before he had a chance to see it.

"Don't be ridiculous," he said. "Look out that window. There's nothing out there. Just a lot of dust and dirt. Are you trying to tell us *that's* England?"

Mr. Wychcote regarded him patiently.

"It isn't," Professor Gull went on anxiously. "It couldn't be. There's been some mistake. Look here, I'm willing to admit that a nuclear missile could blow up a whole country—but it couldn't be kept secret. Albania, perhaps, or an out-of-the-way place like Greenland, where no one goes. But not England."

Other voices murmured in agreement. "He's right. It couldn't be England."

Mr. Wychcote spoke in a low, sad voice: "Do you really believe, gentlemen, that the United States government would go to the trouble and expense of flying you thousands of miles in order to tell you a fairy tale?"

Professor Gull sat down and mopped his brow. The windows were open but the room seemed close. Dust was sifting inside, in little puffs. He wondered dimly what the dust had once been.

". . . The immediate question facing the President and the Soviet Premier was: What to do?" Mr. Wychcote was saying. "They were on the hot line, conferring at once, naturally. What a dilemma. Great Britain and Ireland had been vaporized, but who was responsible? Missiles from each power had been above the Pole on routine patrol . . . but which one had strayed, which one had left systems control? And had it been *forced* from control? The possibilities were endless. The question of blame might take years to answer. It might never be answered. However, this was a secondary consideration. Thanks to the preliminary joint staff work on theoretical accidents, the two statesmen were ready with a plan. At all costs, secrecy had to be maintained. Suppose the world knew what had happened? Can you imagine the wave of horror and hysteria that would sweep from continent to continent?"

Mr. Wychcote's heavily tranquilized audience blinked at him and stifled yawns.

"Think of the outcry, the tensions," he continued. "America and Russia would be forced to accuse each other. Lacking proof, they might have to invent evidence. In such an atmosphere of fear and suspicion, anything could happen. Provocation, response, counterprovocation—an incident, perhaps, and then—escalation." Mr. Wychcote tapped the floor sharply with his pointer and several nodding heads jerked up. "For the sake of all humanity, therefore," he went on, "the accident had to be kept secret. Britain and Ireland had to be isolated, but in a way that would attract no special attention. Hence, *every* nation had to be isolated, or rather, to ameliorate the crushing economic effects of a moratorium, permitted to trade with its immediate neighbor only: America with Canada, France with Spain, Russia with Eastern Europe, etcetera—and Britain with Ireland."

Professor Gull asked another question. "Would you mind telling us where we are? I mean, exactly where we are at this moment?" His voice sounded unusually loud. "In the Highlands?" he added.

Mr. Wychcote shook his head. "Not the Highlands. Not Scotland. We are in England." He gestured toward a window. "This is Oxford. To be precise, we are in the grounds of All Souls College."

"Oxford?"

"Oxford," said Mr. Wychcote.

"You mean, it *was* Oxford," someone said.

"*Is,*" said Mr. Wychcote firmly. "We must think positively, progressively, creatively." He extended his wooden pointer toward the window. "That tower out there, gentlemen. That is Merton College."

"You mean it survived the blast?"

"It is being built. It is being restored. That is why you have come to England." Mr. Wychcote raised the pointer like a cavalry saber. "This is Operation Phoenix. We and the Russians are restoring—everything."

Professor Gull mopped his brow again. Then he noticed that he was using not his handkerchief but one of the travel pamphlets. It was titled: *Visit Historic Shrewsbury in Storied Shropshire!* He laughed once, wildly, and then fell silent in embarrassment. But no one even glanced his way.

Mr. Wychcote was succeeded by representatives of other executive departments, who brought with them charts, graphs and maps studded with colored pins, to explain in detail the program for rebuilding Great Britain. The professors sat dully in their seats, struggling against the effects of sedation. Some fell asleep from time to time and had to be gently wakened by an attendant posted there for that purpose. Professor Gull was not sure whether he was napping or not; the voices of the speakers seemed tinny and distant, their faces slightly blurred, and he could not quite read the numbers and lettering on the charts. The idea of reconstructing Britain struck him merely as being clever, and he envisioned it as all taking place in miniature, tiny model buildings being glued to a board on a worktable.

There was a break for tea. Professor Gull drank two cupfuls, and this roused him to the sensation of growing dismay. He sought out the last speaker, a plump little State Department functionary, and plucked at his sleeve.

"Do I understand that everything is being restored?"

"Everything." The man smiled at him and nodded pleasantly to the other scholars nearby.

"But it's fantastic."

"In a sense, perhaps. It is certainly ambitious."

"What about London?"

"Of course London," said the State Department man, taking a bite out of a tea cookie. "London, York, Canterbury, Bristol—all of them, to be sure."

"And the villages and towns?" someone else asked.

"Every village," said the State Department man equably. "Every town and city. Every monument and castle, every church and cathedral, every forest, glen and vale."

"This is incredible," said Professor Gull.

"Every stick and stone," continued the State Department man, good-humoredly, "every blade of grass, every hedge and bush, every mansion, palace, hut and hovel. *Everything.* Stonehenge and the crown jewels, the Old Vic theater and Holyrood Palace—"

"Fiscal madness," interrupted the Harvard economist, who, like Professor Gull, seemed suddenly to have awakened.

"The money is there," the State Department man assured him, reaching for another tea cookie. "As the Treasury man told you, the space race has been abandoned." He seemed to realize that the group of humanists around him did not share his casual mood. He frowned and spoke in more sober tones. "There is a new priority, you see. Total restoration, gentlemen. The United States and the Soviet Union have made an absolute commitment, a solemn and secret pledge, to expunge this terrible entry from the ledger of history." He replaced the cookie on the tray and folded his arms. "The Cold War has been forgotten. The restoration of Great Britain is the task of our lifetime."

No one said anything.

"England will rise again," the State Department man continued. "It must rise. It will. You will help restore it. Scotland, too. Ireland," he added, "is not budgeted at present." Still there was no response. The scholars were rubbing their eyes, glancing up uneasily at the charts and graphs at the front of the room.

"What about the people?" one man asked.

"You were told about that by Labor," the State Department man reminded him patiently, wishing that the tranquilizer dosage could somehow be reduced. It made briefing sloppy. "New generations will be bred, born and reared," he said. "There will be people in the towns and cities, there will be birds in the forests, deer in the parks, and foxes in the fields. Insects, too, and even vermin. Nothing is being left to chance. Everything is part of Operation Phoenix. Hundreds of specialists from both nations are here now, and many hundreds more will follow. You are but one small group, valuable as you are. Already, as you have been told, the first villages have been erected, the first trees planted—"

"Impossible," someone said.

"Difficult, yes. Time-consuming, naturally. And expensive. But impossible?" The State Department man permitted himself a slight smile. "After all, the Dutch rebuilt Rotterdam in a few short years, and the Germans repaired their shattered cities almost overnight. New York itself is constantly being reconstructed. No, gentlemen, the physical job is the easiest. It is the planning that is hard." He glanced at his watch. "But it's time for your little tour of Oxford; then you'll come back here to see where you fit into our system. Don't forget—at the first sign of anxiety, ask for more pills. We've got plenty."

For the next hour, Professor Gull and his forty colleagues were led from one hut to another through the dust of old England to view the plans for the new. Oxford, it appeared, was the headquarters of the American effort, and York was the Russian command center, but since the project was bilateral, there were Russians everywhere in Oxford, whizzing by in staff cars and jeeps with their American counterparts, working on blueprints and designs in the architectural tents, and arriving or departing in helicopters, which stirred up great clouds of dust. Merton College, meanwhile, grew visibly during the afternoon, as stone after stone was raised into place, and surveyors already were hammering in stakes nearby for Corpus Christi College.

Back at the briefing hut, the new group was shown an enormous organization chart, headed "Operation Phoenix." At the top were two squares side by side, one labelled "U. S. National Security Council," and the other "Presidium of Supreme Soviet Council." Descending from these was a complicated network of lines and boxes, indicating the ways in which the strength of the two world powers was being disposed for the restoration of Great Britain.

"Here's the Historical Policy Planning Group," said the instructor, pointing to one box. "That's where the basic decisions are worked out for approval by the Inter-Branch Coordinating Group"—his finger jumped to a higher box—"subject to review by the Executive Committee and the Priorities Board. . . ." His voice droned on and his finger hopped expertly from box to box; several of his listeners, still bemused by drugs and weary from their trip, snored in their chairs.

A bell rang. An attendant began to pass out assignment slips, instructing each man where to report for duty.

Professor Gull was handed a slip bearing his name and the notation: "Assigned to Future Section, Hut 12–B." A similar slip was given to his neighbor, a dapper little scholar named Hoop, who sported a neatly trimmed white mustache and a goatee. "That's odd," said Dr. Hoop. "I'm a specialist in Norman Britain. What could that have to do with the future? Come to think of it," he added, as he and Professor Gull left with the others to find their duty station, "the idea of having a Future Section at all is not clear to me. The purpose of the project is restoration, is it not? Then how is it possible to restore something that has never existed?"

"There is a section on prehistoric Britain, I believe," said Professor Gull.

"True."

"Then perhaps there is equal justification for one on post-history," said Professor Gull. "At this point," he added, "I would not be surprised at anything."

Hut 12–B was a scene of intense activity. Some twenty men were working at long wooden tables strewn with papers, typewriters and telephones. Professor Gull and Dr. Hoop were escorted to a private office at the far end of the hut, where they were introduced to the section chief, a husky and vigorous young Yale man named McAmis.

"Welcome to Future Section, gentlemen," said Dr. McAmis heartily. "We're at the end of the day now, but tomorrow we'll get you fitted in bright and early." He grinned, showing perfect teeth. "We're primarily a planning and coordinating section—"

"I'm sorry," said Professor Gull, "but there's one question which wasn't covered in our briefing. We've been told that Britain has been destroyed—and I can't quite believe that—and we've been told that it's going to be restored—and I don't really believe that, either—but I still can't understand exactly *why* it's to be restored."

Dr. McAmis seemed puzzled. "Why? Well, good Lord, we've *got* to restore it. We can't just let it all go down the drain and forget about it."

"But it's *gone* down the drain."

"Of course. That's the terrible thing. That's the problem we're up against. But we can't simply sit still and mope about it. We've got to put our shoulder to the wheel," said Dr. McAmis, "and rebuild it as quickly as we can. We've got to restore it completely, down to the last little detail. The Moratorium can't drag on forever, you know. It's got to end sometime—and when it does, England's got to exist. Otherwise, the whole theory's shot to hell."

"It's all incredible."

"Take some more tranquilizers," suggested Dr. McAmis. "And then lose yourself in the work. It's the only way to get through the first days. After that—well, you'll find yourself caught up by new ideas, by the professional attitude of enthusiasm and good workmanship we've got here, and then you can bear it. We're all horrified, gentlemen, but we can't let ourselves be torpedoed by it. We've got a job to do, schedules to meet, deadlines and priorities. It's a staggering responsibility. We've got to rebuild Britain just the way it was, and in record time and in secret, to boot. Secrecy *and* authenticity—those are our watchwords."

Professor Gull shook his head. "How can you possibly talk of authenticity? The whole thing's a gigantic fake."

"I must caution you not to think negatively," said Dr. McAmis.

"Restoration is wholly different from fakery. The British themselves restored ancient buildings damaged by the blitz. We are simply carrying out a program of restoration on a huge scale. And think of the alternative. Can you really imagine a world without England?"

"I must admit I cannot."

"It's a terrific task, of course. The pressure is awful. But we've got to do it, gentlemen. The decision has been made at the highest levels, and it's one in which every civilized man must concur. We have no choice. And besides," Dr. McAmis added, "it's given the humanities their proper role at last."

"Really?" inquired Dr. Hoop. "What do you mean by that?"

"Well, with the space projects canceled, the scientists and engineers have been kicked out of the driver's seat. They're nobodies now. In Operation Phoenix, the humanists are the ones who are in charge. The challenge of our generation has arrived—and the humanities alone can meet it!" Dr. McAmis winked at his visitors. "As for Future Section," he continued, "the basic idea is simple. It will take thirty or forty years to get Britain back on a self-sustaining basis, repopulated and rebuilt to the point where it can start producing its own history again. But in the meantime, we've got to do that job ourselves."

"Produce history?" asked Dr. Hoop.

"Right. We can't have a history gap. It's one thing for the other project sections to build a city here and a village there, with all the old medieval trimmings the way things were, but time doesn't stand still for us. In our section, gentlemen, we deal with everything that happened *after* the Accident."

"But *nothing* happened after the Accident," said Professor Gull.

"Correct. So we must create the kind of events that would have happened if there hadn't been any Accident, because the whole theory is to demonstrate that there *wasn't* any Accident."

"There'll always have been an England," said Dr. Hoop.

"Very good! You see, you can't have the future population of Britain poking around in the history of this period and finding nothing, can you? No, they've got to find all of the things that make up their past, in an unbroken continuity. They've got to read about who was Prime Minister and what acts the Parliament passed, and moreover, they've got to have the documents to prove it. They've got to find their old copies of the London *Times* and *Punch*, too."

"Good Lord," said Professor Gull.

"The burden is fantastic," Dr. McAmis went on. "And the planning that goes into each step!" He shook his head and sighed. "Take publications alone. We have to devote a lot of effort to this aspect. We plan the issues here, but the actual printing is done in London, where the presses are. There's a tremendous backlog. You don't turn out two years' worth of the *Times* overnight, you know. Then there's *The Guardian* and all the others. We don't have to print many copies of each issue, fortunately. Just enough to be able to stock the future libraries. But here's an example of how complicated this business is. Take just one issue of the *Times Literary Supplement*. Let's say it carries the reviews of thirty books. Do you see the implications?"

"No," said Dr. Hoop.

"Well, my friend, what about those thirty books, eh? Where are they? They've got to exist, too, don't they? Of course, they do. So we have to produce them. Novels," said Dr. McAmis, "biographies, political works, economic studies, memoirs."

"Poetry?" asked Professor Gull.

"Of course, poetry. Actually, poetry's the easiest. You can rig a computer to write poems—and that's what the Operations Research boys have done for us—but not novels. In view of the work load, we're putting heavy emphasis on poetry right now. To future generations this will be known as a poetic age."

Professor Gull looked at Dr. Hoop, whose mustache was working as if he were about to sneeze; then he looked at Dr. McAmis, whose handsome, boyish features reflected sincerity and purpose, and then he glanced at the window, which framed a portion of the endless brown plain.

"And what will we be doing, exactly?" he asked.

"Writing history. History of the future. It would be fairer to say you'll be going beyond the traditional role of the historian. You'll actually be *creating* history."

"Creating, perhaps, but not history. Not true history, anyway."

"It will be the only true history. Look at it in a positive way, as a challenge. You and your colleagues in Future Section will be creating the only absolutely indisputable history that has ever been written in all of—well, in all of recorded history," said Dr. McAmis. "You will be amply supported by whatever facts you want. The Documents Section is equipped to produce state papers, speeches, private correspondence, official testimonials, magazine articles and even photographs; we can also provide statuary and films. Your job is merely to make future history natural and plausible."

"I have never found history plausible."

"True. Therefore we must create plausibly implausible history. You'll be interested to know, Professor Gull, that Policy Group has scheduled a Liberal Cabinet for the second future decade— you'll be doing planning work in that area, naturally. . . . Well, I can tell that you both have had an exhausting day. We'll call it quits for now, I think," said Dr. McAmis, rising from his chair, "and get to work in the morning. Don't be discouraged, gentlemen. It's a huge job, it's true, but we've got to be patient and take on one thing at a time. Rome wasn't built in a day, you know."

"What do you think of all this, Hoop?" asked Professor Gull. They had eaten supper in the mess hall and were sitting on their bunks in one of the tents, waiting for lights-out.

"It's remarkable," said Dr. Hoop, who had removed his shoes and was meticulously wiping them free of dust. "They've gotten a lot done in a very short time, haven't they?" He held one shoe at arm's length, eyeing it critically. "Someone told me at supper that Stratford-on-Avon will be virtually finished by fall, except for the trees and grass."

"That's not quite what I meant." Professor Gull watched the dozen other occupants of the tent, who had settled down to games of cards or chess. A few were reading, and others were industriously reviewing papers they had brought from their offices. "Doesn't this seem—dishonest?"

"My dear fellow," said Dr. Hoop, unsnapping his cufflinks, "it's the only possible solution. Put yourself in the President's position. The frightful thing occurs—*wham.*" He dropped the cufflinks on his pillow and gave Gull a good-humored wink. "The President's job is to prevent an even bigger disaster. What reasonable alternative did he have?"

"I'm not sure. I've never been President. I only know that, as a historian, I don't think I can sit down at a desk in Future Section and start making things up. Truth is something precious, Hoop. It shouldn't be tampered with."

"Truth must serve the purposes of life, Gull. Life comes first."

"Men have given their lives for the sake of truth."

"Have they? I wonder," said Dr. Hoop. "Men have died for many things, I know, but I really doubt that truth is one of them. In any case, if we don't rebuild Britain, the Russians will do it alone—and make a shoddy job of it, too, I daresay." He took a coat hanger from the wall locker and examined it closely before hanging up his tie. "Why don't they have mirrors in these lockers?" he complained. However, he carried a small mirror in his wallet and used that in order to inspect his goatee. "I suggest we turn in, Gull. You'll feel better after a good night's sleep."

But Professor Gull did not get a good night's sleep. He was bothered by the snoring of the other men and by the howling of the wind outside the tent. For a long time he lay thinking about the England that existed now only in his travel folders. He thought, too, of the future Liberal Cabinet he had been promised, and wondered distractedly how he could find enough Liberals to staff the Ministries. Then he remembered that he would have to invent these Liberals himself. He could invent plenty of them if he wanted—tough, dark little politicians from Wales and the Marches, say, who would be fiery in debate, wily and irresistible at council tables; he could see them storming in and out of Commons. . . . His imagination plunged forward. He, Gull, might well resurrect the Liberal Party. He could restore its former fortunes. He might bring it to greatness, even. His future Liberals, what brilliance they would have, what wit, what energy, what genius—how proudly they would lead Britain into a new golden age!

He sat up, perspiring and ashamed. What right had he to speak to Dr. Hoop of historical truth, when the moment he closed his eyes he began spinning these self-serving fancies? He grimaced and rubbed his head. No matter, it was all folly, all dreams. He listened for a time to the snores around the tent. The devil of pride was puffing the egos of those peaceful sleepers, too.

The snores oppressed him. He put on his bathrobe and picked his way across to the entrance flap, opened it, and stepped outside.

The wind-whipped dust had swollen the moon and tinted it lavender. It shone like a bruised but benevolent eye on the dark clumps of tents, huts and vehicles, and on the heavy mass of Merton College. Across the plain, the winds raced and danced and scooped up more dust, sometimes blowing it into shapes that hung for a moment in the lavender light like the ghosts of the old colleges—spires that fell into towers which sank or soared or drifted away and then rushed back again as domes, as crumbling mansard roofs with toppling chimneys that stiffened, unpredictably, into spires again.

Another man was strolling nearby. Noticing Professor Gull, he approached with a polite series of coughs to make his presence known, and commented earnestly on the weather. "It is much milder here than in York," he said.

"You've been working in York?" asked Professor Gull.

"Yes. I am Russian. Lately I have been assigned to your Roman Ruins Section, as an observer."

"I see." Professor Gull looked at him with some interest, although it was too dark to see him clearly. The Russian was smoking a cigar; Professor Gull wished he had brought out his pipe. "Tell me, does your government have the same attitude as ours about this, um, project?"

"Oh, yes."

"There is no difference?"

"Very little. We are perhaps more serious. We need to be, you see, because we are more remote from British traditions than you. You will notice that although my English may be a bit stilted, my accent is—I trust—acceptably Oxonian."

"It's very good."

"Thank you," said the Russian. "That is the result of incessant practice. I spent a month at Leningrad at a special school before I came, being turned into an English gentleman—or perhaps I should say an English gentleman of Slavic descent. It was a bloody hard drill, I can assure you. We read, spoke and thought in nothing but English, day and night. For us, *Burke's Peerage* was light reading matter. It was kippers for breakfast, scones with our tea, and a game of footer every Saturday."

"That's thoroughgoing training for specialists who are just going to do a job and then leave."

"Leave? But we can't leave, old chap. We can hardly come in and build a facility with a capacity for sixty million people and let it stand idle. We've got to stay on and operate it as caretaker Englishmen until the new generations come along."

Professor Gull shivered as a sharp gust blew around the edge of the tent. The first light of dawn was reddening the Merton College scaffolding. "I don't intend to stay," he said. "They brought me here under false pretenses. This has nothing to do with me."

"It has everything to do with you," replied the Russian. "Who blew up Old Blighty? You did. And I helped. And who must restore it? *We* must."

"I didn't blow up England."

"You paid your taxes?"

"I had no choice."

"Ah, then you *did* blow it up."

Professor Gull was not disposed to argue the point. "Even granting that," he said, "it doesn't mean I have to restore England."

"Why not? It is a purely creative act, the restoration. And there is a practical side to it. Operation Phoenix is absorbing tremendous social forces that otherwise might be diverted to warlike ends. At least the funds spent on York Minster will not be used to place rifles in the hands of Islamic guerrillas. The restoration of England has already had a salutary effect on international tensions. Ultimately, it may become desirable to vaporize and then restore one nation every generation. That would ease the population pressure and provide a harmless outlet for human energy both at the same time."

"You're joking, and in bad taste."

"Stranger things have happened," said the Russian, "and in even worse taste."

"I think it is immoral to speak lightly of such matters."

"Today's jests are tomorrow's realities, sir. But morality, at least, does not enter into the question. It is, first of all, a matter of logic. The vaporization of Britain was the culmination of a logical historical development, was it not? History does have its logic. A terrible logic."

"It has no logic whatsoever."

"Think what you are saying!" the Russian exclaimed. "Without historical logic, what becomes of fatalism? And without fatalism, we are adrift!" He tossed the butt of his cigar away. "No, I cannot accept such a gloomy view. To my mind, the vaporization of Britain was logically necessary, in order to express the dual impulse of our age—vast devastation coupled with equally vast reconstruction. It jolly well *had* to happen. Too bad it wasn't Albania," he added, "but better luck next time."

"No good Marxist would talk that way," said Professor Gull severely. "As a matter of fact, this entire project must be an outrage to Marxist principles."

"Not in the least. That is the beauty of it. The good Marxist-Leninist believes in the primacy of environment over heredity. He knows that man can create the classless society. And what is the purpose of Operation Phoenix, sir? Merely to use this great truth in a different way. We are *re*creating the *class* society. A triumph of Marxism-Leninism!"

There was the stir of morning activity inside the tent as the occupants yawned and stretched and began to dress for the day. Professor Gull went back to his bunk, noticing that the canvas walls were decorated with travel posters, pinup pictures of nudes, and such oddments as a hotel "Do Not Disturb" sign. The humanists were full of banter and high spirits. A pillow fight was under way in one corner, and in another, two scholarly figures in striped pajamas were playfully tying ribbons in the beard of a slumbering colleague.

"Gull, let me introduce you to Dr. Knowles," said Dr. Hoop, presenting one of their tent mates. "Dr. Knowles is in genealogy. He was telling me about the maternity program."

"Repopulation program," Dr. Knowles corrected, with a smile. "We have six hospitals set up already, Professor Gull, each with a full obstetrical staff in attendance. Current output is only about a dozen a day per hospital, but we're building up fast. Hospital Six—that's at Leeds, and in fact at the moment it *is* Leeds—Hospital Six got its last consignment only yesterday. Five hundred young mothers-to-be from Denmark, and I can impregnate each and every one with the contents of a single test tube from the lab."

Professor Gull could think of nothing to say.

"I wouldn't, of course. We can't have five hundred little ones from the same sperm donor." Dr. Knowles selected a shirt from his wall locker and put it on. "We've got it all planned out, I can assure you. We mix them up according to a complicated program we worked out on the computer. Got to have the right proportion of Saxons and Vikings," he said, tying his tie, "and Danes, Norman French, and so forth." He buttoned his cuffs and winked at Professor Gull. "With a bit of Greek and Dago thrown in here and there."

"Are these, um, mothers under contract?"

"Of course. They get a good wage just for staying healthy."

"But what happens to the babies when they're born?"

"We've got villages here and there, you know. The first crop will go to Stratford. They're just a year old now, more or less. And the mothers can go with them, too, if they want to. We encourage that. It's not only a question of having a heart," said Dr. Knowles, "but of needing foster parents. We don't have fathers, of course, but in the modern home, the mother is the chief thing. You've got to have mummies."

"I'm sure you're right."

"The hospitals aren't our only source of supply. They're the controlled source, but we do import quite a few little chaps born on the wrong side of the blanket, as the saying goes, provided we can ascertain the father's identity and be sure he qualifies."

"You mean bastards," said Professor Gull.

"Right. Come to think of it, the whole damned future population of Britain will be bastards. But so was William the Conqueror. Pretty apt, isn't it."

"Everything seems apt," said Professor Gull.

He grieved for England. His heart was heavy and his head felt light, strange, and empty, as if a part of his brain had been vaporized, too. At night, he would take his travel folders from his locker and thumb through them sadly as he sat on his bunk. In the late afternoons he would tramp off into the Oxfordshire wasteland, to climb the naked slope that was Boar's Hill, or walk beside the sluggish Isis, choked with silt, and there he would sob aloud. He was alone. No one else seemed to care. Everyone was busy, serious, and working zestfully.

"This is all madness, Hoop."

"Life is mad, Gull." Dr. Hoop was cheerful. He had been assigned to write leaders for the London *Times* and found it much more stimulating than his Norman period.

"It's an insult to the memory of England."

"Imitation is the sincerest form of flattery."

"Besides, secrecy is impossible," said Professor Gull. "These babies in the new villages—as they grow up, do you think they won't find out? The project won't be half-finished when they reach manhood. What are they supposed to think when they see the construction squads putting up Blenheim Palace, say, or erecting the Marble Arch?"

"They'll think like true-born Englishmen, Gull, because they'll have been reared that way. If the history books and the teachers tell them that Blenheim was completed in 1722, that is the date they will accept, regardless of the evidence of their eyes."

"Brainwashing."

"Possibly. But that's the way the young always have been brought up. You and I, too, Gull. Why do we accept 1722 for Blenheim?"

"Because it's true—or was true."

"Because we've been trained to accept it. The new generations will accept it with equal readiness."

"Some won't," insisted Professor Gull, without conviction.

He tried the antidote proposed by Dr. McAmis. He plunged into his work. He invented dozens of Liberal leaders, painstakingly drafting their biographies, providing them with parents, wives, children, schools, managing their brilliant careers, sprinkling in some plausible setbacks—here a divorce, there a crippling illness, bankruptcy or scandal. His creations should have appealed to him as the sons he never had, and the rise of the Party should have offered him vicariously the triumph life had withheld. But it was like a game, and one he was not playing well. For his fiery young Liberals, he could write only dull speeches. Their stabs of wit were blunted by his pen. Their lightning raids on Tory and Labor constituencies became interminable sieges, and their savage political articles, boring tracts.

"I'm sorry," he told Dr. McAmis finally, "but I can't go on."

Dr. McAmis looked sympathetic. "You need a break, Gull. How about a week at Brighton? They're finishing up the Royal Pavilion. It's quite a sight."

"No, I don't mean that. I want to go back home, to America."

Dr. McAmis toyed with a pencil. Summer had arrived; the open windows admitted the racket of jackhammers from the Sheldonian Theater nearby. A truck went by, loaded with young trees for the Magdalen College deer park.

"I can't bring myself to have any part of this," Professor Gull added. "It may be all for the best, I don't know. I doubt it, frankly, but—well, I've decided to resign my grant. Immediately, if possible."

Dr. McAmis doodled on a pad of paper and said nothing.

"I'd be ready to leave today, in fact," said Professor Gull.

"You can't," said Dr. McAmis.

"Can't what?"

"You can't leave. No one can leave."

Professor Gull stared at him.

"Sorry, Gull," Dr. McAmis added.

"You're . . . joking."

"This is war, Gull," Dr. McAmis said, thrusting his jaw forward. "Thank God it's not a shooting war, but it's a war all the same. Call it a world emergency, call it anything you like. The point is that we are soldiers. And soldiers can't just pick up and quit whenever they feel like it."

"Do you mean that I'm not free to leave? That's . . . that's illegal detention, McAmis. No one mentioned anything of the kind in connection with the grants."

"Obviously secrecy forbade that."

"This is ridiculous." Professor Gull's head began to throb. He took off his glasses and thrust them into his breast pocket. "You simply cannot force me to stay."

"We're all in the same boat, Gull. You're a bachelor, but I've got a wife and three children back in New Haven. It'll be at least another year before families can be brought over. Do you think I enjoy being separated from my loved ones?" Dr. McAmis sighed deeply. "But I realize that this emergency requires certain sacrifices—and I'm prepared to make mine."

Professor Gull was breathing heavily. The jackhammers seemed to be beating at his skull. "I'm not a soldier," he said in a choked voice. "I'm a professor of history. I have dedicated my life to the acquisition and teaching of historical truth."

"So have we all, Gull. You know, some men just aren't right for Future. Maybe you're one of them. You might be happier in pre-Accident work. Suppose we transfer you to the Victorian Section? You'd be reconstructing there, not creating."

"What's the alternative?"

"There are dozens of alternatives. You might prefer Elizabethan or Jacobean. Then there are the Medieval Sections, or—"

"I mean, if I refuse to engage in any perversion of the scholar's creed, regardless of historical period."

Dr. McAmis looked reproachfully at Professor Gull. "I'm a scholar, too, you know. I and ninety-nine percent of the humanists in Operation Phoenix are dedicated to something a little bit higher than our own personal crotchets and preferences. We are serving the needs of mankind."

"Well, what about the other one percent?"

"They are assigned to the Service Branch—planting the forests, clearing the ponds and streams, maintaining vehicles. You wouldn't like it, Gull."

"Work gangs," said Professor Gull. "Forced labor. Concentration camps."

"That's no way to look at it. Look here," said Dr. McAmis, "I'm pretty sure I could get you a job in one of the Document labs. That would keep you off your feet."

Professor Gull thought of his pride and his corns, and said nothing.

"What are you doing, Gull?"

"Packing, Hoop. Leaving." Professor Gull began putting shirts and ties into his suitcase. "I'm saying good-bye to the future. They've had me transferred to the Documents Section, in London."

"We'll miss you."

"I'm afraid I haven't contributed much to group morale. Even now, I take small comfort in the thought that I will no longer be a liar and a cheat, but merely a forger."

"Ah, Gull. You are a perfectionist. That's your trouble. History has always been a mixture of true and false, you know, and forgery is not unknown to it. Each generation of historians has spent half its time correcting the distortions and errors of its predecessors. Even we, plowing virgin soil, will undoubtedly sow a crop of boners for our followers to harvest."

Professor Gull snapped his suitcase shut. "Oddly enough, that thought cheers me, Hoop. Future scholars will find our discrepancies. Bit by bit they will be able to piece together the real story of what happened."

"I quite agree."

"Well, doesn't that convince you that what you're doing is pointless?"

"Not at all. By that time it won't matter. England will have its continuity firmly established. The discovery of the Accident will cause quite a furor, comparable to Darwin's first assertions about the origin of man, but it will make no practical difference to the British people. No, Gull," said Dr. Hoop, "let the future take care of the past. In the present, we've got a job to do."

There were several other passengers in the plane for London. Like Professor Gull, they were being transferred because of their refusal to serve the project in their professional capacities. Heartened by the realization that at last he was among comrades, Professor Gull struck up conversations here and there in the course of the flight.

"I gather you're opposed to the restoration," he remarked to one scholar.

"Totally opposed. It's an outrage to humanity."

"I couldn't agree more."

"What an opportunity! America and Russia had a clean slate.

We could have done marvels in city planning. We could have produced a truly modern and scientifically engineered society—and what are we doing? Putting up the same old insanitary and inefficient facilities. It's an act of irresponsible folly."

Professor Gull responded sympathetically, but as soon as he could he moved to another seat and questioned his neighbor there.

"Why am I opposed?" the man replied. "Because it's an insult to my integrity as a scholar."

"Ah," said Professor Gull. "My feeling exactly."

"My position as the leading authority on Gladstone is unassailable, if I say so myself," the man continued. "And yet who is made chief of the Gladstone Subsection? A young upstart, one of these political climbers, a toady, a fellow of no distinction whatever." He glared at Professor Gull. "Obviously, I could not agree to serve under such a man."

"I see," said Professor Gull, excusing himself. With the others, he found similar stories. One man had been offended by the rejection of his plan to produce a biologically perfect society. Another, an expert in Irish history, was making a protest against the failure to budget Ireland, and a third was nursing a grievance against a refusal to consider his proposal that Britain become an international refuge for minority groups.

"What's your position?" the latter asked Professor Gull.

"I think the truth should be told," said Professor Gull. He himself was surprised. "The truth," he repeated. Yes, that was it. So simple, so inevitable. Just the truth.

"You don't say," the man commented. He suppressed a yawn and turned his attention to a magazine.

Professor Gull moved to a seat by himself. Looking out, he saw evidences of activity on the broad, bare plain. Tiny puffs of dust rose from the jeeps of surveyors who were laying out a road, and in the distance a working party was erecting a creek bridge. Then he noticed more than that. He saw now that a ghostly map of old England was sketched on the burned earth. Dark lines marked the routes of the highways. The towns had left blotchy scatterings of shadow and traceries of street networks, and there was a sharp straight streak where a railroad once had run. But of the people who had once lived in those towns and traveled those roads there was no sign nor trace. Professor Gull shivered in his seat. They had vanished—and so, it seemed, had truth.

Yet the truth should be restored, too, should it not? It ought to have some claim to be included in Operation Phoenix. After all, thought Professor Gull, the scholars who manned and directed the project were dedicated to the truth. Surely it was not absurd to suppose that they would honor that allegiance, if the question were brought to their attention. Or would they dismiss it as being irrelevant to the great task that so absorbed their energies? Professor Gull sighed. He did not know the answer. He was perplexed, and his head still ached. He gazed down at the Thames as it wound through the desolated land, past the shades of former towns. Would that one be Henley? There was a village, a real one, a new one, patched green with new grass and hopeful with young trees. Its cottages might be empty now, but surely next year or the year after that, the first children would be sent there, to grow and then to learn—but who would teach them, and what would they be taught? There would be two histories—one that would appear in the books and be read in the schools; another that would persist as subterranean myth and legend, whispered from one generation to the next, ignored or ridiculed by scholars, yet remaining alive, an unslayable heresy, until some future day—

"London Airport," announced the pilot over the loudspeaker. In a few moments, the plane landed.

The passengers were loaded into a small bus which bumped off through the billowing dust stirred up by the arrivals and departures of other aircraft—helicopters, heavy cargo planes, quick little jets carrying busy project officials, and old-fashioned transports moving technicians to and from all corners of Great Britain.

The road to London was paved. The city itself was lost in a haze of dust, but as the bus pounded toward it, Professor Gull seemed to see a distant structure familiar to him from countless photographs and drawings.

"Good Lord," he exclaimed, "that looks like the Tower of London."

"What did you expect?" asked the Irish expert. "The Taj Mahal?"

"But—that's incredible, to have built it so quickly."

"It took even less time to knock it down."

London was rising in an agony of construction. Its rebirth was like a great battle. Battalions of work crews charged into the dust and smoke, supported by the armor of trucks and tractors, and from time to time there came a heavy cannonading of dynamite touched off by excavation squads. The brown Thames held a navy of barges, and overhead hovered helicopters from which architects and engineers peered down, directing their forces by radio. Some streets were surfaced; others were muddy tracks; most did not yet exist. Everywhere were workmen knitting together the fibers of new structures, scores of machines digging, scooping, lifting, hammering, and supervisors speeding by on bicycles, motorbikes or in jeeps, with blueprints clutched in their arms.

Professor Gull's bus driver seemed to be lost. He swore loudly, shook his fist at vehicles which drummed across his path, and leaned out the window several times to ask directions, but without apparent satisfaction. The bus blundered about, and the passengers were treated to an impromptu tour of London and a succession of bewildering, contradictory sights.

St. Paul's was a stockpile of stone and timber, awaiting construction. On the site of Westminster Abbey, two architects were arguing over a blueprint, up to their ankles in mud. Nelson's monument lay on its side at Trafalgar Square, waiting for cranes to raise it. The Tower was the only major structure which was, to outward appearances, finished; it even displayed a Beefeater in full dress at the main gate and clipped ravens slouching on the green, but it stood alone at the edge of a vast plain stretching to the east, where not even a surveying party had yet ventured. Several blocks along Fleet Street had been virtually completed, too, and a pub there was open for business, serving thirsty laborers. Occasionally the ground trembled: the subway system was being restored, too.

Professor Gull gazed in fascination at the vision of London's restoration. Here was the Strand, a trough of tire tracks and construction refuse, and in its center was the church of St. Clement Danes (minus its tower), being used as headquarters for the Russian and American military police charged with traffic control. A Soviet officer stood smoking on the steps. Beyond, on the site of the Courts of Justice, dozens of lions were stockpiled—lions of stone, of metal, of concrete, painted gold or silver, lions of all sizes, some couchant, some rampant, some in bas-relief, and others in high relief. A workman was sanding one down, presumably to give a weathered effect. Elsewhere were rows of stone gargoyles and colonnades, stacks of hitching posts, traffic signs, piles of Portland stone labeled "18th Cent., Pre-Aged," iron gates and fences, bricks, streetlamps, fire hydrants, and a pissoir, shipped in by mistake.

The bus driver at last found his way to his destination in Kensington Gardens and began discharging his passengers at various Quonset huts there. Professor Gull was let off in front of one marked "Documents, Personnel." Inside were banks of filing cabinets attended by six or seven clerks, and several desks, at one of which sat a young man who politely beckoned him to be seated for an interview.

Professor Gull was weary and confused. He wanted a cup of coffee and a quiet place to take a nap, and he found himself struggling to give clear answers to the questions of the interviewer. The filing cabinets depressed him. They seemed to be a more imposing proof of the irreversibility of Operation Phoenix than the Tower. Within each drawer were dozens of dossiers. There were hundreds altogether; the sum of human energy and ambition they represented was beyond reckoning—and this was just one section.

"In view of your academic background, sir," the interviewer was saying, "we're going to assign you as a supervisor. You'll be in charge of a group of technicians who actually make documents. The requisitions are sent in by the various sections—Victorian, Jacobean and so forth—and these are distributed to the supervisors. The supervisors work out the details with the parchment men, the draftsmen, the aging experts and whatever other specialists may be needed to meet the requirements, and then the work proceeds. Finished documents are reviewed and approved by the supervisor in charge, and then are dispatched to the section which made the requisition."

"A supervisor has quite a responsibility."

"Yes, indeed. You've got to have a sharp eye and a clear head. Familiarity with history is a great help, too. We've got a fine bunch in Documents, Professor Gull, but even so, there are mistakes sometimes."

"What kind of mistakes?"

"Wrong dates. Wrong names. That kind of thing. Sometimes the parchment isn't properly aged."

"Do you correct these things?" asked Professor Gull.

"Lord, yes. We can't let any goofs get through."

"But I suppose that there are some errors which no one discovers."

The interviewer looked uncomfortable. "We don't concede that. We aim for perfection. We have to, sir. Anything short of total authenticity is—well, it wouldn't be good for the project. It would make us look ridiculous."

"That would be terrible," said Professor Gull. The thought refreshed him. He glanced more cheerfully around the hut. "But some documents can't be authentic, can they? You can make a perfect reproduction of the Magna Carta, say, because there must be hundreds of facsimiles, but what about the more obscure documents, which existed only in the original?"

"These present problems," admitted the interviewer. "We do the best we can on them. We build up composite specifications from all available sources—the memories of professors who had read them, paraphrases and quotations printed in extant books and manuscripts, and the like."

"But the end product cannot be authentic. It may be a sound job of scholarship, even a brilliant approximation, but not authentic."

The interviewer frowned. "All documents are officially declared authentic, Professor Gull."

"What about those for Future Section?"

"Those are even more authentic than the others."

"Of course." Professor Gull smiled. He felt happier than he had for weeks. The logic of Operation Phoenix demanded faultless authenticity, and as that was impossible—for nothing whatever could be authentic—then the logic fell apart, and so, reasoned Professor Gull, should the project itself.

"I suppose Documents has a review board to examine all finished work before it is sent out," he said.

"Only in special cases," the interviewer replied. "We can't make a practice of it. The volume of documents is too great. We must rely on the expertise of our supervisors, and, of course, on the judgment of the scholars in the various sections."

"Yes, I see." Professor Gull exhaled a sigh of satisfaction. There was a crack in the ramparts of Phoenix. Perhaps it could be widened. Errors had crept in from time to time inadvertently; what would happen if they were pumped in deliberately, generously?

"Do you have any particular questions?" asked the interviewer.

"No, no. Everything sounds perfect to me." Professor Gull felt renewed. He rubbed his hands together; then, more soberly, he reflected that he should not exult but rather should maintain an attitude of gravity and dedication. His aim, after all, was to keep faith with the soul of England and with truth. It was a solemn obligation. Nevertheless, he could not repress a feeling of ebullience, even of gaiety. His opportunity had come, and he resolved to make the most of it.

Professor Gull bided his time. For several weeks he devoted himself to his duties as a Documents supervisor. The technicians under his command sedulously produced whatever the requisitions called for: account books for medieval estates, parchment records of Plantagenet law cases, diaries of rural parsons, letters, bills, vouchers, Roman tiles, modern Cabinet minutes, village church registers, even graffiti on the walls of public conveniences. Professor Gull learned his new trade thoroughly. He gained the respect of the technicians and the confidence of his superiors. As a mark of esteem, he was allowed to do five pages of Holinshed's great chronicle, on which the section leaders particularly commended him, and hinted, too, that he would not be forgotten when the time came for the next major project, the Shakespeare Folios.

His birthday fell in November, and he chose it as the occasion for his first creation. It was a short note from Dr. Johnson to Boswell, of no particular interest, except that it referred tantalizingly to portions of Boswell's journals which had never been found. The technicians did a neat job on Dr. Johnson's note, and

Professor Gull tucked it into the package for Oxford containing some Johnsoniana which had been requisitioned. Then he set to work drawing specifications for his next production—some shredded but still legible fragments of the missing Boswell journals. These were followed by others, in quick order: a diary kept by King John, including some sour reflections on the Runnymede barons; forty-three love sonnets by Isaac Newton; a parchment letter in Latin written by a provincial lord, providing contemporary evidence that Richard the Third did murder the little princes after all, and an Elizabethan playbill, flaking with age, announcing three plays by Shakespeare which no one then or since had ever heard of.

Professor Gull had seldom been so alert and tireless. The imagination which had stumbled over the future Liberal Cabinet was racing forward now, as he dispatched fraud after fraud to Oxford. How many could he produce before they stopped him? It did not matter. That playbill alone would be enough for his purposes. Still, a week passed, and nothing happened. There was no inquiry, no message, no telephone call. Professor Gull became bolder. He turned out documents that proved that Bacon wrote Shakespeare and that the Earl of Oxford wrote Bacon, that William of Normandy was no bastard but that Queen Victoria was, that the Spanish Armada actually defeated Drake, that Gladstone was a bigamist and, finally, that Cromwell was a woman.

The expected summons came at last. The section deputy stopped by one morning. "How are things going, Gull?" he inquired pleasantly.

"I'm forging ahead," said Professor Gull.

"By the way, the Chief of History Branch phoned me a few minutes ago. It seems he wants to see you up at Oxford. He didn't say why, but he said he hoped you'd catch the afternoon shuttle."

Professor Gull nodded and began closing his desk. He thought that the others might as well close theirs, too, and then reproved himself for unwarranted optimism. Operation Phoenix was too big a dragon to succumb to one blow—and he, alas, was no St. George. Even so, he whistled cheerfully all the way out to the airport and lightheartedly blew a kiss toward London when the plane banked and headed northwest.

The towers of Oxford caught the sunlight. He could see them shining in the distance. He counted seven colleges—and others were rising. Several streets had taken recognizable shape, and there were a few patches of green turf, with young trees braced against the winter winds. Beside the airstrip in Christ Church meadow was a wooden sign in Russian and English which announced to incoming passengers that Oxford was seventeen percent completed as of November 15 (with a footnote reporting that Cambridge was only three percent completed).

The office of the Chief of History Branch was in the Bodleian Library. It was a small room paneled in aged oak, with a tiny fireplace above which hung a portrait of the founder, Sir Thomas Bodley, glistening where the paint had not yet fully dried. Professor Gull recognized the occupants of the room, who rose politely as he entered. They were all section heads, eminent historians; among them was his former superior, Dr. McAmis of Future. They were wearing academic robes (those of the History Chief being supplemented by an ornamental chain) and were sipping port as if they had been Oxford dons for years.

This gathering of robed majesty was solemn and impressive. Professor Gull muttered to himself, "Courage!", and shook hands all around.

"Some port, Gull?" asked the History Chief.

"Thank you." He took a generous swallow. On a table near the window, he noticed, some of his productions had been laid out as exhibits—the Boswell journal pages, the Latin letter about King Richard, and the bogus autopsy report on Cromwell.

"Well, now, Gull," the History Chief said, when the amenities had been concluded, "we've called you up here out of deference to your past standing in the academic community. The ordinary Documents supervisor would merely have been transferred and downgraded, you see, but you are, after all, a full professor. We're a bit curious to know just what was on your mind with these, ah, inventions of yours." He gestured toward the table. "I mean to say, take this business about Cromwell. Isn't that going too far, Gull, even as a little joke?"

"It wasn't a joke, sir," replied Professor Gull. He was interested to see that the History Chief had undergone an Anglicizing process in recent months, and so, to some extent, had the others.

A Russian who headed one of the Medieval sections affected a monocle and kept exclaiming "By Jove" at intervals.

"Not a joke, eh?" said the History Chief. He blinked and gave his nose a thoughtful pull. "Well, what in blazes is it? What are you trying to prove, then?"

"Nothing. I am merely being faithful to the spirit of Operation Phoenix."

"The spirit of Phoenix is authenticity, Gull," said the History Chief. "You can't square that with these pranks of yours."

"I'm surprised to hear you say that, sir," said Professor Gull. "You accuse me of playing jokes, but I assure you that my documents are valid—"

"Ridiculous," broke in the Chief of Stuart Section, who was particularly offended over the Cromwell report.

"—and since you've asked me about it, I'll be very glad to prove to your satisfaction that everything I've turned out is properly within the scope of Operation Phoenix."

"My dear fellow," said the History Chief, "we do appreciate new ideas and initiative and all that, but you can't expect us to swallow these monstrosities of yours. Love poetry by Newton, and this slur against Gladstone—these are out-and-out phonies, Gull."

"My documents are as authentic as most," said Professor Gull. "What about the ones which have to be approximated? Those aren't authentic. They're fakes."

"That's scholarship, Gull, not fakery. Those documents have a solid basis behind them."

Professor Gull turned toward Dr. McAmis. "What about the documents for Future Section? What basis do those have?"

"Those are creations, of course," said Dr. McAmis.

"So are mine."

"But yours are fabrications, deliberate whoppers."

"There's a difference between past and future, Gull," the History Chief said. "You can't justify your fakes with this kind of reasoning."

"My documents aren't necessarily fakes," Professor Gull insisted. "They are contradictory to other documents of the past, it is true. But so are many which you have specifically requisitioned."

"I know what you mean, Gull, and it's another false trail. You're referring to source material which brings into question the accepted interpretation of certain historical events. But those are not bogus. They existed before the Accident. The case of the little princes in the Tower is an example. There is evidence both for and against King Richard. There are discrepancies, I admit. But, dammit, these are old and established discrepancies, Gull. You had no right to invent *new* ones."

"Didn't I? But what about the documents that were never discovered?"

"Eh?"

"How about the documents that hadn't been found at the time of the Accident?"

The History Chief gave Professor Gull a hard look. "See here, Gull," he began.

"Suppose there hadn't been any Accident," said Professor Gull. "That's the whole theory of the project: that the Accident never happened. Well," he went on, "don't you suppose that old documents would have kept turning up from time to time in the attics of manor houses, in old chests and cupboards, or stuffed into holes in the walls, and so forth?"

"Perhaps," said the History Chief.

"You know they would. They always did. Hardly a year would pass in the old days without some important find. And not a few of these were contradictory documents, in the sense that they forced scholars to revise their views about past events, did they not?"

The History Chief began to fiddle with his chain. "In some cases," he muttered.

"Well, then, what about these old undiscovered documents? Where are they? What provision does Operation Phoenix make for them?"

The robed scholars shifted position uneasily and glanced at one another.

"There isn't any provision," Professor Gull continued. "So in my small way, I was trying to fill the vacancy. You may not approve of my initial selections, but you must admit that my idea is sound."

The History Chief blew out a big breath. "I admit nothing of the kind, Gull. There's a certain surface plausibility about your argument, but—well, dammit, it's wrong underneath."

"Where?" asked Professor Gull. There was an uncomfortable silence in the room. The History Chief frowned at his fingernails and the Russian medievalist uttered another "By Jove."

"My documents may not have existed," said Professor Gull. "I'm willing to concede that. My point is that they *might* have. And even if they didn't, comparable documents certainly did, and they would have been discovered in the course of time if the Accident hadn't intervened. Surely the claims of such undiscovered old documents to be reproduced now for the use of historians should not be denied merely to satisfy a narrow interpretation of Operation Phoenix. What about the Lost Plays of Shakespeare?"

"There weren't any," said the History Chief, wiping his forehead.

"How do you know there weren't? Just because none had been discovered before the Accident doesn't mean there weren't any. What do you think Shakespeare was doing at Stratford the last few years of his life? Suppose he'd been writing some new plays. A dedicated playwright just doesn't drop his pen, you know. Shaw was still writing at the age of ninety. Shakespeare might have written a dozen plays up there. His memoirs, too, for all we know."

The Chief of Elizabethan Section gulped his port.

"Take the Boswell journals," Professor Gull continued.

"Those were *found*," said the History Chief.

"True. But suppose they hadn't been found before the Accident? What a terrible loss to history and literature that would have been—and what a responsibility to future generations you would have borne, gentlemen, for having suppressed them."

"How the devil could we suppress something no one would have known about?"

"Ah," said Professor Gull, "but it would have been your job to find out. That is your job now. No one else will if you don't. Your failure to deduce the probable existence of undiscovered documents and to produce them amounts to suppression, as I see it. Inasmuch as it is not unlikely that Shakespeare wrote several Lost Plays, your attitude is nullifying what were perhaps the Bard's greatest works."

"The Lost Plays don't exist!" cried out the Elizabethan Chief.

"They don't now," agreed Professor Gull. "But—did they *once?*"

The Elizabethan Chief began to twitch at the corners of his mouth.

"Getting back to Boswell," Professor Gull said, "we know that not all of his journals were recovered. Where's the rest, I'd like to know? Why isn't somebody working on it?"

A moan came from the Chief of Mid-Hanoverian Section. "I'd give my right arm for it," he exclaimed, "but we can't just sit down and make it up, can we?"

"Of course you can. You must. It's part of Operation Phoenix. The restoration of Britain won't be complete without it. You can't leave these gaps—and it's now or never, gentlemen. I'm surprised," said Professor Gull, "that this aspect of the project hasn't been covered before."

The History Chief, sweating visibly, intervened to ask for a break in the discussion. "Well, dammit, there's more here than meets the eye. I'm going to take a walk to clear my head. We'll resume in ten minutes."

During the recess, Dr. McAmis approached Professor Gull. "Forgive me for speaking bluntly, Gull, but your line of reasoning is based on an absurdity."

"I quite agree."

"Deliberate fakery of documents—that can lead to all sorts of things."

"Exactly."

"Once you begin adulterating the truth," Dr. McAmis said, "there's no telling what will happen."

"My very point," said Professor Gull.

"The project could be made to look foolish."

"True."

"I mean to say, who could tell the difference between truth and falsehood? The whole business would become confused and dubious, and no self-respecting scholar would want to be associated with it."

"Precisely. I'm glad you see that." Professor Gull glanced around the room, where those Chiefs who had not gone for a stroll were whispering urgently together.

"Why do you keep agreeing with me, Gull? Weren't you sincere in your arguments?"

"Of course not. If I'd been sincere, no one would have listened.

I had to make a little *cause célèbre* with my Cromwell and Gladstone to get a hearing." Professor Gull winked at Dr. McAmis. "But now it's all right. I've made my point, and once it sinks in, everyone will realize the basic trouble with the project, just as you do now."

Dr. McAmis seemed pained. "You weren't sincere?"

"Not in the slightest."

"Oh." Dr. McAmis pondered Professor Gull's insincerity. "I begin to see what you're driving at, then. But even so, you did have a few good points. This matter of the Lost Plays, for example. It *would* be a shame if—"

The History Chief returned to the room and took his chair. "Gentlemen," he said, and the others sat down, too. He blew his cheeks out and adjusted his spectacles. "Well, Professor Gull, we're indebted to you for a stimulating and provocative session. You've made us all think anew about the meaning of Operation Phoenix, and we're grateful for that. For my own part, however, I can't begin to adopt your extreme position. Oh, we might agree to do a little bit of reconstruction work on the missing Boswell journals—that's not so hard—but the other things—definitely not. That business about Gladstone is out of the question."

"Excuse me, but do you mean to say you'd consider accepting my Boswell but not my Gladstone?" asked Professor Gull in amazement. "But what's the difference between them?"

"I didn't say we'd accept *your* Boswell. If we accepted any Boswell, it would be a Boswell turned out by a committee of our top Boswell men. You'll be the first to admit that Boswell's not your period, Gull."

"But the principle—!"

"Yes, yes, the principle. I daresay we couldn't accept anybody's Boswell except Boswell's Boswell. It wouldn't be right." The History Chief turned to the Mid-Hanoverian, who was a leading Boswellian. "Would it?"

The Mid-Hanoverian moistened his lips and said nothing.

"No, it wouldn't be right," continued the History Chief. "It would be fun, though," he added thoughtfully. Then, feeling that he had been betrayed into an impropriety, he blushed and cleared his throat. "Do you have anything further to add, Gull?"

Professor Gull stood up anxiously. "You don't seem quite to have gotten my point. I thought you'd see it at once, but—"

"Pardon me." The head of the Jacobean Section also rose. He was a corpulent man whose florid face was now dominated by a knowing smile. "If you'll allow me to speak in your behalf, Professor Gull," he said, "I may be able to clarify matters. I do believe that I'm beginning to see what you mean." He gave Professor Gull a friendly nod, and Professor Gull, much relieved, sat down. The Jacobean rubbed his meaty hands together and surveyed his audience with a practiced and good-humored eye. "Gull's been having a bit of fun with us, gentlemen," he said, "but he's got a serious point. In fact, it goes right to the heart of Operation Phoenix, doesn't it, Gull?"

"Absolutely," said Professor Gull, further relieved.

"Right to the heart," repeated the Jacobean. He turned to the History Chief. "Let us set the question of Boswell aside for the moment, and look at the big picture. By 'big picture,'" he added, "I mean nothing less than the purpose of the project itself. What is that purpose? Is it not, sir, to maintain the continuity of British history?"

"In a sense, I suppose," said the History Chief.

"And what is this continuity of history?" inquired the portly Jacobean, obviously relishing his role as Professor Gull's spokesman. "Isn't it an unbroken chain of events reaching from prehistory all the way through the latest future years being planned on the drafting tables of Dr. McAmis's section?"

"Well, yes," agreed the History Chief.

"And doesn't this continuity consist of two parts? The restoration, in the past, of the history that *was*—and the creation, for the future, of the history that *would have been?*"

"You might put it that way," conceded the History Chief.

The Jacobean began portentously to pace; the floorboards creaked beneath him. "History is truth, is it not?"

"Ah, yes. Ideally, that is."

"And the work of Future Section is to create the truth."

"Well—"

"The truth that would have been true?"

"I can't disagree with that," said the History Chief.

"Let's call it a *presumptive* truth," said the Jacobean. "How about that, Gull?"

"All right," said Professor Gull.

"Very good," declared the Jacobean, giving Gull a wink and a jowl wag. "Presumptive truth it is, then. And since the entire project is unified, and since history is an unbroken chain of events, presumptive truth is the basis of all of it."

"Well, now," said the History Chief uncertainly.

The Jacobean turned his abundant bulk in Dr. McAmis's direction.

"Dr. McAmis, would you mind telling us the name of the British Prime Minister?"

"Um, it's Donaldson," replied Dr. McAmis. "You know, Conservative."

"Thank you. And why was Donaldson picked?"

"It was a committee decision," said Dr. McAmis, defensively. "He seemed to be the most logical choice."

"That is to say, if there had been no Accident, Donaldson might very well have made it. On the basis of presumptive truth, we have Prime Minister Donaldson. And, to take an example from the past, inasmuch as there is no present proof to the contrary, it is also presumptively true that William Pitt was Prime Minister in 1800."

"What do you mean, 'presumptively true'?" asked the History Chief.

"I mean that all historical facts—past and present—are presumptively true unless proven otherwise."

"Dammit, Pitt *was* Prime Minister. You cannot possibly prove otherwise."

"Exactly!" rumbled the Jacobean. "That's what Gull has been driving at all along. Logically, Pitt and Donaldson exist in history on an identical basis—that of presumptive truth—and yet we defy this logic in our actual practice. Right, Gull?"

"Right," said Professor Gull.

"What do you mean, 'defying logic'?" asked the History Chief.

"Shall I tell him, Gull?" asked the Jacobean.

"Please do," said Professor Gull.

"Very well." The Jacobean stepped back a pace and folded his arms. "Gentlemen," he declared, "we have frozen history."

No one said anything. Professor Gull wiped his palms on his trouser legs. The History Chief opened and closed his mouth several times, and one of the Russians took a pinch of snuff. The Chief of Plantagenet Section was the first to speak.

"Would you explain that, please?"

"It's simple," said the Jacobean. "By refusing to consider the reconstruction of documents which hadn't been discovered before the Accident, we are denying the validity of the whole project. Worse than that, we are drying up history itself. Research will become meaningless. Nothing new will be found, naturally. Where will doctorates come from?"

"Good Lord!" exclaimed the History Chief.

"Who will want to devote their careers to such history?" asked the Jacobean. "I certainly wouldn't. Who will even want to study it? No one. And finally, who will even *believe* in it?"

"Stop—no more," said the History Chief in agitation. "Look here, you may have uncovered something. We don't want to be hasty, but maybe we'd better set up a committee to work this thing over and come up with a report."

"I'll vote for that," said the Mid-Hanoverian. Several others expressed their assent, too.

"There's one thing that appeals to me right now," said Dr. McAmis, "and that's this business of contradictory documents. As far as Future Section is concerned, we'd better have some of those. I'm not thinking so much of the degree candidates—although I agree that we can't forget them—but what about the realism of the thing? We can't have history down too pat, can we? It would look odd."

The meeting broke up into a babble of individual voices as the Section Chiefs began to discuss the relative merits of Professor Gull's arguments. Gull himself sat in his chair, wiping his spectacles and blinking around in confusion. Things had not gone as he had planned. Far from having been slain, the dragon seemed to have sprouted a second head.

The Jacobean came over and clapped him on the shoulder. "We've carried the day, Gull. I was worried for a moment, but— well, how did you like that bit about presumptive truth?"

"Your logic was remarkable," said Professor Gull. "But the conclusion you drew from it wasn't quite what I—"

"No false modesty!" the Jacobean admonished him, in playful reproof. "The credit is yours entirely, Gull. I was merely seconding your motion, so to speak. I was glad to be of service." He chuckled, and waddled off to find the port.

Professor Gull was wondering what, if anything, he could do, when the Elizabethan Chief approached with a confidential smile.

"Your views are refreshing, Gull," he said.

Professor Gull suddenly felt like weeping.

"This freezing of history," the Elizabethan continued. "It's a telling point. For example, several years ago I was over here on my sabbatical—that was before the Accident—and I ran onto a clue to the existence of some letters by the Earl of Oxford. Unfortunately, I had to return before I found them, but"—he cleared his throat and lowered his voice—"just between ourselves, Gull, do you really believe that Shakespeare was capable of writing the tragedies? Some of the comedies, perhaps, and most of the histories—but *Lear* and *Hamlet?*"

Professor Gull mumbled a noncommittal response.

"It's always been my dream, you see, to establish the real authorship," the Elizabethan Chief went on. "I'm not pledged to the Earl. Not a bit. My mind is open. And I don't have any truck with the theory of examining the plays themselves for internal evidence. You can prove whatever you want that way. No, the only thing is documentation. Cold, hard contemporary stuff, eh?"

Several of the scholars were inspecting Professor Gull's exhibits. The Mid-Hanoverian was fingering the Boswell journal fragments speculatively, and the Russian medievalist was examining the parchment libel against King Richard. From the group around the History Chief came excited phrases:

"Gull's right. It's all very well now for us to play it safe by restoring only established documents—"

"But later on, what? We've got to think of the future of the past."

"We're creating a rigid image. History must be flexible at all costs."

"And as Gull said, it's now or never."

"Very well, dammit," came the voice of the History Chief, "but how can we control this thing? I mean, you can't turn every mother's son loose on his pet project. It would be chaos."

"Set up a review board—"

"—a commission—"

"Committees in each section—"

Professor Gull could stand no more. He tugged at the nearest robe. "You don't understand," he cried out. "It's all a lie—the whole thing! That's what I was trying to tell you!"

The circle around the History Chief opened to admit him. Friendly faces beamed at him. "My purpose," said Professor Gull, breathing heavily, "was to show you the dishonesty of the project itself—"

"You've done that, Gull," said the History Chief, reassuringly. " 'Dishonesty' is not the word I'd choose, however. 'Incompleteness' would be better, I think."

The Stuart Chief reached out and shook Professor Gull's hand. "I want to apologize to you, Gull," he said. "I behaved rather badly over that Cromwell autopsy, I'm afraid. That was small of me. I failed to grasp your idea."

"You've grasped it too well," said Professor Gull, with a sinking heart.

"We owe you a great debt. You have given the project a new and compelling justification."

"So I fear."

The Stuart Chief smiled. "Oh, you needn't worry that we'll buy that business about Cromwell's being a woman. That example is far-fetched, of course, but there are some rough spots in the old boy's career that need smoothing out, document-wise, and I think we owe it to our successors to do what we can."

Professor Gull nodded. Then he turned away as the historians resumed their discussion of the best practical means of administering this newest program. His shoulders quivered and his chest was heaving. There were tears in his eyes, but he could not help chuckling, and when he glanced up at the damp portrait above the hearth, he laughed outright. Sir Thomas Bodley was gazing down, with one eyelid slightly lowered, as if caught in a supercilious wink. Professor Gull winked back.

"Welcome home, Gull," said Dr. Hoop.

"Thank you, but I won't be staying more than a few days." Professor Gull sat down on his bunk and unlaced his shoes. With the onset of cold weather, the humanists had been moved out of tents and into permanent structures; Dr. Hoop and his tent mates had been assigned to the Sheldonian Theater. Space heaters had been installed, but most of the warmth rose instantly to the giant dome.

Professor Gull wrapped a blanket around his shoulders to ward off the drafts. He told Dr. Hoop about his experiences in London, his documentary inventions and his plan, and how the History Branch chieftains had, unexpectedly, adapted it to serve their own purposes. "Now I'm something of a hero," he concluded. "They've even asked me to serve on the review board they're setting up to issue grants for new documents."

"Success often comes when it is least expected," agreed Dr. Hoop.

"I was a fool, Hoop. That's the size of it. I underestimated the agility of human imagination. I blundered."

"You blundered brilliantly, at any rate."

"True. It is a fanciful thought, but I have come to think of myself lately as a kind of repository of British virtues. Possibly the sole repository." Professor Gull shivered in the chill air and hugged his blanket more tightly. "My life has been an undistinguished one. I have labored quietly and to small effect. And yet when the occasion arose and I found myself in adversity, I was equal to it. I became a British lion. I was, if you will forgive me, magnificent. I roared, Hoop. And although I made matters decidedly worse, I can take some satisfaction in the spirit of my performance."

"Perhaps it is all for the best, Gull."

"You may be right. But whatever happens, my moment has come and gone."

"What are your plans?"

"I shall retire," said Professor Gull firmly. "They cannot deny me that. I shall demand it as my reward." He sneezed, and the sneeze echoed delicately high in the dome. "I always wanted to retire to England. It was my dream. I shall, at least, be granted that. . . . Would you care to take a stroll before lights out?"

"No, thank you. It's too cold for me."

Professor Gull wrapped his scarf around his neck and pulled his cap down over his ears. Outside, a frigid mist drifted in the streets, shrouding the stars. The stone masks of the Caesars that orna-mented the Sheldonian's exterior were wet as if with tears, and a solitary cyclist creaking by made a black track on the shining pavement. Professor Gull wandered off in the fog, pausing only to wipe his glasses and to blow on his hands. He saw, dimly, Oxford arising—the old colleges struggling up where they had stood before, some of them already lighted and sheltering scholars, as they always had; soon enough undergraduates would be back, pimpled and chattering, and old dons would be nodding over their wine, and American tourists would be snapping pictures of the deer at Magdalen, and there would be crowds for Eights Week.

He leaned against the massive base of the Radcliffe Camera, staring up at the dark towers of All Souls. Who could tell? Perhaps it had all happened before. Suppose this were the second time—or the tenth? The England they were so diligently copying now, that might have been bogus, too.

Professor Gull did retire. He became Britain's first pensioner. Although he was provided with a snug cottage in a Cottswold village, he spent most of his time traveling around. For years there was hardly an important public ceremony he did not attend. When Salisbury Cathedral was reconsecrated, Professor Gull could be seen kneeling reverently in the nave; at the raising of the final monolith at Stonehenge, he appeared on his bicycle, with his lunch in a paper bag; at the coronation of young Henry X, he was in the first row of Abbey seats allotted to commoners; when the London-Edinburgh railway was opened, he purchased the first ticket (second-class). He was a frequent visitor to the spas. At Cheltenham he drank mineral water and walked the Promenade in plus-fours; at Brighton he bathed in the Channel, and at Black-pool he played golf. In time, he became a minor authority on rural church architecture, and saved the designers from many an in-felicity. At home, he gardened as actively as his increasing years would permit, maintained a housekeeper and a dog, and read widely in history and literature (although he declined to examine the complimentary copies of the Lost Plays as, one by one, they were brought out, handsomely printed and meticulously anno-tated).

He still maintained his interest in the Liberal Party and wrote papers for the historical journals, all dealing with Liberal events early in the century. As for the modern Party, revived and reaching once again for power, he kept a dignified silence, following its fortunes in the *Times*, but eschewing all opportunity for comment. His public appearances became less frequent. The last one of note was a lecture on politics at Eton, in which he spoke feelingly of great men of times past and refused, when pressed by his youthful listeners, to compare them to present-day leaders. "We must await the judgment of history," said Professor Gull solemnly. Then he chuckled, descended from the platform with a flourish of his cane, and, still chuckling, hobbled off in the direction of Windsor Castle nearby, which he had resolved, he told everyone, to see once more before he died.

Neighbors

¶ The new people moved into the Sutter place so quietly that they were settled there almost before the town knew they had arrived. One minute, it seemed, the old house was empty, just as it had been for nearly ten years, with its shutters closed and the yard all overgrown with weeds; and then, as quick as a witch's charm, there were lighted windows, and a woman moving in the kitchen, and a tall man standing out on the half-rotted front porch, squinting around in a calculating way at the weeds he would have to cut and clear.

Mrs. Grant, down the road, was the first to pay a call. It was dusk, but she hurried out anyway, carrying the pie she had intended for her husband's supper, shielding it with her apron from the autumn dust and whirring bugs. Her husband had grumbled: "Leave 'em be till morning," but Mrs. Grant knew better. In the morning, there would be half a dozen women trotting over to meet the new neighbors. Yes, Mrs. Grant told herself as she struggled through the heavy weeds, it was necessary to call at once—now—so they would know that they were among friends.

"How d'you do?" she called out to the tall man, who still stood on the porch, now watching her labored progress.

He raised his hand to his head, but he wore no hat and so simply smoothed his graying hair.

"Yes, ma'am," he said politely.

Mrs. Grant pushed her way through the last of the weeds, twisting her head aside from the high ragweed tufts so that her seamed cheeks swung. The man stepped down to greet her, his long hands describing the beginning of some courtly gesture which remained incomplete, as though he had been preparing to assist her to descend from a carriage.

"My name's Nettie Grant, just a neighbor woman," she said, panting a little from her exertion. She whipped the apron flap from the pie. "Don't want to bother you folks, moving in and all, but I know how it is, things all upside down, and maybe your wife'd like a little bit of pie I thought I'd run over, that's all."

"Well, that's very kind of you, ma'am." The man looked soberly at her face. "Our name's Taylor," he said. He glanced back briefly at the house, where the floorboards could be heard creaking beneath footsteps. "Well, now," he said, "won't you step in and meet my missus? She'll sure be glad to see you."

"Oh, I couldn't, not but just a minute."

"She'll be mighty glad," the man repeated, with the beginning of a smile. "Watch your step, ma'am," he added. "This porch is rickety." Again he spread his hands delicately, in a tentative welcoming motion that was the more flattering to Mrs. Grant's sense of gentility because it was never completely defined. As he paused to hold the door for her, she glanced up into his face. It was grave and heavily lined, but the angled jaw gave it a mildly sardonic cast. A withdrawn man, but kindly, she thought, and she resolved she would repay his dignity by making her visit short.

"Mother, we've got a neighbor lady visiting," Taylor called out.

His wife came quickly in from the direction of the kitchen, deftly smoothing her hair. Younger than her husband, she was handsome in an unobtrusive way, with the calm yet abstracted manner of an experienced and competent mother. She, too, was polite and dignified, yet deferent enough to satisfy Mrs. Grant, who was conscious of her position as an older woman come to call with a practical gift.

"Ah, you've got a little one," Mrs. Grant remarked at length, eyeing a playpen surrounded by unpacked boxes in one corner of the room. Its mat was littered with an assortment of rubber toys and blocks.

Mrs. Taylor smiled. "Yes, a boy." She glanced up at the ceiling. "He's asleep now, poor dear."

"With the moving and all, oh yes, I know," put in Mrs. Grant, although she had, in fact, lived all her long married life in the same house. She thought for a moment that Mrs. Taylor might take her up for a peek at the sleeping child, as an evidence of trust, but there was no invitation.

"How old is he?" she asked.

"Eighteen months." It was the man who spoke. His deep voice resounded hollowly, as if the dim room, not yet attuned to life's resumption, still were casting echoes from its years of emptiness.

"Eighteen months," said Mrs. Grant. "That's good. There are several his age in town. He'll have plenty of playmates."

There was no response. Mrs. Taylor's smile remained, and her husband nodded his long face courteously. But Mrs. Grant felt out of place. The room was not lighted, and as the sky darkened, the objects around her became less distinct, the room itself a shadowy uncertainty, seeming almost to be not quite a part of the house; by contrast, too, the soft spread of light from the hall that led to the kitchen glowed more emphatically, silently beckoning the couple to their supper. Mrs. Grant made her farewell.

Taylor saw her out to the road; as they paused beside his old pickup truck, she took the liberty of gently touching his sleeve. "It's so nice to have people living in the Sutter house again," she said. "It brings the place to life. And especially with a child."

"Yes, ma'am."

The wind was cool. It picked a slow rustling path through the overgrowth like a timid animal seeking a place to lie. Mrs. Grant touched the man's sleeve once more.

"It's a nice town," she said. "You'll like it here, I know."

"I'm sure of that, ma'am."

She had a further impulse then, to touch him or to say something, whatever might draw from him once more the odd despairing elegance which his hands had vaguely shaped before, but she did nothing, and he stepped back, a dark figure now, waist-deep in weeds, all movement cloaked by the quickening night.

"Good-bye," she said.

"Much obliged, ma'am."

And she hurried along home, glancing back just once at the house, which glowed brightly at the one end, with darkness at the other; a house not yet revived, it seemed, but slow in waking to the new life within it.

A week went by. All of the other women had paid their calls, had brought their gifts of cookery and offers to help with house-cleaning chores. Most of the men had met Taylor at the hardware store, where he was the new clerk and accountant. They had seen him, too, working steadily at dusk to clear the yard, and they also had offered to help.

But the Taylors had declined, politely, firmly; the wife with her self-sufficient maternal smile, the husband with his grave, ironic air.

"I don't half blame the woman, though," said Mrs. Gaylord to Mrs. Grant. "She probably hasn't made her mind up about arrangements, things like that."

"She don't want to have people around till she gets the place fixed up," put in Mrs. Spence.

The women were having midmorning coffee in Mrs. Grant's kitchen. From the window they could see the Sutter place, its peaked roof speckled with new shingles, its yard half-mowed. Out back, scrubbed clothes fluttered brightly on a line.

"Then, some people like privacy," said Mrs. Gaylord. She was a small woman with hair like coarse-combed cotton, a doll-woman, fast-aging into wrinkled uncertainty. When she said "privacy," she allowed her eyes to widen and her withering lips to purse, suggesting that she might have had an altogether different word in mind.

"A pretty woman," said Mrs. Spence with honest envy, for she herself was as heavy as marble, and as veined. "Is the child pretty, too?"

"I haven't seen him," said Mrs. Gaylord. "Have you, Nettie?"

"Not yet," said Mrs. Grant. She gazed at the far-off line of clothes that gravely waltzed to the music of the wind. They moved with mournful grace through slow unfinished patterns, like the inconclusive gestures of the man himself.

"There's one thing we can do, though," said Mrs. Spence suddenly. "Why didn't we think of it before? We can mind the child and free her for her work."

"Of course," declared Mrs. Gaylord. "We could easily take turns. And I could send my girl over after school."

Mrs. Grant moved to the stove for the coffee pot, but she kept her eyes on the distant dancing clothes. From where she stood they looked like children's garments—little shirts and trousers, tiny skirts and towels and sheets. She frowned, vaguely troubled. Then she turned with the pot. The Taylor woman was proper cleanly, she thought. A washing almost daily for a week—what could be wrong with that?

". . . the one thing to do," Mrs. Gaylord was saying, working her little mouth between phrases as if testing and rejecting alternative statements. "She can hardly refuse that kind of help."

"Why should she refuse?" asked Mrs. Spence.

Mrs. Gaylord fluttered her eyelids. "Some people tend to be shy. Or proud."

"But it's only neighborliness to help," said Mrs. Spence.

"Of course," said Mrs. Gaylord, nodding her close-curled little head. "Helping, that's what neighbors are for. And in a small town, we're all neighbors."

She smiled tightly at Mrs. Grant, encouraging a response. Mrs. Grant said nothing, but glanced around the room in a worried way, as if something had suddenly slipped askew. The sight of her familiar kitchen objects reassured her—the stove, the sink and pump, and on the opposite wall the portrait of Lincoln, simply framed, bought years ago at a church bazaar. "Oh, yes," she said at last, but her eyes lingered on the brooding full-face view of sadness that she reverenced, almost worshiped, and she shivered slightly, although the room was warm, for she thought then she knew what had drawn her to the tall man from the moment she had seen him standing quietly on the porch. It was a shadow of that same soul-grained darkness which, when she sensed it in some living man, was as if some spring of sorrow in herself were touched.

"I'll go up straight after lunch," said Mrs. Gaylord. "Why don't you come with me?" she said to Mrs. Spence. " 'Twas your idea."

"I will," said Mrs. Spence, stirring her bulk, ready to set off that instant.

"Nettie?" asked Mrs. Gaylord. "We could make it almost like"—she pursed her lips in a wry smile—"like a committee."

"No, not today." Mrs Grant rose and went again to the stove, needlessly. "I want to help, of course. But not today. I've got mending. Mending and things."

She stared out across the rusty fields to the bright line of laundry. She could not trust her memory, although she had gazed often at that line, in musing inventory of the new neighbor's things. She could not trust her memory, no, but intuition pitilessly rose—shirts, she had seen shirts, the gray thick work shirts of the man, and overalls and socks, and the woman's garments, too—all of that; but never, no, not once had there appeared a single thing belonging to the child.

John Hollander, who owned the hardware store, had studied Taylor's application for employment with some care, for the man had moved around a lot—ten jobs in four years, all in different places. But there was no black mark anywhere, the references were good, and Hollander had decided that it would be a relief to have a mature man in the store for a change.

Now, after two weeks, he was glad he had hired him. Taylor not only was quicker with figures than any of the previous book-keepers, but, as a clerk, he had a quiet manner that impressed customers. Some actually bought more than they had meant to, simply to make it worth Taylor's while to wait on them. Besides, Hollander had come to like the man.

So, at closing time one day, he expressed a natural impulse to friendliness, clapped Taylor on the back and invited him and his wife to dinner.

"We don't dress up or nothing, just everyday clothes," he added, suspecting the reason for Taylor's hesitation.

"I'm sorry," said Taylor, slowly. An odd expression, almost of mirth, twisted the edges of his saturnine face. "I'm afraid we can't. No, sir, I'm real sorry."

"Hope your wife ain't sick," said Hollander.

"Oh, no."

"Or your little kid."

"No, sir. Nothing like that."

"Well," said Hollander uncertainly. He felt an irrational embarrassment, as if he had asked some prying personal question.

"We're not much for going out," Taylor said.

"Sure. Well. Some other time, then."

"Much obliged, sir."

Hollander knew he should feel irritated, if anything. He had made a generous gesture; it had been declined without satisfactory explanation. But as he hurried home, he felt only the sense of having trespassed—and that the trespass had been expected. Why should he feel this way? He grumbled to himself and then dismissed the whole affair without thinking much about it, as was his custom with troublesome matters.

When he told his wife of Taylor's refusal, he spoke shortly, in the tone he used when he did not want to discuss a subject at length.

"That's strange," said his wife. "Very strange."

"If he don't want to, he's got a reason. He's a good man."

"You know what I heard?" she asked.

Hollander turned away from her.

"I heard from Mrs. Gaylord," his wife continued, "Mrs. Taylor won't let anybody see the baby. Fact is, nobody's seen it once, even."

"Could be sick."

"Something may be wrong with it. But they haven't called the doctor in. They ought to call the doctor."

"Maybe religious reasons."

"No," she said. "They're just regular Methodists. Nothing like that."

"Maybe nothing a doctor can do."

"Always something a doctor can do, even if there's not much money. You'd think they'd try—"

"We know nothing about it!" Hollander turned with an angry look.

"Somebody should do something. I mean, if the child is crippled or something—"

"Their business!"

"We could help. There are lots of people who'd like to help, but where there's pride—"

"It's their business," Hollander repeated, and left the room to avoid the enticement of listening further.

He rubbed his hand across his eyes, as though to erase the image of the man as he had last seen him in a quick backward glance from the store's doorway. The muddy light of day's end had been atomized by floating dust, and the tall man standing meditatively still in the center of the store had seemed composed of countless varied points of drifting light, a two-dimensional figure without depth, an accident of aimless dust eddies in the dying of the day.

"Their business," Hollander said again softly, to no one.

Frost came early that year. It hardened the roads and paths, gathered silently beneath the bushes and in the long shadows of trees, then spread in the sharp nights to whiten the bronze-bearded weeds in vacant fields throughout the town.

"A hard winter coming," said Mrs. Spence, whose full cheeks had been scourged red by the bitter air.

"Come near the fire," urged Mrs. Gaylord. It was her parlor; she was hostess to the coffee group, which in past weeks had grown from an informal gathering of three or four to a definite twice-weekly meeting of eight or ten. She glanced at the other women with satisfaction. It was like a club, and she was chairman.

"Is Mrs. Taylor coming?" asked Mrs. Lamb, staring into her cup, aware of her audacity.

"She said she was afraid she couldn't," said Mrs. Gaylord, with emphasis. Some other woman echoed: "Couldn't."

"Had to stay with the baby, I suppose," said Mrs. Lamb softly.

In one corner of the room, Mrs. Grant shut her eyes and tried to think of something else. The thought, the words would not come.

Instead, she heard Mrs. Gaylord speak her name. "Nettie, what do you think? About the Taylors?"

Mrs. Grant opened her eyes. Dear God, she thought, what to say?

"You live closest," said Mrs. Gaylord, her little face crinkling. "I mean, within sight of the house."

The other women looked at Mrs. Grant.

"I don't watch them," Mrs. Grant said huskily, in a voice that betrayed her lie.

"Well, I think something ought to be *done*," Mrs. Spence grumbled.

"It's a crying shame," declared Mrs. Lamb.

"May I ask a question?" said Mrs. Field, a small woman with a nose that quivered when she spoke. "May I ask who's actually seen the child?"

Mrs. Grant trembled, but her voice was clear. "What do you mean?"

"I've gone there several times myself," said Mrs. Gaylord. "He's always been taking a nap."

"Babies nap a lot," said Mrs. Grant.

"I ask you," persisted Mrs. Field, "who has seen the child?"

"Who's even heard it?" asked Mrs. Lamb. They all glanced at Mrs. Grant. She felt the lie in her mouth, but could not utter it.

"If the child is sick—" Mrs. Lamb began.

"Isn't that their affair?" asked Mrs. Grant.

"We've been all through this before, Nettie," said Mrs. Gaylord. "We've got to think of ourselves." She paused, working her lips as if her teeth were loose. "There may be some contagious disease."

All the women looked up at this.

"Just think of it," whispered Mrs. Lamb.

"It's not a question of meddling," Mrs. Gaylord went on. "We've simply got to know, for our own peace of mind. Is the child ill or not? That's all. One look."

"The doctor should do it," put in Mrs. Spence.

"Absolutely. We'll take the doctor."

"A question of public health," said Mrs. Field.

"Just one look."

"Who could have an objection to that?"

"We try to be friends—"

"Pride, that's all. But who's to know what's being hid?"

"We've got a right, we all have young ones—"

Mrs. Grant remained stiffly seated, gripping the cup hard, unable to speak. The room was rank, packed with fire heat and body smells. She felt a dizziness that forbade her to rise and leave. Would she dare to warn the man? She shuddered. How could one warn of this? And then, he would know without warning, that man, for it would have happened before, perhaps a dozen times, in a dozen different towns. The only question for him would be— how long would it take here?

She turned her head from the circle of faces sharply flushed with heat and noticed that the door to the rear of the house was ajar. A child, a girl of ten, was standing there, listening.

Mrs. Grant raised one hand defensively, thinking that the child must not, must not hear, when one of the voices began to shape what she dreaded above all.

"Mary, I'm just wondering if maybe—"

"What?"

"It seems completely—well, I hardly know how to suggest."

"Go ahead."

"Well, no one has seen the child or even heard it. Doesn't that—? I mean, suppose there *isn't* a child?"

"No *child?*"

"It sounds outrageous, but—"

"I've heard of cases—"

"No *child!*"

Mrs. Gaylord's sharp voice cut above the others. "Whatever may be, it doesn't change our duty. We've got to know, we've got a right!"

Home again, Mrs. Grant sank into the worn rocker beside the kitchen stove. She felt heavy with age, with weariness; she closed her eyes and rocked for comfort, but the chair's patient creaking beneath her weight was somehow a painful sound. She stopped and glanced fearfully outside.

It was noon, but the frosty wind had stretched thin clouds out across the sky, and the whitened sun was small. No washing flapped at the Sutter place. The old house seemed drawn up tight, hard-wrapped into itself, waiting. . . .

There were children there. Mrs. Grant sat up straight and rubbed her eyes to clear them. Children, then; crueler than she could have believed. Children already, loosed as if arrows. She moaned aloud and rocked, clasping her hands. Three or four of them were edging around the house; two, bolder, creeping up on the front porch.

The wind gossiped at the window-pane, taunting her with whispered relays of those shrill voices chanting there now at that poor creature—

"Where's the baby? Where's your baby?"

No, it was too far to hear. But the words were in her mind as surely as they were now in the wind there beyond hearing. Flute voices, high and clear, echoing the words of the women that had been so swiftly carried to the children through the agency of that little girl. Echoes of the women, but echoes, too, of what murmured ceaselessly within her as well, what mocked and scorned her, pressed her in her chair, kept her from running up there to scatter them all with broom sweeps.

Her echoes, too. She could do no other now than whimper, foolish old woman, and shut her ears against the teasing wind.

Hollander's breakfast coffee was black and hot, like rage.

"She wouldn't let them in," his wife repeated.

He made no response, but kept his eyes fixed on his cup. He did not want to look at her, neither did he wish to hear, and yet he did not, could not stop her, nor stop himself from listening.

"Six of them went up there," his wife went on. "They took the doctor with them. All very polite. You know Doctor Phillips. He wouldn't hurt a fly, the sweet old man. Who could be afraid of him?" She sighed and gently rubbed her nose. "Well, they went up and the doctor and Mrs. Gaylord, they went up on the porch

and the other ladies told the children to go home—there were
some little ones up there, playing in the yard—and they knocked."

She paused, but Hollander refused to prompt her with a
question.

"Well," she said, "after a bit the door opened and it was the
woman, of course, and they—the doctor, I mean—he kindly explained the idea. That is, to just have a look at the child to be sure
it was all right, to ease the minds of the mothers, you see, and she
listened and nodded her head like she was going to let them in,
but what she said was only that the baby was sleeping and she was
afraid she couldn't wake him up at this particular time for an
examination and besides, she said, he was quite all right. Oh, she
was very pleasant, they said. That's what made it so hard. And
then she begged them to excuse her, speaking very nice and
nodding her head out at the other ladies in the road who were
waiting, and then very soft-like, she closed the door."

Hollander shut his eyes. It was useless; his very silence asked the
questions.

"And that was all," his wife said. "They couldn't very well force
their way in—you know old Doctor Phillips—and they had to go
on away. But there's talk now of getting a warrant or something, I
don't know what. But anyway, there's a kind of law, public health,
and Mrs. Gaylord's getting her husband to look it up and maybe
they'll go to the judge. Oh, it's a terrible business, really, and I
don't want any part of it, but those women have a point. I mean,
it would be so much easier if the Taylors would just open up a
little and satisfy everyone that it's all right."

Why? Hollander shuddered with fury—at whom? He did not
know.

His wife's voice came at him now with an insinuating cautious-
ness: "John, you know what they're saying—about there not being
any child at all." He did not answer. "Well," she said, almost
whispering, "I just wondered if you happened to notice on the
man's tax forms, his withholding forms, whatever you call them, if
he marked down for three exemptions or just two."

He gave her a quick, savage glance. "I got no idea," he lied. He
felt the sweat gathering beneath his arms.

"Well, I just wondered."

He stared straight down into the cup. The dark trembling surface of liquid reflected his features, distorted and swarthy, transforming his frown into something sly, something knowing. . . .

"One of the children claims to have seen it through the window yesterday," his wife said. "The baby, I mean. Said she was carrying it around in the house in her arms, wrapped in a blanket. They asked him did he actually see the baby and questioned him about it for a while, and he said finally that he didn't really see anything except"—she hesitated, with a sigh—"except something wrapped in a blanket."

Hollander pushed back his chair and stood up.

"I got to go to work," he said.

Outside in the frosty air, he spat into the silver grass and kicked dead leaves as he strode. God damn them all, he thought. But as he reached his car, he slammed his fist against the metal door. From that very first day, the seed had been in his mind, too, after seeing the paper where the man had listed but the two exemptions.

Yes, from the very first day. The seed, hidden, but grown now beyond ignoring.

In his own mind. No one else had put the wondering there. No one else could be blamed for that.

The children came creeping back the next day, and the day after that.

Mrs. Grant watched from her window, shivering in the threads of chill air forced through the cracks. The children seemed bigger than before, as if they had grown, but she saw that there were simply more of them, and older ones, too, now. From that distance, she could not recognize the faces; she bent forward, straining to see, until her breath fogged the pane and the far-off figures faded.

She wiped the glass with her hand. They were ringing the house, hardly pretending to hide any more. And it was beginning to snow; white dust shaking down, cold and bitter, blown sometimes by wind gusts like a lace curtain whipped aside, but always fluttering back, endlessly, impossible to stop.

She could watch no longer. Her hand on her heart, she turned heavily to look at the portrait of the sad-faced man which she cherished. That would never change; yet she saw now that there was change somewhere. Her old cheeks quivering and wet, she sat staring at the square of paper on the wall, seeing it as a token only, black marks printed on white, useless without any answering grace within herself.

That first evening when she had seen the lights up there, her own husband had said it all: "*Leave 'em be.* . . ." Ah, she had known better, she had. But suppose she had waited; by morning, perhaps, they would have moved that pitiful little crate of a home-made playpen upstairs out of sight. Then she would not have said the words now haunting her: "*You've got a little one.* . . ."

And perhaps none of it would have happened. If she had only waited.

But the man himself had invited her inside. Dear God, *he* had known it was no use but to submit to whatever was to come.

There was a furious hammering at the front door. Mrs. Grant sat straight, then pulled herself up and went to answer it.

Snow blew in past a red-cheeked boy, hot-eyed and stammering. "They—they're movin'—movin' out!"

He whirled and ran off. Other children now were dashing by, straight in toward town.

"They're movin' out!" A girl's shriek, clear as a gull's scream, dying as she rushed on. More of them came running through the stinging grainy snow to spread the news in town.

Moving out.

She made her way slowly back to the kitchen, her hands touching the walls of each room as she passed through, not for support but for simple reassurance. The air seemed so cold, her body shook so with chill, that she could hardly be sure she was inside her own home and not out in the blowing snow, not herself cast out.

A tiny cloud of light enveloped the old pickup truck, a spume of snow crystals spun into brilliance by wind and sun's reflection. The cloud dissolved in an updraft, reappeared across the road and then was sucked like smoke into the dark woods.

Wisps of ice clung to the tall man trudging back and forth between the house and the truck. He was hatless, and his hair was whitening to stiffness with snow specks, and his ungloved hands, seeming swollen by the strain of the things he carried, became ever redder, as if whipped by the lash of frost until the blood had broken through. Still, he moved without haste, ignoring the pain, the chill, his burdens and the few scattered children who remained beyond the yard's edge covertly watching, in an aimless pretense of play.

Once, on the way to the house, he halted, rubbed his hands along the glassy sides of his wool jacket, and for a moment gazed down the road in the direction of the Grants' house. The children shrank back and uneasily moved a few steps away, but he was looking above their heads, perhaps even above the other house. The motion of his hands ceased. He simply stood, as if awaiting some long-expected event, and the snow that whirled around him from all sides sheathed him quickly in a glittering coat that remained even when at last he moved once more.

Larger figures now were visible in the distance; hidden at times by snow gusts, then reappearing closer, like statuettes stealthily advanced by an unseen hand. Near the Grants' house, the foremost paused, their heavy coats and scarves white-patched with clinging snow. Then some advanced farther, followed at intervals by others, in twos and threes, an erratic straggling column of townspeople, mostly women; and when the first few came within a stone's throw of the yard, the children there trotted back to them, like dutiful pickets glad to be relieved of their posts.

As the first ones moved closer, they slowed their step uncertainly, so that those strung out behind caught up, and the column became a shifting formation, stamping on the road for warmth, but only gradually advancing. One man came quickly from behind; Hollander, his cleated boots stinging the frozen dirt, a brusque red hunting cap jammed on his head. He brushed his way through. Near the front, he heard a child's voice that shook with self-importance: "They ain't brought it out yet, I swear they ain't. I watched!"

Hollander swung around so that he was staring down at the line-webbed rose-cold skin of Mrs. Gaylord's face.

He shouted at her: "Why'd you come? Why don't you go home?"

She stepped back from him, her mouth working without producing speech, but the words came from a woman behind her:

"We come to help—"

Hollander twisted away and strode ahead to the yard, where he stopped and looked back. As if emboldened by his example, the people were shuffling forward. He was in the middle now, between those huddled human forms and the tall man, whitened from head to foot, who still walked his round without ever a glance to the side.

Hollander stepped several paces on, then stopped in the man's path. "Taylor," he said, and from his pocket he took out an envelope and extended it.

The man paused and with difficulty took the envelope in his stiffened fingers.

"I heard in town," said Hollander. He licked his wind-raw lips. "I brought your pay out, anyway. It's got the Christmas bonus in it. You earned it."

He tried to say more. He scourged his mind for words. But could he say anything beyond what the others had already perverted, *"Come to help"*? To help—

The man's face was carved with cold. The lips parted:

"Much obliged."

As if by common assent then, they parted, Hollander turning back, the other man stepping woodenly toward the house.

The wind blew up with sustained power, so that they all bent from its force, blinded by the spray of snow. Hollander slipped, almost fell; he struggled upright, facing the people whose heads were bowed against the snow blast, and felt his fury freeze and lock his throat. Impossible to roar them away. The wind would outshout him. He staggered into their midst, his numbed arms swinging in protest, but no one noticed even this.

Across the yard the tall man walked steadily, not yielding to the push of wind, his arms holding with great care something that seemed at first to be a ladder, oddly folded into sections, but which, as he gently lifted it into the truck beneath the trembling canvas top, was recognized as the playpen. Then he turned once more, with heavy steps returning to the house. He did not enter this time, but merely held the front door open for his wife, who stepped out onto the porch, her arms crooked under a burden impossible for the watchers to identify through the shimmering veil of snow.

All stood staring then, even Hollander, even Mrs. Grant, who had struggled up alone to the rear of the crowd, sucking her breath in gasps, her body shuddering with cold.

The woman stood quietly on the porch, her head inclined so that she could gaze down at what she so carefully held in her arms, waiting while the man closed the door, locked it, and slipped the key beneath the snowy doormat. He straightened up, then took his wife's elbow and helped her down the steps and slowly across the yard toward the truck. They looked to neither side, just forward, their heads held straight despite the tearing of the storm, their bodies protectively close and touching, but their progress was so retarded by the wind's fury that it seemed they might never pass quite through the driving snow.

One figure broke loose from the watchers and rushed into the yard. It was a child, beating its way ahead with flailing arms.

The man and woman stopped and gravely turned. The child lost its balance, fell down before them, almost at their feet, then scrambled up, swung around and dashed back. By the time it reached the others, the truck door had opened and then closed again.

Mrs. Grant fought past the surrounding bodies, her brittle fingers stretched out as though desperate to seize the child, to choke its words.

It was the girl she had seen before in Mrs. Gaylord's house. But she could not reach her. Too late now, as before, even though the girl's first words were lost in the roar of the truck's motor.

The child's face was blue-edged with cold. Her eyes were brilliant and her voice, when she repeated what she had said, was shrill:

"Toys—that's all she had, just toys!"

Twenty yards away, the truck lurched forward, bucking, its wheels skidding.

"Look!" the girl cried, twisting away from the hands of the men who supported her.

She pointed not at the truck, now bumping off along the road away from town, but at something small that had fallen near its starting place.

Hollander walked toward it wonderingly. The others followed.

He stooped and picked it up. It was a rubber duck, a baby's toy. Turning, he held it high in his hand above the people gathered behind him, then flung it among them.

Someone muttered: "Where is it, then—?"

They all looked toward the house, dark now and closed, as it had been before, a heavy sullen square with edges blurred by snow. The question seemed to echo in sudden stillness: "Where is it, then—?"

Mrs. Grant pushed her way clear and faced them. "You wanted to find out, didn't you?" she cried out. "Well, you know about it now—"

She trembled so that her knees gave way and she sagged down into the snow.

"You found out!" she shrieked, beating wildly at the hands that sought to help her rise. "You found out about it, so why don't you go away? Don't you believe it yet?"

They began to back away, murmuring.

Her voice still struck at them. "If you don't believe it, then go look—go look for it in the house! And if you don't find it there, then get shovels—yes, get shovels!—and go out and dig!"

They were turning away now, back toward town, the wind pushing them urgently.

"Dig! Why don't you dig!"

She sobbed and fell face forward in the snow, and would have stayed there, if two of the men had not finally gone back to pull her up and help her home again.

The Glory
of
G. O'D.

¶ He was disturbed by the public controversy concerning the death of God. True, it did not seem to be a personal attack on God, but rather—and he had to confess that he was a bit hazy in his understanding of it—an attempt by certain young religious philosophers to revitalize Christian beliefs. Even so, he did not think it was fair. Surely it would have been enough to propose that the popular image of God be brought up to date. One could readily tolerate the notion of God clothed in a charcoal-gray business suit instead of the conventional clouds and robes, and perhaps dispensing divine justice from behind an executive desk— but to insist on God's death? That was carrying it too far. He felt not only uneasy but in fact individually threatened, inasmuch as for the past forty years or so, ever since his childhood, he had— quite privately, solely to himself, never making any fuss or uproar about it—considered that he was God.

Yes, literally God. When he was unusually tired or depressed, he found it had a tonic effect on his spirits to gaze into the mirror and remind himself, "Well, after all, you know, you are God," and give himself a wink and square his shoulders. But he knew he could confide in no one. He had to keep the matter to himself. Really, a man could not go through the streets proclaiming he was God nor could he safely chance as much as an ambiguous reference or even a little jest at some social gathering. People would take it amiss. They were still touchy on the subject, as though this were a form of eccentricity which could not be countenanced for a moment.

But he was not an eccentric. It was not just a wild fancy. He had some special evidence. He was, first of all, a foundling. He didn't know who his parents were. Granted, there were lots of foundlings in the world, but how many of them had been named George O'Donnell? G. O'D. He'd gone back to the orphanage not long ago to try to find out how this name had been chosen for him, but the old nuns couldn't remember. One of them thought perhaps he'd been named after a popular janitor who'd died at that time, but she wasn't sure, so that G. O'D. was at liberty to assume that his name had been selected under divine influence.

Then there were the Biblical codes. G. O'D. had worked out a system of numbers based on the letters in his name (G being the seventh letter in the alphabet, E the fifth, O the fifteenth, R the eighteenth, and so on) and by applying these numbers to various sacred passages and writing down the words thus indicated, he had been astounded at the results. While it was true that some of the messages so deciphered were too mysterious for him to evaluate, he did uncover several which tended to affirm his unique status, and in the course of time, often laboring far into the night over the great book, he added many more. He amassed such a body of evidence, in fact, that he was sometimes tempted to send extracts anonymously to some leading theologian, and subsequently seek a means of learning that expert's opinion, without revealing his own identity.

But he never did. He was too timid. He feared mockery and ridicule. The only safe course was to maintain a strict silence, and try to conduct his life in accordance with the lofty precepts appropriate to a person in his peculiar position.

Even so, he could not repress a hankering for recognition. Sometimes he indulged himself by holding an imaginary press conference or magazine interview, which he fancied might run more or less along these lines:

Q: When did you first discover you were God, sir?

A: Oh, a long time ago. I was about five years old when the idea hit me, I think.

Q: And you had no doubts about it?

A: It seemed pretty obvious.

Q: Still, you didn't reveal yourself publicly.

A: I did tell some of my playmates at the orphanage, but their reaction wasn't too encouraging. They beat me up, actually. And then later on, as I was growing to manhood, I decided that this wasn't the kind of thing a person goes around advertising—at least not until conditions were right for an announcement.

Q: And now you've spoken out at last.

A: That's right. I wanted to put an end to this business about God being dead.

Q: You've certainly done that, sir. Can you give me an idea of your future plans? That is, I'm assuming you'll take a pretty active part in public life.

A: [chuckling] Oh, absolutely. I'm offering my services to various governments.

Q: The governments of Christian nations?

A: Not only those, young man. I'm going to be available to any monotheistic society, bar none.

Q: Israel?

A: Of course. And the Moslem nations, too. I make no distinctions along those lines. But I'm definitely not going to run after anybody's business. I'll let them come to me.

Q: What about the Communist world?

A: I have no prejudices against any form of government, but I don't want to overcommit my energies. There's such a thing as spreading oneself too thin.

Q: And your program?

A: Oh, world peace. Brotherhood. Justice. It's pretty clearly spelled out in the Bible, I think.

Q: How about performing a miracle?

A: A miracle?

Q: Just a little one. My photographer would like a nice shot to go with my story.

A: Oh. Well, I suppose I could manage one, if you insist. Here. I'll stand over here and, um, change this lamp into a burning bush or something. . . .

G. O'D. was five feet four inches in height. He was plump and growing bald. Because of defective vision, he wore glasses. An ulcer denied him rich food and strong drink. Realizing at an early age that he lacked both personal charm and physical attractiveness, he had never sought the companionship of women. He earned his living as a clerk in a municipal agency, working at a paper-piled desk in a huge office where there were dozens of other clerks at similar desks doing similar jobs. He lived by himself in a rented room. He spent his leisure time alone, too, occasionally treating himself to a movie, sometimes taking walks, but usually remaining in seclusion poring over works of philosophy and taking neat notes in a careful hand.

Certain propositions he encountered in his reading powerfully supported his conviction that he was God. He was particularly interested in those idealist philosophers who suggested that reality existed only in one's thoughts. The universe, therefore, was only an idea—and an idea, moreover, that existed only in the mind of G. O'D. Hence, the death of G. O'D. would be the end of everything. As for the notion that anyone else could entertain the same claim to omnipotence, G. O'D. reasoned that other human beings were nothing more than ideas in his head, too. "When I die, all creation dies," he wrote in his notebook. "Therefore my existence is the only fact of any importance. In a word, I am You Know Who."

At other times, G. O'D. was plagued by doubts. God should be joyful—and he was not. God should be vibrant with power and strength—and he was a weak and pitiful creature. God should be beautiful—and he was repulsive. He was not God, after all. He was just pretending. It was a childish masquerade—and dangerous, as well, for although it did help him over the worst feelings of helplessness and inferiority, it might in time become a mania. He might become a victim of his own fantasy—if it was a fantasy— and society would find it necessary to place him under restraint.

Often he laughed bitterly at himself. What a fool he was. If he had any sense at all, he'd drop the whole business and take up stamp collecting. And yet . . . and yet! God could fill any vessel, could He not? External beauty meant nothing. Flesh was temporal matter, soon to dissolve. What greater proof, indeed, of God's spirituality than His choice of such a humble exterior—of course! God would know He'd be safe from prying eyes if He were hidden within G. O'D. No one would think to look there.

Thus G. O'D. would spend his nights—arguing with himself, flipping through various texts, seeking new proofs by means of his Bible decoding system, gesticulating before the mirror, pacing his threadbare little room in excitement or despondency, sometimes gloomy, sometimes exalted, sometimes in such a frenzy that his ulcer would snap at him and he would roll groaning on the bed. Even out on the street or sitting at his desk in the office he would be seized by joy or stricken by uncertainty, until he feared that his self-control might give way. In public, he moved in anxiety with downcast eyes, as though unbuttoned. He shunned conversations, lest some damning word escape his lips. He left off eating lunch so as to reduce social contact with his fellow clerks (who, it must be recorded, did not notice his absence), and began paying his monthly rent by mail in order to avoid seeing his landlady.

Being God was not easy. Still, he thought, this burden could not be laid aside. It was his fate, was it not? If a man turned out to be God, he couldn't help it. It wasn't the sort of thing one could simply stop. But G. O'D. was becoming weary. He had big pouches under his eyes, a stomach in revolt, head buzzing with little circling thoughts, and a growing tendency toward flatulence most troubling in crowded elevators. It was all most un-Godlike. When would it come to an end—or would it grow worse?

G. O'D. suspected that he might be going to pieces. The signs were already ominous. He found himself alighting at wrong subway stops, forgetting to wear socks to work, entering stores for no reason and then having difficulty finding his way out. Once he tried to eat a napkin in a restaurant, complained to the waiter that it was underdone, and then, having realized his error, sat for some time staring down at his untouched plate. He knew that his loneliness would ruin him. He had needs that must be met. Human contact was essential, without delay. He had to speak to

someone frankly and fully. Could he go to a priest? Impossible!
No priest could condone what would seem, at first blush, to be
blasphemy. A psychiatrist, then? Too risky—he might be locked
up. His fellow workers likewise were out of the question, his landlady would evict him at the mere mention of the subject, and he
had no friends. He must unburden himself to a sympathetic
human soul and in anonymity—and yet how?

He began to wonder if there were others who suffered in the
same way. It was unlikely, but there might be a few. Just one
would do—if he could think of some way to find him. He puzzled
for weeks over this problem before a possible solution occurred to
him. He would place a classified advertisement in a newspaper! He
sat down at once to compose the notice, carried it down to the
newspaper office and paid for it to be run for a week.

> Anyone honestly believing himself to be
> God, kindly write full particulars to
> Box D-44.

He stopped by the newspaper office the next day to inquire
about responses. There was nothing for Box D-44, nor was there so
much as a postcard the following day. G. O'D. was depressed; then
he realized that his correspondents would need time to write their
replies and post them. He returned to his room to study his advertisement for the hundredth time. It was clearly written, he
thought, and yet it was buried in the middle of a page, just one
of scores of miscellaneous notices set in tiny type. The newspaper
might have several hundred thousand readers—but of these, only a
small percentage would scan the classifieds at all, and fewer still
would come upon his handiwork. How many—a thousand? Five
hundred? Two hundred? And from such a limited audience, how
could he hope there would be even a single one who would bother
to answer? It seemed hopeless. He thought of placing a huge
display advertisement that would command wide attention or,
alternatively, of canceling his notice altogether. It was a familiar
predicament. Should he, or shouldn't he? Was he God, or G. O'D?

On the third day, the first mail was waiting for him. It exceeded
his wildest hopes. Box D-44 had no fewer than fifty letters. And
that was only the beginning. The responses came in thereafter by
bag and by pouch, in the hundreds, in the thousands, a regular

storm of letters. There were so many that G. O'D. had to hire a
taxi to transport them back to his room. In a panic, he canceled
the ad, but it was too late. By the end of the week his quarters
resembled a mailroom at Christmas-time. Letters were piled in the
corners, shoved beneath the bed, stuffed into the closet, heaped on
his table; they littered his floor everywhere in great toppling stacks
among which he wandered bemused, holding huge wads of them
in his hands. It was incredible. And down at the newspaper, he
knew, still more would be flooding in for him to collect. But he
had not opened a single one. He lacked the courage. He feared the
worst—they'd all be from cranks, from pranksters, from slippery
salesmen who preyed on the manias they found in agony columns,
from shut-ins seeking pen pals, from indigents requesting hand-
outs, from foreign students wanting language practice, from every
source, in fact, except the one he'd hoped to tap.

And yet . . . and yet! G. O'D. chose one letter at random and
opened the envelope with his fingers. The sheet of paper inside
was of fine quality. It had an expensive smell to it. The text of the
letter was typewritten, with no errors or strikeovers, and was in
proper form. He glanced at the signature—his heart leaped, he
exclaimed aloud in joy, and began eagerly to read:

Dear Box D-44:
  I do not have the privilege of knowing your name, sir, but
when your advertisement happened to come to my attention, I
realized that it was intended to be read by me and only by me,
and therefore I feel it my duty to respond.
  You inquired as to "full particulars." There is little to say.
As a child I underwent the usual imaginative progression, fancy-
ing myself to be in turn a dwarf possessed of magic powers, the
Dauphin of France, Sir Launcelot, the reincarnation of Houdini,
a combination of Babe Ruth and Rudolph Valentino, etc. It was
not until I had outgrown this frivolous nonsense that I began
slowly to realize the truth; namely, that I was in fact the Supreme
Being, Who had happened to select, as His earthly habitation, the
mortal flesh of a human male of a certain height and weight,
with hair of such-and-such a color—in short, the self I had
always supposed myself to be. Naturally, I was highly elated by
this discovery, which, at the same time, I determined to keep to
myself, inasmuch as my temporal career in investment banking
would not be advanced by such a disclosure.

Although my decision was the correct one, it has cost me great anguish over the years. For that reason, I have felt great satisfaction and relief in the process of writing this letter, being the first time I have made even an anonymous acknowledgment of my status.

Yours very truly,
GOD

G. O'D. was in a transport. He clasped the letter to his chest and danced about the room, scattering the stacks of envelopes with his heedless feet. A human soul had addressed him at last! Finally, rapport! He was no longer a lone visionary! Even if all the other thousands of letters were from cranks and fools, this one he'd plucked up by chance had given meaning to his life. And it was from a man of substance, a distinguished and successful man, a man of power and influence—a banker! It seemed to add a certain tone to being God.

He resolved to answer the letter at once. He, too, would pour out his heart and his dreams—and then he realized that the banker had deliberately omitted both name and address, just as he, G. O'D., had protected his privacy behind the shelter of Box D-44. Perhaps there were others who had not been so cautious. He began opening more letters. Although not one bore a return address, he read them with a mounting excitement, for all had been written in obvious sincerity, and—to judge by the quality of the prose and from various little hints within the texts—many of his correspondents were men of attainment, like the banker. Taxi drivers, yes, and clerks like himself, and also tenant farmers and unemployed stevedores, but likewise there were professional men, university professors, and industrialists! The favorite signature was "God," but occasionally other titles were employed, such as "The Lord," "The Creator," "The Deity," "The Most High," "The World Soul," and "The First Cause." Many letters enclosed cash; G. O'D. soon found these unsolicited donations piling up in such stacks that it was clear he had unwittingly collected more by his one tiny advertisement than he had been paid in salary for the past year. It was a windfall, manna from Heaven, so to speak, and yet he set the funds impatiently aside. The messages were what commanded his attention. Each was like a long-pent sigh of release, a great secret confided, a soul relieved, a heart unburdened.

Dear Box D-44:

Your ad was like a flaming beacon. I cannot describe to you the joy that possessed me when I saw it and realized that after all these lonely years, someone had sensed my presence and was seeking to acknowledge my divinity. Yes, Box D-44, your message has been received! I reveal myself to you and to no other! Even though I cannot yet make my true nature known publicly (my patients, some of whom are in deep analysis, would not be likely to understand), I am compelled to express to you my heartfelt thanks. . . .

Dear Box D-44:

I was stunned to see your notice. By a series of mathematical calculations which only three other men in the world would be capable of comprehending, I established proof thirty years ago that I am God (I have since obtained confirmation by computer programming), but I kept my worksheets under lock and key and did not breathe a word to anyone. The time is not yet ripe for disclosure. However did you discover it? If only I could glance at the calculations you used. Surely you must have stumbled onto the exact method I devised, for there could be only that one way—and yet I cannot safely visit you nor permit you to know my earthly name. Even so, I salute your genius. . . .

Dear Box D-44:

Permit me to congratulate you, sir. My duties in the field of law enforcement require me to be much in the public eye, and therefore it has been difficult for me to suppress the real facts about myself, for my enemies would like nothing better than to find a means of embarrassing me. It is a great pity we can never meet. Nor would it be prudent for me to employ the methods at my disposal for learning your identity, for although I have no doubts as to your loyalty to me and your country, nevertheless it might somehow lead to the compromising of the Top Secret relating to my person. Hence I am able at this time merely to pen this word of sincere appreciation. . . .

Dear Box D-44:

Excuse this scrawl. I must use my left hand, to disguise my writing. You know the truth—but the world must not know. One of my aides brought me your ad as a jest, hoping it might lighten my somber duties. I laughed with him, dear Box D-44, but when he had left, my laughter ceased, and I sat at my desk in humility and thankfulness. The considerable powers at my com-

mand would be insufficient to recompense you for the great
spiritual benefit thus conferred upon me. . . .

G. O'D. kept opening letters. His hands trembled with emotion
as he tore at the envelopes, and often he had to brush away his
tears of joy so that he could read their contents. There were no
cranks, no pranksters! All were deeply sincere! He sat on the floor,
surrounded by the great heaps of mail, reading avidly, perspiration
beading his forehead and misting his glasses. No longer was he
alone. He was in the center of a multitude of grateful and
admiring friends who were sharing with him—only with him—the
most profound of all experiences. He had been chosen as confidant
of a secret too great to be told to wives, parents, associates, con-
fessors—and did this phenomenon not constitute the greatest
proof of all that God existed? If the belief in personal divinity
were so widespread, then surely this amounted to a statistical
demonstration as convincing, say, as the relationship between
cigarettes and cancer.

The night wore on. G. O'D. worked feverishly at his mail,
opening, reading, counting, jotting down numbers on a piece of
paper. Several times he fell asleep on a mattress of discarded
envelopes; waking in sudden fear that it was all a dream, then
sighing in relief as he saw the mountains of letters and stacks of
cash all around him. More, more! His fingers ached, his eyes
burned, but as the day arrived he forgot about his breakfast, his
job, everything. He had to finish his mail. He could not leave a
single one unread.

It was late afternoon before he was through. Red-eyed and un-
shaven, he went out to a cafe to eat. Only with difficulty did he
prevent himself from dancing along the street and blowing kisses
to passersby. His mind was in a whirl of delight. His senses tingled.
He was dizzied by visions of destiny. Each mouthful of spaghetti
was a miracle to him. The grubby girl behind the cafe counter
seemed a seraph of grace and serenity; the movement of her hand
as she surreptitiously picked her nose described a divinely perfect
arc. G. O'D. smiled upon her, upon his fellow customers, smiled
upon his greasy plate and stained coffee mug. All was glory in his
eyes. The way was clear now. He would advertise in newspapers

from coast to coast, from Canada to Mexico—and what torrents of belief would not then flood forth! He chuckled aloud. Even his ulcer, leaping like a salmon, did not disturb him. He would be able to silence the yapping of those theologians. His own puny efforts and proofs could be laughed away or ignored, but not the testimony of all those letters. He would uncover the fundamental reality of faith compared to which all else would be like straws in the wind!

He rose from the counter, paid his check and went to the public telephone booth. He wanted to make one little calculation before putting his plan in operation. Calling the newspaper and finally obtaining a connection to the proper department, he asked what proportion of the readership was estimated to examine the classified advertisements, according to the most recent surveys. When he was given the answer, he hastened back to his room to apply this estimation to his own figures.

The result was astounding. G. O'D. was flabbergasted. Of those who had been exposed to his little notice, no less than 93.4 percent had responded! His pencil fell from his fingers and he stared dumbly at the great masses of mail around him. He felt as though he had stumbled into the hidden grotto, as it were, and come unexpectedly upon the sacred fire . . . America, America! He had heard its heartbeat, knew its secret dream. This, then, was what caused men to leap from their beds in the morning, gobble down their breakfasts, and dash to their offices, their factories, their stores and shops! Had he supposed the conviction of divinity to be widespread? Ah, it appeared to be all but unanimous.

G. O'D. quit his job. He moved to more spacious quarters, hired a housekeeper, purchased a new suit, a typewriter, and several huge file cabinets. In order to defray his expenses while gathering and organizing future correspondence, he hit on the notion of an I-Am-God Club. His classified announcements would offer membership for the modest fee of five dollars per annum, in return for which he would produce a monthly newsletter, to be mailed in brown wrappers to box numbers listed by his anonymous subscribers. Yes, he thought, that would be suitable. He would cut the stencils himself and turn the crank on the mimeograph machine with his own arm. The housekeeper could help with the mailing.

The I-Am-God Club was an immediate success. Cash memberships came in by the thousands daily, from every corner of the country, and soon G. O'D. was able to have his newsletter printed on glossy paper. It contained quotations from the letters of club members, as a means of exchanging relevant personal experience; G. O'D. wrote a column of his own, answering queries and providing counsel on various matters; he included selections from appropriate works of theology and philosophy, and he even devised a topical crossword puzzle.

G. O'D. became wealthy. His enterprise flourished. He hired clerks and secretaries, assistants and aides, retained law firms and accountants, wisely invested club monies in the stock market, contributed generously to charities, and found time to make personal visits to hospitals, where he comforted the ill and alleviated their suffering with little acts of kindness and words of cheer. G. O'D. was a builder, too. To house his expanding operations, he erected the God Building, the tallest skyscraper in the city; soon thereafter, he constructed a village in Florida for the benefit of club members wishing to spend their retirement years among congenial companions. Although he shunned public life, he was nevertheless sought out for advice by many of the leading figures of the day, and more than once the name of G. O'D. appeared on the guest list at White House functions.

His proofs of God grew enormously. Millions of personal testimonials were on file, carefully cross-indexed, and preserved against loss by being recorded on microfilm stored in the deepest vault of the safest bank. He often wandered through the giant file rooms of the God Building and let his fingers trail across the smooth, cold cabinets or paused to open a drawer at random and skim through a folder or two. One day, he thought, he would have enough. Until then, he must labor unstintingly. Often in the early evening, after a busy and fruitful day, G. O'D. would stroll out on the balcony of his penthouse high atop the God Building, and there, full of thankfulness and contentment, he would gaze benignly down at the thousands of twinkling lights below and raise one hand gently in benediction.

The Persecution
of the Colonel

¶ A chill spring storm burst across the meadow and shook the heavy-headed trees beyond. It blew in with the dusk, and the first raindrops seemed black, like bits of night torn out of the sky.

The young man limped toward the Hall. Its upper story was tightly shuttered, but some of the ground-floor rooms were lighted, and one window was touched with the soft irregular coloration that suggested a warm fire within. There was a cascade of thunder. The sky split, wild and bright. In the flash, the young man noticed a figure standing behind one of the unlighted windows; but it vanished as the lightning died.

Anxious to accomplish his mission, the young man hurried ahead, reached the massive door, and knocked. Almost at once the inside bolt was drawn and the door swung open.

"Come in, Mr. Smythe." The Colonel's voice was hearty and the handshake that accompanied it was firm. "Nasty turn of weather, eh? Ah, you've caught a bit of rain, I see. Come, I've got a fire. You'll soon warm up. And we'll put that coat of yours on a chair nearby to dry."

The young man readily removed his coat and stood before the fire. The paneled room, he judged, had once accurately reflected the solid prosperity of a successful landowner, but that must have been many years ago, long before the Colonel's time, for the rugs were frayed, the upholstery well-worn, and the tables dull from lack of polish.

"You'll have a drink, Mr. Smythe? . . . Of course!" the Colonel declared. He kept the bottles handy on a table near the hearth, and as he poked among them for the particular one he sought, the fire made the shadows of his fingers do a clumsy dance on the opposite wall.

"Here we are!" He grunted with satisfaction as he plucked the bottle up. "Well, sir, if you'll accept that chair, we'll draw up snug-like, see, and get to business." He puffed as he eased himself into his own chair and then cleared his throat noisily. "But first," he said, with a wink, "we'll have a toast. To neighborliness, eh?"

"Gladly," said Smythe.

"Capital!" the Colonel responded. He tilted his upraised glass and drank with gusto. "Um!" He smacked his lips, then gave his visitor a thoughtful look. "Sounds as though you had a bit of a cold, sir. Your voice is thick, I mean."

"I'm afraid so."

"Ah, well. This is the medicine for it, eh? You can't go wrong with a couple of doses of this prescription!" The Colonel chuckled and drank again. He was elderly, but as sturdy as a draft horse, and his fleshy face was stained by years of weathering. He was an avid hunter, it seemed, for guns and rifles were hung on the walls or leaned in corners, each weapon glistening with fresh oil.

"Now," the Colonel barked cheerfully, as if he were convening a regimental officers' meeting. "You phoned me, sir, about my cows?"

"Yes. I'm afraid they found a gap in your fence and wandered into my meadow—"

"Ah, so you informed me, Mr. Smythe. Well, the problem

seems a simple one, eh? Come morning, I'll trot down to have a look at that fence and then get it patched up, that's all."

"I'd be much obliged, sir."

"No problem at all, Mr. Smythe. Never a problem between neighbors if there's fair dealing and honesty, is my opinion." The Colonel nodded in self-agreement and the firelight winked on his bald dome. "It's an honest county, this," he added, "though I've known it but a few short years. And yet, I'm not such a newcomer as yourself, sir, since this is your first season, eh? Strange about those cows, though," the Colonel rambled on. "Old Towsley, he's my dairyman—my whole staff, to tell the truth—he mumbled something about the beasts, come to think of it. Said of the eight, he counted but seven. In short, one missing."

"Oh, I say, really?" Mr. Smythe seemed taken aback. "I was almost positive I'd sent the lot back through—"

"Undoubtedly you did, sir, undoubtedly you did! Old Towsley's half blind and can't handle numbers besides. You could have driven a dozen of your own to my barn and the old chap wouldn't have noticed!"

"But, seriously, sir, I shall certainly have a talk with my men first thing tomorrow—"

"Think no more about it, Mr. Smythe!" The Colonel chuckled heartily. "I mentioned it simply to illustrate old Towsley's muddled ways. No indeed, sir, it isn't a question of one cow more or less, but of neighborliness, as I have said." He paused; then, with an embarrassed glance at Smythe, he added: "Excuse my thoughtlessness for referring to Towsley's eye troubles. I meant no personal allusion to yourself—"

"Not at all, Colonel," Smythe said hastily. He removed his dark glasses, gave them a quick polish on his sleeve, and replaced them. "I've had a sensitivity to light, ever since childhood."

The Colonel made a clucking sound. "Pity!" He rose to replenish their drinks. "Neighborliness, Mr. Smythe, that's the drill in these parts, and I can honestly say I'm delighted to have such a considerate young man as yourself next door to me. Your glass, sir. Ah!" He sat down again. "I treasure such a relationship all the more, you see, because I had an unusually nasty experience in the opposite way five years back, when I was living up north. A rotten show it was, all the way through!" He leaned toward Smythe confidentially. "Had a chap adjoining me who was one of these odd quirky types—paranoia."

"Really!" remarked Smythe.

"Worst of it was," the Colonel went on, scowling at the recollection, "that nobody in the village had the decency to warn me. No, not them! They'd let the trusting old fool march in and buy his bit of land to settle down to a modest country existence—and not a word from them, not one! I had to find out for myself. 'Twas like living on a powder keg!"

"Good heavens," said Smythe. "What happened, sir?"

The Colonel took a healthy swallow from his glass. "Ah, it began quietly enough. That's the way with those chaps. To look at 'em, you'd never suspect a thing. Fellow rapped at my door one day, polite as pie. He told me in a roundabout way that one of my dogs had slipped over and killed a fowl of his. Oh, he was full of apologies. Could hardly bear to disturb me about it—that kind of thing. But I caught a glint in his eye, and I said to myself, 'Oho! Something's up here!' But naturally, I returned his politeness with my own."

"Of course," said Smythe.

"For the sake of appearances," the Colonel continued, "I went over with him to investigate, but I knew straightaway there was something odd, because neither of my pups had a taste for fowl. Good dogs both, they were. I suggested the presence of a fox, but the fellow claimed that one of his men had seen the culprit fleeing, and could swear it was a dog, and a collared dog at that. So what could I do but defend my own, eh? I denied it was possible. A dog, perhaps, but mine? Nonsense!"

"Did your neighbor become—er—violent?"

"Ah, not him!" the Colonel declared grimly. "That's not their way, you see, sir. They're clever, these creatures. Oh, he had a disarming way about him. A young chap, several years your junior, I would judge, Mr. Smythe; a bit slenderer, too, and with a rather high-pitched voice. When I spoke my little piece, he simply bowed his head a bit, as if he were accepting a challenge almost, and again I was struck by the look in his eye." The Colonel shrugged and shook his head. "I've been through some sticky places in my lifetime, I can tell you, but I'd never before seen a slyer, more ingratiating devil than that chap up north!"

"What did he do, Colonel?"

"Mr. Smythe, that was the very question that troubled me. Rather, I wondered what *would* he do? Not that I thought he was a loony then, but I can assure you I was a bit uneasy." The Colonel pursed his lips reflectively. "First, I decided to find out more about the man. I went to the village and made inquiries. I spoke to the banker and to some of the tradespeople. Right off, I could tell that this neighbor of mine had them scared speechless, for they claimed to have heard nothing bad about him, and on the contrary vowed that he was an altogether pleasant person. Not only that, sir, but I got the distinct impression that these poor folk would side with him in any dispute—out of sheer terror, you see. Why, in a week's time, they turned positively hostile toward me!"

Smythe nodded in response, and thoughtfully stroked his close-cut brown beard. "And then, Colonel?"

"Then the game broke out into the open," said the Colonel. "A day or two later, the fellow appeared again at my door, still pretending civility, you understand. He told me he'd lost a second bird the night before. I looked him in the eye. 'What's that to me, if I may ask?' I said, as any honest man would, and he dropped his gaze then—couldn't brazen it out, you see—and mumbled some kind of apology and off he went. But it gave me the shivers to see the way he slunk along, casting his eye left and right, for it put me in mind of the way a hunter will study the terrain where he intends to ambush his prey."

The Colonel paused to blow his nose. His listener remained silent, staring down into his glass.

"'Twas then," the Colonel went on, "that I smelled danger. I thought at first the rascal might try to poison my beasts—and then it occurred to me that he would hardly be satisfied with that. No, once these chaps get a grudge started, there's no easy ending, that I knew. Well, sir, I made a second foray into town, and I was a determined man by then. I cornered the banker and this time I held on. I wouldn't be shaken off, sir! For hours I worried at him, presenting the plain unvarnished facts, you see, and finally he had to admit, sir, that I was right. He seemed shocked and amazed, Mr. Smythe, and not a little frightened."

"You convinced him you were dealing with a madman?"

"Ah, not convinced, Mr. Smythe. He had known it all along, of course. No, I merely forced him to concede the truth, although he still pretended that this was the first hint of trouble that had come to him. Bankers are crafty that way, sir!" The Colonel set down his glass and fumbled in his pocket for a pipe. "He told me something about my neighbor's background. It seems that the young fellow was an orphan, of indifferent stock, who had got some kind of education and scraped up enough money to come to that county and buy his piece of land. Ah, in another type, such a story would be admirable, Mr. Smythe, but with this fellow, his struggle to succeed had merely puffed up his wild suspicions of the world until he had gone clear over the edge! The banker confided in me further. The young man, he said, had overextended himself some-what and was even then applying for a loan to see him through. Without it, he might be in deep trouble with his creditors.

"The opening was too obvious not to be seized. I said to him, 'Surely, you're not going to approve the loan?' And he replied, 'On the contrary, Colonel, I believe we will approve it.' The blindness of some folk! I argued with him, as you may imagine, saying that here was a heaven-sent opportunity to get rid of this creature. 'Deny the loan, sir, and you'll topple him,' I cried. He was un-certain at first—and I could hardly blame him, for a banker is by nature a timid animal—but after I had been at him for another hour or two, he agreed that the time had come for firmness. Yes, Mr. Smythe, I managed to stiffen his backbone. He promised he would turn down the application."

"Admirable," muttered Smythe.

"But there was much else to do," the Colonel continued, stuffing his pipe with tobacco. He brought it to his lips and struck a match, glancing sharply over the flame at the face of his guest. "I had to make certain of it. So in the next few days I visited each of the important tradesmen in turn, those who had extended credit to my neighbor. I didn't waste time in trying to overcome their terror of the lunatic. No, with them I pursued a subtler course. After gaining their confidence, sir, I let it slip, as if by accident, that the chap's attempt to get a loan from the bank was being turned down."

"A clever stratagem," said Smythe.

The Colonel inclined his head in acknowledgment. "The effect was like one of these chain reactions, sir. First one creditor called for payment of his bill, then another, then a third and fourth, and sure enough, within a few days that young devil was beating a path to the bank, hoping to speed up his loan. I happened to be in town that day myself. As a matter of fact, I had just visited the banker, for I anticipated what would happen. I wanted to put some more iron in his nerve, you see, so he wouldn't back down at the last minute. I drew myself up, sir, to full height, and I told that banker in no uncertain terms, sir, that if he turned tail and approved the loan, I could not be held responsible for the consequences."

"And he followed your—ah—advice?"

"He did indeed, Mr. Smythe! I was standing near the bank when the young chap came out. Oh, you could tell he had suffered a blow. He thought he had the village under his thumb, like some feudal tyrant, you see, and then all of a sudden—" The Colonel brought his hands sharply together and laughed shortly. "He was ruined, sir! He staggered toward me, pale and trembling. He gave me one glance—ah, the hatred in it, Mr. Smythe!—'twas like the mask of a demon, sir! But like a coward, he said nothing, and passed on by. The next day his land went on the market!"

"You had finished him, then," remarked Smythe.

"Not quite! Ah, but there was another factor I almost forgot. It seems that my intervention had prevented a great tragedy, sir. The young schemer was engaged to marry the daughter of one of the other landowners, a lovely girl she was, and naturally, when his bankruptcy came to public notice, the engagement was canceled—"

"Naturally."

"—and the girl herself, saved from a life of horrors, was dispatched by her family to France, to avoid the villain's revenge. These chaps will stop at nothing, Mr. Smythe! But I should tell you of that look he gave me there in the street outside the bank. As plain as day, sir, that look spoke an unutterable passion for vengeance, as if that young devil had screamed aloud his intention of murdering me, of hunting me down, sir, no matter what the cost, no matter how long it might take—"

"Ah," remarked Smythe, "but he appears to have been unsuccessful, thus far."

The Colonel chuckled. "True enough, sir, true enough! I was too quick for him, I think."

"You sold your own property and moved down here, I would gather."

"Correct, sir."

"To remove yourself from the possibility of being shot down by this—this madman," said Smythe. He reached over to feel his coat. It was quite dry now, except, it seemed, for the area around the shoulders.

The Colonel watched his movements. "Well, sir, not precisely for that reason," he said slowly.

"Don't mistake my meaning, Colonel," said Smythe quickly. "I don't imply that you had any personal fear—"

"Understood, sir!" boomed the Colonel. "No, let me tell you. It was a rather unpleasant incident, and at its conclusion I chose to move away, for there was some hard feeling among ignorant persons up there.

"Well, sir, the morning after the scene at the bank, I was out walking along the edge of my property, when I thought I heard a noise nearby. It seemed to come from the direction of the lunatic's fields, so I slipped across the fence to investigate.

"Over a rise, I saw him. He was on his knees in the meadow, sobbing. A fit had taken him, Mr. Smythe. I could tell that he was nerving himself to some desperate deed, and I saw with alarm a bulge in his coat pocket which I took to be a pistol, but which actually was a knife. One of these little fold-up affairs, sir, but capable of carving a man to ribbons!"

Smythe reached again toward his coat. "How frightful, Colonel. And did he attack you?"

"He would have, sir, he most certainly would have!" The Colonel puffed heavily on his pipe, and the smoke obscured his face. "But again, I was too quick for the chap. I pulled out my revolver—and fired!"

"You disabled him, sir?"

"Not exactly, Mr. Smythe." The Colonel paused. "No, I killed him, sir. Killed him on the spot. There was some nastiness about it later, but the jury at length agreed it was clearly self-defense on my part. It was after that, Mr. Smythe, that I moved here. . . ."

The Colonel's voice faded and the echoes of his last words whispered along the walls. The dying fire glowed fitfully with little resentful spikes of reddish flame. The room hardened in silence. The Colonel's features seemed fleshier than before and his eyes were drawn into a squint.

When he spoke, his voice was thick, and it had a querulous tone. "But about our business, sir. About that so-called gap in my fence. Strange, most strange. I had not noticed it before you moved in, sir. Nor had my man Towsley, sir, and he's got a keen pair of eyes, Towsley has. . . . What—leaving so soon, Mr. Smythe? Come now, sir, is that quite neighborly? And before your coat is dry?"

The Evening Guests

Just how it all began, no one seemed to know. It may have been a savage quarrel, a series of nasty scenes, or simply a misunderstanding which their mutual suspicions had hardened into an unforgiving hostility.

Whatever the cause, it could not possibly have been so grotesque as the result, for George and Sylvia continued to live together—not as man and wife but as enemies. They refused to consider any of the civilized solutions which their friends urged on them. Reconciliation was out of the question, and separation likewise. Divorce was not to be mentioned.

Indeed, *nothing* could be mentioned. That was the ludicrous part of it. They ignored each other. They did not speak. Yet they continued, obstinately, to share the same house. And nothing passed between them, not a glance, not a gesture, not a single word.

Each was unwilling even to admit that the other still existed, and as if to fortify this defiance of physical reality, they went on spending their evenings in the living room—George in his easy chair near the hearth, his magazines and pipes close at hand, and Sylvia on the sofa with her books and her knitting, not twenty feet away.

Night after night they sat thus. The only sounds to be heard were the rustling of pages being turned, the scratchy sucking of the pipe, and the quick little snaps of the knitting needles. Weeks passed this way, and months. Never once did they speak.

It might seem unlikely that a man and wife could indulge themselves in such an impractical domestic arrangement for more than a day or two, but for George and Sylvia, it was not difficult. They already had separate bank accounts, separate bedrooms, and separate personal servants, so that when the trouble began, the cook needed merely to prepare their plates in the kitchen (however, they continued to eat together at the dining-room table, staring coldly at the silver service).

Neither would give up. Neither would be the first to yield. Sylvia would not visit her sister in Chicago, for that might imply flight, and George would not sleep at his club, for that might suggest that he was surrendering. Their friends persisted for a time in their well-intentioned efforts to bring about some rational course of action, but without the least encouragement. The name "George" seemed to have no meaning for Sylvia. She looked puzzled whenever she heard it, and changed the subject. As for George, the mention of his wife merely caused his eyebrows to peak a little, as if the speaker had uttered an impropriety. He would not recognize that there was anything to discuss. At length the friends stopped trying altogether. George and Sylvia were simply impossible; the whole thing was too ridiculous, too annoying. It made everyone uncomfortable, and so, one by one, the friends dropped away.

The passage of time only served to make the silence more profound. George and Sylvia continued to spend their evenings together. The lines around his mouth deepened; her brows were drawn in a perpetual frown. His hair thinned, and hers took on a silvery touch. Yet even this foretaste of age did not deter them.

They seemed bound to the prospect of a lifetime of silent evenings. Nothing, it seemed, could change their ways.

And then, one night, Mrs. Mayway appeared.

Inasmuch as she was Sylvia's friend, George did not see her. That is, he characteristically refused to see her, and indeed he resisted every impulse to turn his head her way. The fact that Mrs. Mayway had come to visit Sylvia was enough for him; he resolutely denied Mrs. Mayway's existence, too.

It was a stormy evening, with intervals of heavy thunder. George did not hear the front doorbell, nor was he aware that one of the servants had answered it to admit a caller (he was not alert to such a possibility, for no friend had visited for a good ten months). He sensed that Sylvia had set aside her knitting, had risen, had crossed to the entrance to the foyer, and was actually in the process of welcoming a guest. It was remarkable, being the first time in more than a year that he had heard her voice—detestable whinnying that it was!—raised in social tones.

"Mrs. Mayway!" Sylvia was saying, "How absolutely delightful of you to have come! And in such terrible weather! How terribly brave you are—and what a joy it is to see you!"

This shattering of the long-accustomed evening silence was shock enough to George, but to have it accomplished by the most hateful sound in the world—his wife's voice—was an outrage. He sat quivering in his chair, too confounded to hear Mrs. Mayway's reply. And who was this Mrs. Mayway? He could not recall such a name. It must be one of Sylvia's new acquaintances (he assumed that she had some, for she undoubtedly continued her idle daytime round of shopping and bridge parties). He squirmed uneasily behind his newspaper, gnawed at his pipe-stem, and vowed to maintain his outward composure at all costs.

Sylvia's voice, having smashed the silence, seemed now to be pricking him with the broken pieces. He clung to his newspaper, his eyes searching the columns for some story that would command his attention. But his consciousness was prisoner to Sylvia's voice, which swallowed up all other sounds—the drumming of the rain, the crackling of the fire. It even seemed to smother the responses of the other woman.

George's annoyance swelled up like a boil. He coughed and rattled his paper. The effrontery of this Mayway woman! It was positively indecent of her to sit thus in his presence, actually abetting Sylvia in what could only be a plot to torment him. Even if Mrs. Mayway let Sylvia do the talking—and good Lord, how Sylvia talked, as if the dam of silent nights had broken out a flood of words—it was the grossest insolence to have invaded his house, his hearth, his privacy. How he hated Mrs. Mayway, and how he hated Sylvia, whose voice dinned into his ears like the screeching of a harpy!

". . . yes, my dear Mrs. Mayway, loneliness is indeed the price one pays for freedom. I quite agree. We who are widows certainly realize that better than anyone. . . ."

George snatched the pipe from his lips and slammed it into the metal ashtray. So Sylvia had widowed herself! He permitted himself a small, savage chuckle, and with great effort kept from turning to glare outright at his wife and her guest. Who did Mrs. Mayway think *he* was, eh? A ghost, perhaps. He snorted, and pressed a button on the wall to summon his manservant. The ghost would drink damnation to them both, then.

The clock struck ten.

"Must you leave so soon? . . . Good heavens, can it be that late? . . . Oh, of course, I will. And *you* must come back again to visit me, dear Mrs. Mayway. I don't know when I've enjoyed an evening more!"

And George was aware that Sylvia had stood up, that she was mincing over to the foyer, and that at long last the detestable Mrs. Mayway was leaving the house. He shuddered in relief. When his manservant appeared, he ordered the drink at double strength.

But the following night, Mrs. Mayway returned. Again there was Sylvia's fawning welcome; again, the interminable gabble of Sylvia's voice; again, her maddening affectation that she and Mrs. Mayway were alone in the living room and that George was of no more significance than the chair he sat in.

It was worse this time. Monstrous, in fact. Sylvia began confiding in Mrs. Mayway certain secrets of her married life—things so delicate that they could hardly be mentioned even between a husband and wife who lived in loving harmony. Yet here Sylvia was blurting them out in George's presence to an absolute stranger!

As if this were not enough, Sylvia refused to treat these matters seriously. She giggled as she spoke; she even interrupted herself to laugh outright, and although at times she lowered her voice confidentially in the course of relating some particularly intimate event, her every word still echoed throughout the room.

George sat as if stunned. How could he stop her? Visions of violence simmered in his mind. Should he rise up in anger and order Mrs. Mayway from the house? Should he drown out that abominable voice by shouting and shouting? Should he seize the poker and smash their pale and pasty female faces?

Fortunately, he managed to remain seated and do nothing. Of course, he realized, this was Sylvia's design. This was why she had brought in this stooge of a Mrs. Mayway. She was determined to break him down, that was it. She knew that if he so much as turned his head to scowl at them—let alone shouted or raged— then she would have won, for, once he admitted her existence, she would proceed stage by stage until she succeeded in driving him from the house.

No, he would thwart her. He would sit still. He would keep his silence, though it cost him a thousand agonies. Let her keep it up; he would steel himself against her voice just as he had disciplined himself to ignore her presence, and soon that whining, screeching, sniggering nastiness that now so bedeviled him would become no more disturbing than the yapping of some moonstruck bitch a block away. Gritting his teeth, he settled back in his chair and forced his eyes to register each separate word in the first block of newspaper print he saw, a soap advertisement. He determined to commit it to memory.

But the struggle continued. Each night at nine o'clock Mrs. Mayway appeared, and for the ensuing hour, George was forced to endure Sylvia's voice. It was with the greatest effort that he adhered to his resolve. Not once did he turn his head, never did he permit a single murmur of protest to cross his lips, nor did he even lift his eyes from the page before him. A week went by in this way. He took a bitter satisfaction in this prolongation of his ordeal. How vexed Sylvia must be that he still held on! He almost chuckled aloud, thinking of *her* temptation—to steal a look at him, to see how well he was standing it. Ah, and if she did—and he knew he would sense it at once—then the victory would be his, not hers.

Nevertheless, by the end of the second week of Mrs. Mayway's nightly visits, George began to wonder how long Sylvia would keep it up and, similarly, how long he could tolerate it without some explosion. His only success was quite limited; he was able to banish Mrs. Mayway completely from his mind. Her speech, if indeed she spoke, could not be distinguished from the rustling of draperies stirred by a draft, and as for her appearance—well, he had not the slightest intention of glancing at her, goaded though he was to commit some such indiscretion by Sylvia's constant prating.

Toward the end of the third week, George noticed that his hands were trembling. He sought to control them, but in vain. The trembling grew worse. Helplessly he cursed his hands for betraying a weakness that might, against his will, spread to the rest of his body and so force him into premature surrender. He clenched them into fists, but still they shook, and the more he strove to master them, the more agitated they became, until at length he had to put his newspaper aside.

He was seriously worried. Was this merely a temporary affliction—or was it the first signal of collapse? He shifted position in his chair and stole a glance at his watch. He had forgotten to wind it, apparently, for it showed but five minutes past nine, and surely Mrs. Mayway had been in the room for a good half-hour.

He sank back, hopelessly. His hands, now jammed uncomfortably in his pockets, still twitched even there. Denied his newspaper, he felt totally at Sylvia's mercy and cast about wildly for some preoccupation intense enough to provide a new defense.

Her phrases seemed to burn on his skin like tiny wounds. ". . . oh, yes, Mrs. Mayway . . . And then let me tell you what happened, Mrs. Mayway! . . . And would you believe it, dear Mrs. Mayway? . . . Mrs. Mayway . . . Mrs. Mayway!"

It was a chant. Mrs. Mayway! In despair, he let his mind suck in the name, the way a drowning man might in the final moment deliberately gulp the murdering sea. Mrs. Mayway! Very well, then, he would turn all of his awareness on Mrs. Mayway. Perhaps by concentrating on her, he might find some release from what was infinitely more abhorrent—that incessant chattering.

He closed his eyes. He would not look at her—never would he do that—and yet to fix his mind on the idea of Mrs. Mayway, he had first to form some vision of her. He turned his head toward the fire. In the flickering play of light he seemed to see her image take shape. A short woman, and stout, he thought. Yes, she would be that, quite the opposite of Sylvia, who was lank and skinny (incredible that he could ever have thought Sylvia to be graceful and slender). Mrs. Mayway would have pouchy cheeks, no doubt, with a wart here and there, and probably a strong hint of a mustache above the corners of the mouth. A regular toad Mrs. Mayway would be!

And almost at once George felt better.

He thought that he could hear the woman's voice as well. It was not sharp and nasal, like Sylvia's; rather, it was the kind of voice one might expect to issue from a potato—a mealy, gurgling voice, full of liquid splutterings and hesitations, a nasty sort of voice, not uttering words but drooling them, in a ceaseless little whimpering about the injustices of life, as if life had not been all too lenient in permitting such a thing as Mrs. Mayway to exist at all.

Thus George sat staring into the fire, fascinated and repelled by Mrs. Mayway. He seemed almost to hear her voice, and to see her lumpy face and squat and shapeless body. The more firmly he fixed his mind on her, the less tormenting Sylvia's words became to him. In fact, he sometimes found it hard to believe that Sylvia still was speaking, for although he could not actually distinguish Mrs. Mayway's voice, he was obsessed with the idea of the way it *would* sound, just as he had become absorbed in the thought that Mrs. Mayway would, in reality, look precisely as he had already imagined her.

His stratagem was successful—marvelously successful. By concentrating on Mrs. Mayway, he had all but banished Sylvia. Yet his hands still trembled. Trembled more than ever. And his arms were quivering, too. Had he made some terrible miscalculation? He looked swiftly at his watch. No, he had not forgotten to wind it. It pointed nearly to ten. He could stand a few more minutes, surely. But what about the next night? What about the one after that?

Sylvia was exultant. She was wearing him down; slowly, to be sure, for he was displaying surprising tenacity, but the end would come soon. Yes, he would be forced out! She could hardly contain her eagerness. How clever of her to have thought of Mrs. Mayway! It had been the perfect choice. And how she had relished, with greedy appreciation, the precise degrees of torment to which George had been subjected—how he had squirmed, how he had silently raged, how he had grown stiff with apprehension—and now, with the end near, how he was trembling!

She was not even tempted to look at him, for the image which she had fixed in her mind revealed his deterioration quite as clearly as would the reality. She could *see* him there—a little man with narrow, uneasy eyes, and growing bald in an obscene, patchy way. Odd that she had once thought him lithe, wry and sophisticated.

Her voice rang out loudly: "*Dear* Mrs. Mayway . . .!" It was her battle cry. "Mrs. Mayway . . .!" It flashed like flame through the room. Let it burn him, she thought. Let it scorch him out. She laughed and scraped her nails along the arms of her chair, waiting for the inevitable scurry of his feet, the spluttering impotent outrage of his squeaky voice.

Ten o'clock sounded. Sylvia sighed. The next night, then, perhaps.

"Oh, dear Mrs. Mayway, how time does fly! And just when I was about to tell you of the time that—oh, well, it will have to wait, dear Mrs. Mayway. Until tomorrow? . . . How delightful!"

Yes, it *would* be delightful. It had been delightful from the very first evening, in fact, when she had escorted Mrs. Mayway into the living room. How flustered George had been! How helpless he was now! She was almost sorry it would soon be over. One more night would do it, she thought. Two at the most, surely. And then she would not need Mrs. Mayway any longer, for she at last would be mistress of the house and free to invite guests who were somewhat more congenial. Of course, she would be everlastingly grateful to Mrs. Mayway. . . .

But the following evening a strange thing happened.

It was ten minutes until nine. As usual, Sylvia was sitting on her sofa, busily knitting while her mind marshaled the hour's worth of sarcasms and innuendoes and gossip she would soon measure out to Mrs. Mayway.

George seemed to be remarkably restless. She sensed that he was already fidgeting in his chair, suffering the presence of Mrs. Mayway in anticipation. Quite probably he had spent a sleepless night and troubled day, rehearsing his passive agony. She smiled down at her knitting, savoring triumph.

Then she became aware that George had risen. He was actually leaving the room.

Sylvia sat quite still, amazed. Was it possible that it was all over? Was he yielding now—in the final moments before Mrs. Mayway's arrival—unable to bear the prospect of another evening?

She heard his voice in the foyer. Of course, he would be instructing his manservant to pack his bag and drive him to the club, that must be it. In her exhilaration, she turned her head boldly and gazed at George's easy chair for the first time in all these many months. It seemed ridiculously small; its leather was as creased as an old man's skin. Sylvia giggled. Perhaps George would send for it. If not, she would have it thrown out . . . yes, she would throw it out and change every lock in the house. Change all the locks, hire new servants and—redecorate!

But George had not left, it seemed. His voice still sounded in the foyer, and surprisingly enough, it was louder than before, as if he had turned her way again. Was it possible that he was coming back? And was he conversing with his manservant—or with someone else?

She wrinkled her face in distaste. How rudely his voice struck her ears, after his long months of silence.

". . . glad you could make it, sir. Quite a pleasure for me, I can tell you. . . . Straight ahead, Mr. Jobber, and we'll pull up by the fire. Nothing like a warm fire on a chill evening, eh?"

Sylvia gripped her knitting needles as if they were daggers. It was preposterous—a visitor for George? She stared angrily down at the heap of yarn in her lap. What nonsense it was. A mere diversion. The man would be inside the living room now (how sickeningly effusive George was being!), but naturally he would remain for only a few minutes, for he would see her sitting on her sofa, and when George failed to make an introduction, he would become quite embarrassed and uneasy and hastily invent a reason to leave.

"Is that chair comfortable enough, Mr. Jobber? . . . Are you quite sure? . . . Splendid! Ah, just let me ring for my man and we'll get a bit of warmth inside as well, eh?"

The French clock against the opposite wall was on the point of chiming nine. Sylvia regarded it in annoyance, wondering whether Mrs. Mayway's arrival might not be postponed for a few minutes, until the other guest was able to arrange his exit. Surely he would not, *could* not stay! And yet she could discern no signs of departure, for George was squeaking away at a great rate—almost a monologue, indeed—so that the poor visitor could find no opening to make his excuses.

"Whisky and soda, Mr. Jobber? . . . Capital! That's just the thing on an evening like this—and easy on the soda, if you'll accept my advice. This whisky of mine, you see, is almost a family inheritance. . . ."

On and on he rambled. Would there be no end to his garrulity? Sylvia could well picture the unfortunate Mr. Jobber poised all the while on the edge of his chair, peering uncertainly in her direction and wondering just how he could remove himself from what was clearly an untenable position. True, she could ease his path by just one rueful, understanding glance. But, of course, she would never do that, for then he might address her directly. No, he must be forced to speak to George about her first, so that George would be placed on the defensive.

The clock struck nine. Sylvia glared at it. Mrs. Mayway would have to wait just a bit, for once.

But Mr. Jobber did not leave. Sylvia sat clicking her needles furiously in a tangle of yarn. Was it possible that he actually intended to stay? By now there had been several opportunities for him to go, but he had remained, listening with evident satisfaction to George's boring stories. Smoking-car stories, too, some of them; most inappropriate in the presence of a lady, and yet Mr. Jobber's chuckles were an echo of George's own.

He must be common, dreadfully common. No gentleman would behave in such a fashion. Sylvia had never heard the name before—Mr. Jobber indeed! Even its sound was vulgar. She determined to banish the fellow from her mind. If he were one of George's new acquaintances, then he was below the notice of any civilized person. He did not deserve to exist.

At ten past nine, she decided it would be quite wrong to keep

Mrs. Mayway waiting any longer. Let the vulgarians swill their liquor and guffaw at off-color stories; she was not to be deterred from welcoming her own invited guest into her living room.

And so, looking neither to one side nor the other, she marched out to the foyer. "Mrs. Mayway? Good heavens, I must have kept you waiting! How thoughtless of me! . . . What? Oh, you're far too kind. . . . The pleasure is mine, Mrs. Mayway. But I mustn't keep you standing here a moment longer!"

In the living room once more, however, Sylvia found that her well-planned series of thrusts and jabs had been upset by the arrival of Mr. Jobber. Her composure was quite gone. Drat the fellow! She sought to bring her thoughts back in order, only to find them tumbling about haphazardly; odd phrases intruded disconnectedly right in the middle of that choice story she had so carefully prepared. Not that Mrs. Mayway would mind—but how *could* one converse rationally under such impossible conditions?

". . . and then, dear Mrs. Mayway, as you may remember, the poor fellow—you know, he absolutely *sobbed* in such a *tragic* way all through our honeymoon—oh, and I was going to tell you, the ridiculous part of it was . . ."

"Marvelous tale, eh, Jobber? Makes you want to explode, thinking of that old farmer's face when he came down from the loft and saw his wife? Reminds me of another one, by the way. About a goat and an elephant. . . . You haven't heard it? Well, it seems there was this goat, you see . . ."

They were all but shouting. Sylvia paused for breath. One of her knitting needles had snapped in her fingers; she tossed it aside. It was Mr. Jobber's fault, she decided. What a brute he must be. Tipsy half the time, no doubt. Probably a big hulking creature with hairy arms and great hands and feet, the kind of lout George *would* bring into her house, just to spite her. Well, she could put up with it for one night, anyway. Surely he would not dare come back again.

But he did. Mr. Jobber came each evening just before nine, arriving precisely in advance of Mrs. Mayway. Sylvia's knitting became hopelessly botched, and her clever little bits of gossip, confused and pointless. Thank heaven for Mrs. Mayway, she thought. But it was not the same, not the same at all.

Oh, how she *hated* Mr. Jobber! He was worse than George, even. An animal—an animal!—totally devoid of any human impulses of decency. And his voice—it was hardly a voice at all. He did not speak. He grunted, he croaked, he issued disgusting guttural noises, like the bubbling of some frightful swamp. It would be out of the question to look at him—one would faint straight away in revulsion!

She trembled so that she could hardly keep up her conversation with Mrs. Mayway. Good heavens, was it possible that *she* would be forced to leave, and not George? That was unthinkable . . . and yet the aura of Mr. Jobber—there, right in the same room with her—was becoming more unbearable each evening. George himself seemed to have faded. She heard his voice but fitfully, as in a dream, so preternaturally was she drawn by her unwilling vision of his guest. Would she break down completely? Would she and Mrs. Mayway be driven out, then?

"Oh, yes, Mrs. Mayway. *Dear* Mrs. Mayway. Tomorrow evening. Of course."

But her voice was a whisper. Even with Mr. Jobber gone for the night, she remained shaken, for the shadow of his presence seemed to linger in the room.

The time passed quickly now. Everything seemed to speed George and Sylvia along their separate daytime ways toward nightfall. Their evenings together in the living room still formed the heart of their existence, but what had been a cold and hostile silence before now echoed with their hasty voices, sounding and resounding without pause. The ritual of the hour of visitation had become unalterably fixed. It seemed impossible that Mr. Jobber would fail to come at his certain time, or that Mrs. Mayway would not arrive at hers, or that George and Sylvia would neglect for a moment to fill the hour with talk.

Thus the rhythm of the evenings assumed an impulse of its own. The talk flowed from them almost without effort, as if they were but the instruments for sounds originating elsewhere.

George heard his own voice and Sylvia's, but distantly, and the words were lost. He was not even sure at times that they were uttering words at all, only sounds—his sounds and Sylvia's. Sylvia was but a voice to him now—a voice producing random noises, and therefore hardly a real voice, simply a noise. But he was no longer concerned about Sylvia. Her significance had dwindled, for that of Mrs. Mayway had increased. He did not need to summon her image; it presented itself now voluntarily. It had acquired, somehow, a force of its own. When it had been but a momentary vision cast up accidentally by the vagrant flames, it was unpleasant enough, but worse was the premonition then of what it might become. Yes, it was that now. Something that had grown independently of his will. Something that was drifting across the boundary of tolerance.

Sylvia was short of breath. She spoke haltingly. She found herself staring at the French clock, urging it on. Suppose it stopped some night at nine-thirty, say? Suppose the servants forgot to wind it? Her voice broke. She coughed into her hand. "Please excuse me, Mrs. Mayway . . ." She hastened on. But there were shadows cast by the fire on that opposite wall. Strange she had not noticed them before. . . . One shadow was fluttering and gray, like that of thin fabric you could almost see through. The other one was black and solid; it did not move—except perhaps to grow slightly larger. And now the first one, she saw, was even more indistinct, fading as the other darkened. She wet her lips and twisted her fingers in the knitting yarn. That shadow, spreading like a stain. It would cover the wall soon. It would hide the clock.

The night was moist and heavy. Through the French windows, left slightly ajar, the fog came gently in. It gathered along the rug and, as more came in behind, built slowly up into a wall and slowly, too, edged forward. Soon George could not tell where the rug stopped, or if it stopped at all, for its edge was hidden by the wall of fog, and the far end of the room had disappeared. Now chairs and tables were vanishing as the fog crept forward, almost as if they were being sucked back out of sight. And the room was growing smaller.

The shadow on the opposite wall was reaching toward the clock. It touched the shining rim of gold. . . .

They left the room together. Doors swung open for them, and the pavement outside rang with their quick footsteps. They hastened along the glistening wet street, not yet aware that they were walking side by side, and as they went, they glanced back from time to time, wondering whether what they had summoned to that house and were now fleeing from would follow them still— or whether it might not already be up ahead, wherever they were going.

Dolley Madison
in Peru

¶ Va and Charles called it their "shack." It was built in the
native style with mud and straw and goatdroppings and other
materials too indigenous to mention, but the living room was fifty
feet long, with great old wooden ceiling beams (timbers from
Magellan's flagship, by local tradition), and passageways branched
off in all directions—to the kitchens, the family rooms, the guest
rooms, the library, the study, and then out to the servants' quarters
and a dozen other outbuildings where they kept the goats, the
horses and the helicopters.

Quite a shack. When Va told her friends about it, she said it
was crude, but the friends knew better. Va and Charles were
incapable of summering crudely. It was not merely their money
that prevented it, nor their unerring taste. It was rather a certain
joie de vivre, an effusion of the spirit, even an Olympian playful-
ness, as if they were Zeus and Hera descended to permit a few
lucky mortals to join in their amusing games.

And so the friends came. Everyone came. Did it matter that the shack was a thousand miles from anywhere? It didn't, not a bit.

Right now things were quiet at the shack. Bunnie, aged four, was in bed getting over a nasty scorpion bite; Deedee, eleven, was off in the window seat taking her Spanish lesson from Pete (the Finance Minister of Colombia, a wonderful person and devoted to Deedee), and the boys—Awful and Kiki, ages seven and ten—had been flown down to Lima in the big 'copter to see a bullfight.

Frau, the housekeeper, asked: "How many for supper tonight, madam?"

"Twenty," said Va. "No . . . thirty. Thirty would be safer. But do tell the men if they need to slaughter any more goats, to take them farther away from the shack this time. Awful is much too interested in blood. . . . Where are the McMinns?"

"The Secretary had to fly back to Washington early, madam."

"Poor Arthur. Did Mrs. McMinn go, too?"

"She went out with the *National Geographic* people to tag jaguars. They didn't say when they'd be back."

"I don't suppose they know when. But it's not important, Frau."

It *wasn't* important. Janice and her six *Geographic* people—or was it eight?—could come in any time, and hardly be noticed. They could even bring back some of their drugged jaguars, if they wanted, and park them overnight somewhere (preferably not with the goats). There was always room for more at the shack.

A buxom woman came in, wearing jodhpurs and sandals, her orange hair wrapped in a bandana. She cried out: "My God, Va. What a place. I've been lost for an hour." She stopped before the picture window. "What's *that?*"

"The Andes. Good morning, darling. Did you sleep?"

"Fabulously . . . and some delicious little Indian appeared with breakfast on a tray. I almost gobbled him up, the sweetheart. He had a sapphire in his forehead."

"That was the maharaja, dear. Charles and I insist on everybody doing a little something to help. Otherwise, this would be too like a hotel. But where are your boots, Rel?"

"I loathe boots," said Rel (everyone called her Rel, the initials she signed at the bottom of her political columns).

"House rule, darling. Because of the scorpions."

Rel jumped up on a chair. Va giggled and clapped her hands together, summoning a servant and sending him off for boots.

"There weren't any scorpions on St. Croix," Rel said reproachfully.

"No, but there were worse things. Tourists. Rel, that last season was frightful. You didn't come then, but we had swarms of them, parading through the yard, feeding the donkeys and taking pictures *all* the time. The Chief Justice was taking his sunbath one day when eight of them—from Iowa, I think—got in somehow with their cameras. It was abominable. Scorpions are a small price for privacy. Besides, St. Croix was definitely not a unique place for summering."

Not unique at all. Va and Charles had realized this after only two seasons. Before that, they had taken a chalet in the Rockies (Va was pregnant with Bunnie then, and Charles was writing his life of Burke) which had been most suitable except that the altitude was hard on guests with heart conditions (like the poor Chief Justice—the predecessor of the sunbathing one—who had overdone skiing and climbing and actually had expired), and before that, a charming cluster of cottages on an island off Maine, which had proved, unfortunately, to be "too available," as Charles had put it the day after the mayor of New York (Democrat) and the governor (Conservative) had arrived simultaneously for breakfast and come to blows. St. Croix had had its tourists . . . but the shack in Peru was working out splendidly.

"How do you find time to write, Va?"

"I simply lock myself away, dear. Marj and I are doing a play, did you know? Henry has promised to produce it this fall. We wired him the first two acts last week."

"But isn't Marj in Cambodia?"

"Ceylon. We collaborate by radiophone."

"Va, is it true that the President is appointing Charles to Defense?"

"Ask him yourself."

"Charles?"

"The President. He's flying in tomorrow, the darling. Oh, it's not a working trip for him, but he won't mind one teeny little question, not from you. . . ."

But was it the President—or the Prime Minister? No, the Prime Minister had arrived last night with Arthur and Janice, and now he was splashing outside in the nude pool. How pink he was.

Other guests were coming down to breakfast, or perhaps to lunch. Va greeted them with embraces, with kisses, with fluttering waves of her lovely hands. On the broad hearth, between the Great Danes, Katzenreich the sculptor was modeling her torso in guano. The heavyweight boxing champion was skipping rope on the terrace, and out of the stable came the jeweled maharaja, galloping a pony toward the polo field, gaily brandishing his mallet.

Someone was kissing Va's hand. It was Charles. . . . Back from Paris so soon? "Darling," she whispered in delight, patting his bald spot as he bent, "what's all this about you and Defense?" Charles chuckled and pinched her cheek. "Not Defense," he whispered back. "State. . . . Where are the boys?"

"In Lima, sweet. Awful so wanted to see a bullfight. Pete brought him the cutest little matador suit."

A scorpion went scrambling across the straw matting on the floor. Someone—Katzenreich?—seized a poker and gave it a fatal whack. Rel screamed. From the goat pens came an answering scream as the men began butchering for supper.

Lady Jane, the soprano, danced in, stunning in vicuña shorts. "Va—all this is so *splendid*. You've done it again, my dear. Whoever else would have thought of Peru!"

"Va is our pioneer," said Katzenreich.

Va kissed Lady Jane. She kissed Katzenreich, the Great Danes, everybody. She even blew a kiss after the goat scream that echoed against the sides of the blue-white Andes. Those mountains—how she longed to climb them, to claim them, to watch from their peaks over her lovely summer shack!

Supper was gay. They sat on the terrace beneath lanterns and stars, eating chunks of roast goat and drinking a rum concoction Charles playfully called "Old Incan." Cool breezes from the mountains blew the mosquitoes away, and General Gonzaga organized a crew with giant nets to bag the vampire bats that flapped up tipsily from the barns.

"*Much* better than St. Croix, Va," someone cried.

It was, much better. But how long would it last? Two summers? Three? Already one heard talk of a road. Then there would be a hotel somewhere, a ski resort in the mountains, retirement villages and all the rest.

"Time for bed, pigeon," Va said to Deedee, kissing her.

Deedee made a face. "Must I, *Maman?* So soon?" She cursed in Spanish (how sly of Pete to teach her that!) and complained: "But everything's so lovely now. And tomorrow they may all be gone."

She went off, finally, after Charles promised to let her keep a jaguar cub, if Janice brought one back. (Where *was* Janice? No matter. Professor Graves knew the jungle like the back of his remaining hand.)

Yes, thought Va, everything was lovely now. And no one would leave tomorrow (or if some did, then others would come to take their places). But still, if it was doomed . . . She had a moment of panic. Charles—she wanted Charles. She found him at the fire pit, helping Gonzaga haul out a bat which had taken a nosedive into the embers. "Charles . . ." She clung to him. "After the shack—what?"

Charles dropped his end of the bat. Va needed him more. "There's always the Antarctic, my dear." He breathed into her ear and nibbled at the lobe, her lover. "And Tierra del Fuego." He chuckled. "Even—the Catskills." Va clapped her hands. Of course. How unique *that* would be. No one else would think of it—until too late. She gave Charles a grateful kiss and whirled back to her guests . . . no, first she rushed into the shack to give an extra good-night kiss to her babies, and a special hug to poor Awful, who had jumped into the bullring and had been slightly gored. Sad little kitten, he had wept so over his torn costume. If only he had more of Charles's good sense, and less of Va's impulsiveness!

How did it all begin—or had it ever begun? Hadn't they been together, Va and Charles, forever? She stood naked in the moonlight that trailed like curtains from their bedroom windows, brushing her hair, listening to Charles as he lay in bed, telephoning Washington, New York, London, Berlin. The soft little light that illuminated the dial glowed up caressingly on his face, making him look as young as when they had first met, skiing on the Zugspitze. She, unpracticed, had done a Christiania across his schuss; they tumbled together, skis snapping like firecrackers, and arose, red-cheeked, angry and in love, seeing in each other's wind-watered eyes the vision of their future life.

But life would end! She sobbed. Charles glanced at her, pausing in midsentence.

"Oh, Charles." She wept.

Charles hung up on the Polish Premier. He swung his legs from the bed and leaped to take her in his arms. "My sweet, my own Va."

"We will die, Charles!"

"Never, Va." He lifted her and stepped out on the balcony. The Andes were shimmering with snow and stars. "We are immortal, Va." He kissed her. Near the stables, a quick shadow moved. There was a burst of light, a sharp report . . . the shadow plunged and fell. "Puma," said Charles. "Gonzaga got him." He chuckled. "Don't worry, dearest. They always go after the horses first."

"I don't care about the pumas."

"Are you and Marj fighting over the play? Tell Charles."

"No, no. . . . Oh, Charles, this will end some day."

"Nonsense. We have barely begun. Just think—State! You'll be my Dolley Madison. We'll wear powdered wigs and take snuff, Va."

"Tell me more, Charles." She clasped him tightly. How strong Charles was, how calm and sure.

"We'll give the most splendid dinners, Va."

"More splendid than London?"

"Much more splendid. I was only Ambassador then." He kissed her again, lightly, on the forehead. "We'll do exciting things, Va, in State. Receptions, parties, balls."

"You can wear your medals, Charles."

"You are my only medal, Va."

"Dear Charles." But still she was not at ease. The Andes troubled her. How superior they were, so massive and aloof. They did not care! "What lies beyond them, Charles?"

"Beyond the mountains? The rain forest. Tribes. Another world, Va, not ours."

"Not ours?" She shuddered, naked in the chill night air. "Then . . . whose?"

"No one's, Va. Does it matter?"

It did matter. Va could not say why. But she could not bear to distress Charles. She hugged him fiercely. "It *won't* end."

"Never."

"And next summer, or the one after that, Charles, when we have to leave the shack and go to—"

"Tierra del Fuego."

"Even then, they won't desert us, will they, Charles?"

"Of course not, Va."

"And our lives will always be full!"

"Always, Va!"

"And unique!"

"Unique, Va."

"Oh, Charles. . . . But what does it mean?"

"This, Va." He kissed her. "To use," he said, "and be used." He swung her around and carried her back inside the room, his mouth on her throat.

"To be uniquely used, Charles," she cried, digging her finger-nails into his shoulders. Scorpion . . . vampire . . . bat . . . puma . . . they stung and clawed each other in their delicious, devouring love.

They were all in little Army planes, threading vapor paths in the sky above the jungle. General Gonzaga had performed wonders of organization, even finding a child's parachute for Awful, who just wouldn't be left behind.

How thrilling of Janice. Two nights in the jungle with her geographers and all those fearful creatures! No one would have worried if Professor Graves's watch hadn't been found in the stomach of the puma Gonzaga shot.

Va was crouched at the open hatch, peering down with binocu-lars. Not a wisp of smoke, not a gleam of metal or patch of ground; just the endless tangle of wet green trees, fairly throbbing with growth. "Do close that bloody door, Va," said the Prime Minister. "I can't light my pipe."

"You aren't supposed to smoke," said Awful from the corner

where he was playing with his parachute. He pulled the emergency cord. The chute, pointed Va's way, vomited nylon. It filled the tiny cabin. "Blast and damn it, boy," grumbled the Prime Minister, struggling in the folds, "you've knocked my pipe away. Unbuckle," he added, seeing that Awful was being dragged toward the hatch as the peak of the chute flopped outside and caught the air. Cursing, he seized Awful by the leg, unstrapped the chute, and let the wind snatch it.

"Look at Mamma go!" cried Awful, in envy.

Va, having been expelled through the hatch, was swinging rapidly down beneath her own parachute. Just before she vanished into the jungle, she waved up gaily, to show that she was all right. . . . Good-bye, everyone! She gazed for one placid instant at the dozen little planes—which one was dear Charles in?—and at Awful's chute, cavorting across the sky like a mad little cloud.

She came down through slimy branches. Wads of damp greenery slapped in her face like mops. The chute collapsed on her, caught on prickly boughs, ripped and gave, ripped and gave, easing her to the dark ground with hardly a bump or scratch. She stepped from the white folds, a jungle butterfly in madras slacks and yellow boots, still holding the binoculars. A snakelike vine was twisted around her thigh. She pulled it away, shuddering. What a stench of decay there was, and what a mess of debris strewn about and rotting away—a badly kept jungle. "Me Tarzan, you Jane," she cried out defiantly, to keep her spirits up. A few yards away, what had looked like a scattering of mushrooms on moss sat up and opened one sleepy eye at her. It was a jaguar, a dart still in its side. "Be a good puss-puss," said Va. The jaguar yawned and lay back down. (Janice never did things by halves. The jungle must be simply cluttered with snoring beasts.)

She picked her way among the greasy trees. Giant flowers mouthed at her, mosses sucked at her boots, plump spiders danced in their webs. But she must not go far. How vexed Charles would be if she wandered off while they were searching for her. She glanced up—but the bits of sky she saw were black, and the treetops were waving. It was storming now; the planes would have had to go back.

Poor Va. Now Marj would have to finish the third act by

herself. Perhaps Henry could stage it as a memorial, with the actors in black, and muffled drums beating. (Were those muffled drums she was hearing now? How coincidental.) And Charles, would he remarry? Yes, of course he would, the darling. But he might choose badly . . . if only she could advise him! Perhaps she could carve the names of the best candidates on the tree beneath which they would find her body. But she had no knife. (Those drums again—the idiots would wake all the jaguars.)

A great bearded spider tumbled down on its silk and swung before her face. She gave a cry and ran through a clump of oily brush, startling something large and brown that had been watching her. It fled. Surely, a man. "Stop," shouted Va. She chased him, following his course as he plunged unseen through the nasty growths, snapping off flowers, leaving great prints in the ooze and moss. The jungle came alive. Snakes fled up trees, monkeys scrambled among the branches, screaming, and birds fought until their feathers scattered down, as Va dashed after her lumbering quarry. She could hear him nearer, gasping, losing ground. He was out of condition, clearly. When she caught him, she would recommend a month at Madame Su's club, plus two sets of tennis before breakfast.

It *was* a man. An oafish young man, tattooed from head to toe, and definitely flabby. She overtook him just as he burst into a tiny clearing, and flung himself, sobbing with exhaustion, on the ground before a fire over which turned the spitted body of what Va rather hoped was a jaguar. The drums were there, too, but the drummer had vanished.

Hovels made of mud and branches were ranged haphazardly beyond the fire. Out of them now hurried gross women, sagging with fat, carrying babies and shooing the older children ahead. They were shrieking and howling. Va, hardly winded, stepped forward with one hand raised, signifying peace, but the children ran into the jungle, and the women, baying in terror, waddled after them. How Madame Su would have clucked at the sight of those wagging backsides and puffy ankles!

The men, it appeared, were drunk. They sprawled in hammocks, cradling clay jugs of home brew, and when Va went from one to another, giving them a shake, they merely sighed or smiled and dreamily scratched their loins. She finally tipped one hammock over, spilling out a guts-tub of an old man who wore jungle roses in his filthy hair and might be the chief.

She spoke to him in Spanish, Portuguese, French, even in German, Swahili and Latin, but the old toper only staggered back and forth, blinking his red eyes, dribbling at the mouth, and shamefacedly adjusting his loincloth. She had come on a jungle debauch, just her luck. Or were they always in a state of wassail? And nobody was tending the jaguar. It would be burned. She went to the fire and gave the spit a turn.

The pudgy young brave she had chased was trying to kiss her feet. Most abasing. She pushed at him with the toe of her boot. Now the men were peering at her from over the edges of their hammocks. She shouted at them, and they ducked down. She supposed they would expect her to be their white goddess and preside at their idiotic feasts and dances. She could well imagine how clumsily they would dance. Even Ravenevsky, who had drummed grace into many a bowlegged diva, would despair of them. Being white goddess here would not be in the slightest unique.

But had she a choice? The storm had blown the planes away. They could never find the place again from the air, and Gonzaga's army could hack machete paths for fifty years through the rain forest without finding her. Could these savages guide her out? Most unlikely. Even sober, they were undoubtedly too incompetent to go more than a mile or two without themselves becoming lost. No, she was doomed. How frightful it would be, wasting her lovely life alone with these buttery louts. Clearly, thought Va, that would be impossible. Good taste alone would proscribe it. There was but one alternative. These creatures were savages. . . . Very well, then they must pull themselves together. They must act like savages. They must be whipped into shape, recast in the noble forms which surely their ancestors had possessed.

But how difficult it was. How frustrating! It took her two weeks alone to make them adopt a sensible slenderizing diet. The men were taken off their home brew, too (Va acting as a one-woman temperance society, smashing jugs and gourds by the dozen), but even so, the vulgarians would sneak off into the brush to glug some in private. How these backsliders would groan at the morning calisthenics—and how ruthless Va was in keeping them at it!

Several times she almost despaired. If only they had some redeeming grace or skill, if only they did not depend on her for everything. Arts and crafts were unknown to them, for she had searched the hovels and found not so much as a basket, let alone a rude painting or piece of jaguar scrimshaw. Their language (consisting chiefly of grunts and sighs) was nowhere evident in written form, and perhaps just as well. Va devised a new one, simple and forthright, relying heavily on signs. The whole tribe went to school each day right after push-ups. No more napping, no more snacks, no more jungle juice!

They were docile. They wanted to learn. They worshiped their Va. She could not be too angry with them, when they loved her so. It was still not unique being white goddess to these bumbling fleshpots, but they were doing their best, perhaps, poor dears. The women had shed pounds, even if they still were blubbery, and it was touching to see how they tried to copy Va's hairstyle with their matted locks. The men, hopeless Falstaffs that they were, had at least a sensitivity to Va's moods. When she praised them, they wagged themselves and beamed, and when she frowned, they moped and slunk about.

Was Va pleased with them? She was. She had to be. No one else could have managed them so well. And yet, if only someone were there to see! How Charles would applaud, how delighted Marj would be (and just a little envious, too, n'est-ce pas?), how thrilling for everyone. Suppose they found her? Suppose they came? What fun to see them, what pride to show them her Indians. . . . But would she not be the least bit annoyed, as well? Her Indians were not sophisticated, perhaps, but they were true to their Va, and they would never leave her (indeed, they had no place to go). When she died, how they would weep, how they would tear their greasy hair and gnash their rotting teeth—and there would be no rival to become Va II. If they were not unique to her, at least it was a comfort to know that she was unique to them, the loyal simpletons.

Noises in the sky! Airplane engines—buzzing, roaring, thundering close! Then, circling overhead, great grasshopper forms of 'copters, with strange white puffs bursting below them—parachutes!

Down they drifted, a dozen and more, crashing through the trees, plunging through the roofs of the hovels, dangling from branches, all roaring out for Va, Va, Va. They had come for her at last, the sweethearts. They simply could not go on without their Va! "Va—how clever of you!" Yes, there was Marj, in the cutest little cap, and dear Charles in goggles, caught twenty feet up in the vines, hacking himself free with a knife, and here came Janice, who'd been found after all, and poor Rel, screaming again, having landed butt-first in the fire embers. "What *have* you discovered, Va? A lost tribe, I'm sure!" That was Lady Jane, floating down hand in hand with the Prime Minister, with Awful not far behind them, still in his matador suit, the brave little trouper. And General Gonzaga was rounding up the Indians for Madame Su and Ravenevsky (how *delightful* of them to have come, too) . . . and here came the President, the darling, thumping to the ground, pince-nez askew and a basket of goat sandwiches on his arm. "Is this next year's surprise already, Va?" Oh, it was, it was. She wept with joy and anguish. They were taking her Indians away before she had finished with the stupid dears. But it *was* a new place, next year's surprise, and here came Charles, trailing vines, to hold her fast in his strong arms. "My darling Va." He saw the gladness in her eyes, saw the pain there, too. He glanced around, he smiled, he *knew*. "Va, you have conquered. My sweet pioneer!" They kissed deliciously. "Don't grieve, my heart," he whispered. "Our jungle, Va. Our Indians. Our world!"

Living
in Sin

¶ Her brother Sam tramped around the room, peering at the stacks of books, the records, the ironing board leaning in a corner, even at the empty fireplace, where dustballs waltzed in the chimney draft.

"So," he said. "Well." He gazed at the flaking plaster ceiling. "You still like it here, then?"

"Sure. Listen—sit down. I'll make some coffee."

"Okay." He sat in the center of the sofa with a look of increasing discomfort, as if the loosened springs were gradually working their way into him. Still his eyes made inventory of the room, searching the clutter for evidence.

She felt like laughing. So obvious.

"It'll be instant coffee," she said, getting up from the armchair. Then she did laugh, and when Sam examined her in surprise, she said: "You look so—so big for a place like this. New York is for little people, didn't you know that?"

He followed her around the corner to the kitchenette, his squeaky shoes conversing with the floorboards. Flatfoot, she thought. Detective. A vice squad of a brother—and so great was the contrast between his majestic inquisitiveness and the pace at which everything had been hidden at almost the final minute, with the very last incriminating male possessions being hurled into the bedroom closet even as Sam's great feet were torturing the first of the four flights up, that she giggled.

"What's so doggoned funny, Mae?"

"Nothing, really," she said, but one more giggle escaped. "I'm sorry."

From elsewhere in the building came wails of children, scrapes of furniture, rattles of radiators, ripplings of old walls running with roaches, tributaries to a river of sound, above which, foamlike, danced the notes of Fineberg's flute from the floor below, played not by Fineberg, but by Goch. Her lover, Goch, impudently piping, sour trills and squeaks, letting her know how close he was—at Fineberg's, right beneath the feet of the suspicious brother—fluting away. In the closet, Goch's pajamas, Goch's wadded shirts and underwear still slowly unwrinkling from their hasty inflinging. And now Goch himself a presence unseen, like Tinker Bell.

Sam watched her pour the boiling water. "Mother's got a bad cold," he said.

"I guess so. She always starts the winter with one." She didn't mean to sound callous. She added: "Poor Mama."

"They'd like you to write more often, Mae."

"I'll try. I do try. Here." She handed him his cup. "But it's hard to find time, with my job. I write oftener than they do."

"Well, they phone you."

"Sure, that's easy. But how can I do that on my budget?"

They moved back into the living room—four paces—and now the fluting seemed to issue up between the floorboards at their very feet, as if Goch, following the creaking overhead, had leaped upon a table.

"You coming back, Mae?"

"For Christmas? I guess so, maybe."

"Well, no. I meant—you know, back home."

"To live?" She shrugged; the flute, as if urging her on, produced a cadenza concluding with a terrific flat. Her brother gazed in wonder at the musical floor. Again, the contrast was too much. She giggled.

"Is it that funny?"

"Well, yes, by God, it is funny." She was suddenly annoyed. In her own apartment, why suppress laughter? "Look, I sweated for a couple of years to get off on my own. Why go back? I *like* it here. Do you think I want to go back and be some jerky secretary waiting for some dumb yuck to ask me to be his goddam blushing bride? So we can sit side by side watching the sun sink into Lake Erie, fully four feet deep?"

Sam looked ludicrous, manifesting silent hurt at her words. Below, the flute stopped as there was a heavy thump—Goch fell off the table?—then bravely resumed, to show her he was all right. Bleeding, maybe; lying broken on Fineberg's floor, perhaps, but like Roland at the pass, with the last breath blowing immortal confidence.

"I didn't know you felt like that about it." Sam stared into his cup, where undissolved brown grains floated. "When you left, you said maybe six months."

"Then I guess I didn't mean it, or I changed my mind. What's the diff, anyhow?"

"Well, for one thing the folks'd like to see you closer."

She shrugged, with just one shoulder.

It seemed to anger him. "They *worry* about you. A girl alone in New York. Is that such a terrible thing?"

"Look, they've *always* worried."

"They want to see you happy, they'd like to see you marry some nice guy. Somebody they know. Listen"—he raised a hand to forestall protest—"I'm not telling you how to run your life, Mae. I'm just saying what the folks feel. As far as I'm concerned, it's your business. Be happy in your own way. You mentioned some New York guy in a letter. If he's the one for you, so be it. I'm all in favor," he went on in trombone tones, his face solemn with insincerity. "Whatever you want, Mae. New York, a life of your own, this guy—what was his name?"

"Goch."

"Yeah, well. Whatever his name is, I'd like to meet him sometime, I really would."

"His first name is Lazarus," she said, probing hopefully for anti-Semitism.

"Well, that's an old Biblical name," Sam said warily. "What's he do? In business?"

"He doesn't really do anything." The flute had stopped; now Goch was singing falsetto, mimicking Mrs. Fineberg, in that lady's presence, doubtless. Puccini, with a Yiddish accent. "He's a sort of student," she added, seeing now, on the mantel, a single tennis shoe—man's, Goch's—which had escaped notice earlier. It vexed her. All that rushing around to hide things had been Goch's inspiration—she hadn't really cared—and, of course, something was bound to have been overlooked. Maybe Goch had left it there deliberately.

"At Columbia?"

"No," she lied. "Yeshiva. You know—the Jewish university"—a dilemma for brother Sam: report Yeshiva back home and risk deeper parental groans, or hold it unspoken inside like something insoluble swallowed in error?

"Oh, yes. I see."

"See what?" She felt the urge to poke, pinch, bedevil, and—now that the serenade had ceased below—to get rid of him before Goch took it into his head to do something else, perhaps to appear tools in hand at the door to repair a nonexistent TV set. Bourgeois apprehensions, possibly, but Goch himself had set the stage by his insistence that the apartment be de-Goched and innocent.

"Well—nothing." Again the manufactured hurt look; an elephant whose toes you stepped on, pretending pain. "You're kind of touchy, Mae."

"I'm tired."

"Well, listen. I've got some stuff to buy before my train leaves. . . ."

Still, for twenty minutes he sat tongue-wagging about nothing, his law studies, his this and his that, no more questions, no more assurances he wanted her to live her own life, but the eyes kept gathering in further exhibits of wickedness neglected by the sinners: the unemptied ashtray with its three cigar butts; the

Argyll sock which seemed to have inched out to view from beneath the sofa, and—worst of horrors—the wire trouser-stretchers that had been left, skeleton outlines of male legs, beside the ironing board.

At last, Sam was at the door, ducking his head as if anticipating a low lintel, but actually to kiss her cheek, and mumbling, "Well, so long, Sis"—the "Sis" designed to evoke memories of the old bonds of family, thus sentiment; thus, perhaps, repentance—but there was no response, for she was preoccupied with Goch's whereabouts. Lurking on the stairs? Probably; so she did not offer to see her brother down, for the two of them together might inspire Goch to a prank.

"Good-bye, Sam. You take care."

She listened at the door to the receding thunder of his descent, then as in a stock comedy, a breath: "Whew!" The whole apartment seemed lightened, expanded. She went quickly into the bedroom and opened the closet to see if the ironed shirts could still be saved, and shrieked, for Goch was there inside, completely nude.

"My God. You nut. Suppose—"

"I heard him leave." He pranced out, plump and rosy.

"But—"

"And if he'd been with you, chicken, I'd have melted into the wall." He struck a boxer's pose on the bed. "Wasn't I sneaky quiet when I came in? Anyhow, I had my story all ready. I'm subletting, see? Poor struggling artist, no money, leasing limited space in apartment. Doesn't a man have the right to privacy, changing his clothes in his own goddamn room, be it closet or what?"

"You left your tennis shoe on the mantel." She found the shirts, hopelessly balled together.

"A minor slip-up. Listen, Marky's coming over this afternoon; he'll bring beer."

"Who's Marky?"

"He's a singer; Markovitz. A Negro folksinger." He flung himself down on the bed and embraced a pillow. "A piercing tenor voice, really great. Mrs. Fineberg will be beside herself. Well, not really a Negro, I guess. With a name like that." He sat up, yawning. "You think that shoe was vital, chicken?"

"I don't care. It was your idea. Look at these damned shirts!"
She flung them at him. "This Markovitz, don't you even know
him?"

"He's a friend of Sara's. She invited him over."

"Well, swell. I'm tired. Why doesn't he go sing at her place?"

She *was* tired. Goch seemed to sense it, and his manner
changed. He began quietly to dress—no more joking—and helped
her pull his things out of the closet. "Chicken, I'm sorry about
your brother. Maybe you were right. And I'll shoo this Marky off
so you can take a nap, okay? My God, they seem to flock to me; I
can't help it, and they just lounge around," he said, in sincere
distress, "making a mess for you to clean up."

"I don't clean up. You do." She sat down on the bed, letting
him pad around the room picking up and putting away, mothering
her with little pats as he passed. "Sometimes," she added.

Markovitz came anyway; no Negro, no singer, just a student
with an ugly pimpled face, amorous when Goch was absent
(getting the beer, which Markovitz had not, after all, brought).

"Look, keep your hands to yourself."

"Sorry; just trying to pass the time." Unembarrassed, undefiant,
unanything. "Say, how'd you ever get lined up with this guy Goch
anyhow?"

"It happened."

"Yeah, I guess. I had a girl to live with last year down on 115th
Street somewhere, I forget. A Puerto Rican girl."

"Tremendous."

"So, it wasn't bad. I was working after school in this cafeteria,
see, and she was on the tables, a nice brown girl like an Indian,
very serious eyes, without hardly one goddamn word of English,
and so one day I . . ."

(*"It happened."*) Markovitz was singing her to sleep with lies
about his Puerto Rican beauty, and she not suppressing yawns but
wondering just how, exactly how, it did happen. How did the
tennis shoe get on the mantel, the Argyll under the sofa, how
come Goch's pink self in the bed? Happened. Perhaps because she
had a job, Goch none; so with his energy undistracted, his
buoyancy unfretted by 9 to 5 (slept till noon), he had over-

whelmed her, *outnumbered* her, beset her from all sides with Gochs—cheerful Gochs, charming Gochs, Gochs like playful cherubs, like brothers mothers fathers, surrounded her with a friendly crowd, all Gochs. And so to bed, where there were more Gochs still.

She awoke. Markovitz was at it again, an unwashed hand patrolling.

"Damn you, cut it out."

"Jesus. You don't have to get sore about it."

"Well, apparently I do."

"Oh, come on. What's the problem?"

"Look in a mirror to start off with, Markovitz."

Unoffended, unabashed, just bored. Fantastic: she, dog-tired on a Saturday afternoon, required to entertain this creep, not even a friend of Goch's.

"Where you from, Mary?"

"Mae. From the old country: Ohio."

"Ha ha. How'd you come to come here?"

"Glory, freedom. I saw you raise your lamp beside the golden door, Markovitz."

"Pretty witty. That the way they talk back in Ohio?"

The phone rang. Markovitz, as if he saved his strength for one act each day and this was it, leaped. "Hello? . . . Well, it's for you," he said, turning, amazed.

The call was from Sam at Penn Station; one last good-bye and he had gotten Markovitz.

They both made it short. ". . . Okay, Sam, I'm writing them tonight and you tell them everything's just fine. . . . That? Oh, um, that was um, Brewster DuPont, um, he's an instructor at Columbia at the Divinity School, he just dropped in with, um, his two sisters for tea. . . ." So *tired*, and the voice was hers but the words from Goch, from the impish harmless little Goch that had somehow gotten inside her head. On the other end, she sensed, puzzlement, suspicion, hurt puffing up the booth. A sigh and a headwag: Good-bye Sis.

She hung up.

"Say," Markovitz complained, "what's this 'DuPont' stuff? You making some kind of anti-Jewish crack there?"

"Yeah, heil."

Goch appeared with the beer, also with Sara, a dark little girl, a family friend, maybe a cousin, who was always worrying at him, even now, as they entered:

"Call your mother."

"Sure." He bellowed: "*Mother!*"

"On the phone, damn you. Call her up. She's very upset she hasn't heard from you for weeks."

"Ye gods, she's fifteen blocks away. She can dial, she can call a taxi. Mae, you got the can opener somewhere?" (Markovitz rose, a human can opener, and went to help with the beer.) "Look, Sara, I'm setting one whole can aside for Mother. She's welcome to it. Let her come, drink, just so she doesn't open her yap."

"Ingrate, she *loves* you."

"Let her love—silently. Here, take this one to Mae. She looks pooped."

A noisy afternoon. *Noisy.* Markovitz giving unconscious performance as Early Man, beer to bathroom and back, each trip announced, pimples in beard stubble like wild strawberries in brush; Sara brooding aloud, self-appointed Big Sister, on Goch's failures as a son, and Goch, oppressed, being snappish.

"You're going over to dinner tomorrow, I assume," Sara said. She cracked her knuckles; a challenge.

"Why ask? I don't know. Stop pestering me. Is she paying you to pimp for her or something?"

"Just because it would make them happy, a little bit happy. Look at Mae. She's a thousand miles from home, but she writes."

"She's independent. She's a thousand miles away. She doesn't *have* to go to Sunday dinners, so why not write? *I'd* write, too. Besides, she's got parents who approximate human beings, probably, not psychotic destroyers of souls—"

"So be independent, then. Earn your living."

"—do you know who sits at the dinner table? Freud. Not only Freud—Jung. Adler, too. He's there. How would you like it to have a bunch of old whiskered characters sneaking around while you're trying to eat your noodles and veal, whispering in everybody's ears, exchanging their goddamn little significant glances, and then, by God, between courses they creep off in a corner and—consult!"

"You're impossible."

"What about you, golden girl? You. You're in love with your father, a fact known to all. Why don't *you* leave home and go a thousand miles away?"

"You pig, I'm at least working toward my degree."

"A cover for your unholy lust."

"Bah. You're just trying to avoid facing up to your own responsibilities. Twenty-six years old, a bum."

"All right, a bum. But a bum has no responsibilities to face. Morally, I'm in the clear. Admit it."

Markovitz rose again. "This stuff goes through me like nobody's business," he said, marveling, and headed off.

That night, Mae was weepy. The shade in the bedroom broke and flopped down when she pulled the cord, and there were new roaches in the kitchen, behind the refrigerator, and the living-room sofa held Markovitz, sleeping.

"Pigeon, what's wrong?"

"Oh, dammit, I don't *know*."

"Period? No, couldn't be yet." Goch was patting her. "That damned Marky. Don't worry, I'll get him out." But he didn't. He did imitations to amuse her, even dashed downstairs for the flute and came back piping; then ran the vacuum cleaner around the room, singing, prancing—a vaudeville for Mae sitting sniffling on the bed.

"You're upset. Your brother—"

"No."

"Something about your parents. They're sick—or well."

"Oh, no."

"Don't deny. Tell Papa. It *is* parents."

"No, it isn't. Why does it always have to be parents? My parents are just ordinary normal people. I can't stand them. I don't think about them."

"Ah, that's the difference. *Mine* are absolute loonies. I think about them all the time—can't help it. They drum themselves into

me; two drumsticks, one for each and me the drum. Listen, I'm
going to rout Marky out this minute." He turned toward the door
decisively, and she could tell somehow that he was planning
ahead: no Marky, an empty apartment, then maybe love to restore
the sense of well-being.

But she was just too tired. "No, I think it is the period. Sometimes I'm ahead. I guess that's it."

"Poor baby. I'll get Marky out."

But he didn't. He wouldn't. He couldn't. She went into the
bathroom, searching for unpleasant traces of Markovitz, knowing
that Goch would wake the visitor from his nap and then, to avoid
the unpleasantness of a direct approach, begin to converse, perhaps play some records, even open more beer—or, if none left,
depart to buy more—and there they'd be till dawn or later than
that, maybe. The last one—Sillman, the indigent painter—had
stayed, ye gods, for a week, a solid week, and even then he had
practically had to fight to escape Goch's hospitality. Throw Marky
out? She fell back on the bed, she laughed, she wept, she clapped
her forehead—Goch's gesture. Why not protest—really protest—
all these Markovitzes? Her apartment. (Well, Goch paid half—or
rather the elder Gochs, the unseen monsters, via Goch's allow-
ance.) Oh, but Goch couldn't help it; tried, but couldn't somehow
seem . . .

She awoke with the light still burning, the vacuum cleaner
moaning—left on, forgotten by Goch, it had sung her to sleep, but
now was dying. She hastily turned it off, and heard from the living
room the flute plus something else—a harmonica, wailing plaid
notes to Markovitz's nuzzlings. An outrage to her. What to do?
March in angry, make a scene, expel Markovitz?

Barefoot, hair wild, eyes wet and red, face puffy, she washed and
while washing listened to the music, each player going in a
different direction, oblivious of the other or perhaps unable to
come together. She listened, wondering. Music, real music, had a
point, didn't it? It went somewhere; it could be predicted, if you
knew enough about it—and that was the joy of it, even when it
was awful, for when your predictions came true, you were satisfied,
happy. And even if you didn't know enough to predict correctly, it
didn't matter; you knew the composer had planned it all out, and

so his happiness in the working out of his plan ran through the music, and that *anybody* could feel.

But this—the squeaking flute, the mumbling harmonica—this was different. No music, no plan, just noise; like the trucks and cars, like the people snoring and moaning, the bugs in the walls, the screams of cats on roofs, of police cars far away, everything bounded by cement and shaking out noise.

Even clean, her face was appalling. A pretty girl, but defiant, angry, looking shrewish. Listening for the sound of beauty, hearing only chaos—two orphan boys, ageless, making music in the night.

And yet, they did create a kind of harmony from time to time, maybe by accident, and so she stayed still, listening. Again the harmony, lasting for a few notes, and carrying with it the tremor of their surprise. Magnificent. Try again, keep trying. All night, if need be. She could imagine them: Goch puckered, arms aching; Markovitz with filthy hands cupped at the mouth. Markovitz the creep, the slug, the nothing—inspired.

That was the marvel. Not to oust Markovitz but to evoke from him, if only for a few scattered instants, a new Markovitz, trembling on the edge of beauty. Unpredictable, pointless, chartless—but who could tell? Even the roaches might be singing beneath the wallpaper, and maybe the whisper of random music might soothe the dreams of Mrs. Fineberg, thwarted diva.

And so she went in quietly to sit where they were playing, to wait along with them for those moments of creation.

One Sunday
after Church

¶ Mr. Haymore, the minister, made a powerful impression on Letty Mellon that Sunday.

She had not paid much attention to the first part of his sermon, but she sat up straight when he suddenly threw his arms wide and declared:

"The wicked *shall* be punished!"

Letty sat up straighter and wiggled her toes inside her shoes. Was Mr. Haymore giving her his answer now, in public?

Mr. Haymore's voice kept rumbling out: "Though they hide their sins behind the cloak of righteousness, yet shall they be found out. . . ."

Letty almost gasped out loud. It *must* be his answer! And Mr. Haymore seemed to be looking right at her, just to be sure she understood.

". . . the wrath of God and man be stirred," cried Mr. Hay-

more, red and angry in his pulpit, "on earth, yes, and in heaven.
. . ."

Letty smiled back at him, to let him know she was listening.
Oh, that *dear* Mr. Haymore!

". . . and against all the gods of Egypt, I will execute judgment," quoted Mr. Haymore, sternly. "I am the Lord!"

Against the gods of Egypt? Letty frowned and swung her feet,
trying to scrape the floor with her toes. Jasper wasn't a god of
Egypt. Perhaps Mr. Haymore was speaking in riddles. He *meant*
Jasper, sure enough. But then he could hardly come right out in
church and say so. "Gods of Egypt" was maybe as close as he
dared come.

He *knew*, of course.

He knew, for Letty herself had told him just the week before.
She had always admired Mr. Haymore, because he was so big and
fat and passed out candy. You could trust Mr. Haymore. Her
mother had said so.

Letty had trusted Mommy, too, and had told her the secret; but
Mommy had only gotten angry. And wisely enough, Letty had
decided not even to try to tell Daddy. Jasper had been ruled out,
naturally, for the secret was *about* Jasper.

So that had left Mr. Haymore.

Letty had gone to the parsonage; she spoke to the minister for at
least ten minutes, and he listened very politely, just as if she were
grown up. She had told him all about Jasper, how he had schemed
his way into the house and had turned them all against her; how
he insulted her and tormented her and chased her in her sleep,
through nightmares—and then, proudly, she had announced what
she had determined to do about it.

"Oh, my child," Mr. Haymore had said. "How can you let such
thoughts enter your head, even in play?"

"It's not in play, Mr. Haymore."

But Mr. Haymore had smiled sadly, as if he had not believed
her. "You must not think such things, Letty."

"I can't help it."

"Then, dear girl, you must seek guidance from God, in
church. . . ."

Guidance? That meant an answer. Letty had taken this to mean that Mr. Haymore was not set against her, necessarily, but wanted time to think it over, perhaps to talk with God about it. He would answer her, then, in church.

And so, on this Sunday, she heard the answer given so boldly, so bravely, in front of everyone, but with its meaning hidden. *She* was to understand; no one else. How wonderful of Mr. Haymore!

"The wicked shall be punished!" Oh, yes, that was clear! She almost wept, she was so happy. When church was over, she broke away from Mommy and dashed up to Mr. Haymore, so excited she could only say "Thank you, thank you" several times, as she grasped his big hand. He seemed puzzled at first, then smiled down at her and winked.

"Thank you," Letty cried out again, and skipped away.

On the way home, she asked Mommy: "When can we get another dog?"

Mommy put on her sorrowful face. "Do you really think you should have another dog, Letty?"

Letty was annoyed. Why did grown-ups have to keep remembering unpleasant things? "But Mommy, I wouldn't do anything to a *new* dog. Not if he was nice."

"I'm sure you wouldn't, dear." But the tone of voice meant the opposite.

"But I *would*n't! Please?"

Her mother sighed. "In any case, Letty, we couldn't get a dog now."

"Why not?"

"You ought to know that, dear."

"Because of Jasper, I suppose."

"Yes, dear. As long as Jasper's at the crawling stage."

"Well, can we get one next week?"

Mrs. Mellon smiled gently. "Dear, I don't think you understand how long the crawling stage lasts!"

"Oh, I understand, Mommy. Can we get the dog next week, then?"

She decided to do it right away. She would go over to Jessamine's to play. They would play a nice quiet game of hide-and-seek upstairs, and then, while Jessamine was hiding, Letty would go to

look for her in that funny old clothes closet near the attic steps—
and she wouldn't find her there, but up on the shelf, way in back,
she *would* find that little box banded in red, with the cute skull on
it, and the label: "Not To Be Taken Internally."

She put on an old play dress with deep pockets. The box would
fit quite nicely there. No one would notice.

But would Jasper mind the taste and cry? Well, if he did, there
was always the pillow handy, and she could use that the way she
had on the kitten that wouldn't stop mewing, the one her parents
didn't know about, the one they thought got lost. . . .

"Mommy, may I walk over to Jessamine's?"

"All right, dear. But be careful. Remember what I said about
strangers."

"Oh, Mommy!"

"It's no joke, Letty," Daddy said gruffly. "Right in the paper last
week, there was a story about a little girl who was, ah"—he cleared
his throat—"hurt by a bad man in a car."

"—so you remember what I said, Letty."

"Yes, Mommy. Oh, Mommy, will Jasper be napping when I get
back?"

"I think so."

"Well, then, I'll just go up to my room without making any
noise. I won't play my records or anything."

"All right."

"Thank you, Mommy."

She let the screen door slam behind her, but stopped for a
moment silently to listen, as was her habit. Her parents' voices
were lowered, but she still could hear.

". . . that horrible, tragic thing! And they don't even know
what he looks like!"

"No. They only know he drove a gray car. That's not much. I
tell you, it worries me a little. But in broad daylight, I hardly
think—"

"Well, anyway, Letty knows just what to do. I mean, in
case . . ."

Letty slipped off. Grown-up talk, all nonsense. What did she
care about men in gray cars? If one of them bothered her, she
would do exactly what Mommy said, and that would fix him, all

right. Besides, men like that were wicked, and hadn't Mr. Haymore said that the wicked would get punished?

It was half-past four when she left Jessamine's house, with her hand in her pocket tightly closed around the funny little box. How *good* she felt! She skipped gaily along the sidewalk, humming as she went. It would be so simple. She would just go up to Jasper's room, and then after that, she would pour the rest of the powder into the toilet and flush it, and then she'd rip the cardboard box into a thousand tiny pieces and swallow them! Well, no, she'd better not do that. Perhaps she should hide them inside the stuffing of that doll she once got angry at and tore. That would be better.

Anyway, she could ask again about the dog tomorrow. Or wait until Tuesday, maybe, because there was likely to be a fuss about Jasper, and Mommy might not be in a good frame of mind. Or even Wednesday, for that matter. She could be patient.

She passed a shop window and paused just a moment to look at her reflection. The effort of skipping had made her cheeks flushed, and the thought of going home to Jasper had put a kind of sparkle in her eyes that reminded her of what Daddy called her, "My little witchling!" That was before the dog, of course. He hadn't called her much of anything since—but that was Jasper's fault, she knew, not hers.

Letty went on, not skipping, but trying different ways of walking. She staggered like a blind man; she dragged one foot like a cripple, and after a while she began to swing her little hips in imitation of those pretty ladies on the television programs, the pretty ladies who sometimes shot people with guns!

Walking like that, she was not at first aware of the car that had come up close behind her, coasting slowly with its motor turned off. It stopped beside her with a tiny squeak.

"Hello there, little lady."

She looked. It was a strange man, but the car wasn't gray. Not really gray. Just a kind of gray, perhaps.

"My, but you're a pretty little lady."

Still, she didn't like his face. He had a funny look, a sort of silly smile, and when he wasn't staring at her, he was glancing up and down the street.

Letty made her mind up. It was time to do what Mommy said: Walk straight into the nearest house and ask the people to let her use the phone to call home.

So, without saying a word to the man, that's exactly what Letty set out to do.

She went through the opening in a hedge, across the yard and up the porch steps. She knocked on the door.

"Let me in, please!"

No one answered. She knocked again, louder.

"Want to go inside?" a voice asked. Yet the voice came not through the screen door, but from behind her. It was the man who had been in the car.

He took her arm and opened the door.

"Yes," he said, "you go in, little lady." He guided her inside.

He laughed. Letty did not like the way it sounded. She didn't like what he said next, either.

"Well, well!" the man declared, still holding her arm. "I never thought I'd find one of you sweet little ladies so anxious to pay me a visit—at my own home!"

He made a noise of pleasure; it was more like a whimper than a chuckle. "It's almost as if fate wanted to bring us together. Isn't it, little lady!"

The
Human Factor

¶ It was a magnificent church, traditionally Gothic in design and yet wholly modernized with the latest technological refinements.

The pulpit was constructed on a hidden elevator, so that the minister could inch toward heaven to heighten the effect of a peroration; the chandeliers, too, could be raised or lowered electronically during the service to suggest, alternatively, the insignificance of man or the close communion of worship. The pews were fitted with adjustable bucket seats, each equipped with an amplifier, permitting the sermon to be tuned to suit individual tastes. The stained-glass windows, being backed with electric lamps, did not depend on the sun for their brilliance, and the aisles could be tilted so as to slope down to provide a subtle physical encouragement on those occasions when the flock was intended to advance to the altar.

Outside the church a vast parking area had been outfitted with miniature closed-circuit television sets, so that those whose wished to pause for worship en route to the golf links and bathing beaches could remain in their cars and still see and hear all that went on within the church. A special feature was a drive-in counseling service open twenty-four hours a day, so parishioners could discuss personal problems with the minister on duty at the window without being required to alight from their cars.

It was, altogether, the most distinctive and fashionable church in the entire city, so popular in fact that it had drawn the patronage of the wealthiest citizens, who vied with one another in their donations.

As it happened, the most munificent gift was made to replace the only element in the church that was not of the latest design—the church organ. The old organ was of splendid appearance, it was true, and there was nothing wrong with it, but the church authorities had for some time wanted something finer that would correspond more exactly to the rest of the establishment. Therefore, they were determined to commission the construction of a special new organ of almost limitless versatility and power. For this project they did not approach the usual manufacturers, for they did not want an instrument that would be essentially the same, even if larger, than the one they already had; instead, they went to the leading engineering firm in the country, one heavily engaged in space projects, and gave it carte blanche.

The church organist, Doctor Alpha, spent several sessions with the engineers, poring over their designs, and although he could not make head or tail of the drawings, their professional enthusiasm was communicated to him, and he had visions of himself exalted to the peak of his career by the instrument being constructed for him. Sometimes he would awake at night in a sweat of trepidation wondering whether he would find himself equal to its demands, but at those times he would take a pill and pace the room and sometimes listen to recordings of great organ masterworks for their soothing effects. After all, he reasoned, an organ was an organ, no matter what frills might be added here and there by the engineers, and the Bach that he would play upon it would still come out as Bach.

Nevertheless, Doctor Alpha was in a highly nervous state on the day when the new organ was brought to the church to be installed, for he feared that he might not have time to accustom himself properly to it by Sunday. There would undoubtedly be a hundred little adjustments to be made by the engineers, problems which would reveal themselves only gradually as the various mixtures were tried in actual practice.

Doctor Alpha hastened toward the nave, where the chief acoustical engineer, Mr. Gill, was busy directing the workmen. "Excuse me," Doctor Alpha asked, "but how long do you think it will take?"

"How long? We'll have it up by the end of the day. Fully installed," the engineer declared, "and ready to go."

"What about testing?"

"Testing?" Mr. Gill seemed surprised.

Doctor Alpha waved his hands over an imaginary keyboard. "You know—adjustments."

"You won't need any adjustments."

"But—suppose there's some slight malfunction. Something's sure to need adjustment from time to time."

Mr. Gill smiled tolerantly. "It's been done already. This organ's been pretested and preadjusted. Do you imagine," he asked sternly, "that we'd install a million-dollar piece of equipment that wasn't in perfect condition, Doctor?"

"It's not that," Doctor Alpha began, but the engineer had gone off to direct the hoisting of several long tubes of metal into the gaps left by the removal of the old organ pipes.

Doctor Alpha fidgeted unhappily in the midst of the clutter. The noise was getting on his nerves. Someone was using an electric drill, which whined piercingly in his ears, and nearby two men were battering away on metal surfaces, creating a fearful din. He made his way out of the nave, heading for his own tiny office, where he spent the remainder of the afternoon with the door shut, reading Bach fugues and singing them aloud to drown out the occasional echoing crashes that came from the main part of the church.

The next morning Doctor Alpha went to the church and cautiously walked to the organ loft, where the only sign of the previous day's activity was a workman's cigar butt to one side of the altar, which had escaped the janitor's attention.

Mr. Gill had been right: The organ—massive, shining with

ivory and brass and steel—was installed. It could not be called beautiful, nor did it have the familiar charm of its conventional predecessor; it had the customary keyboards and pedals and other accoutrements, but the longer Doctor Alpha examined it, the more it seemed to be a machine rather than a musical instrument. But a magnificent machine.

He sat on the stool and lightly touched the knobs and keys, just to feel their cold textures. His fingertips tingled with a sensation of enormous power. He pressed one key down firmly. There was no response. He tried another, without result. He danced his feet across the pedals, he experimented with the mixtures to no avail. Apparently the organ was not plugged in.

He searched all around it to find an electrical connection, even climbing into the loft behind the metal pipes, but he could discover no switch or socket that might answer his purpose. There was a good deal of equipment in the loft, however; an arrangement of little steel boxes linked by wires, rising in staggered rows up to the very top. He gingerly ascended the ladder to inspect them. Every other box was faced with dials and gauges and knobs. Just like hi-fi equipment, thought Doctor Alpha.

He telephoned Mr. Gill and inquired about the organ.

"Don't worry about it," said Mr. Gill, soothingly. "It's absolutely A-OK. All systems are Go."

"But I can't play it."

Mr. Gill uttered what sounded like a chuckle. "You've got nothing to worry about," he repeated. "I'll be over in the morning and check you out on it. Roger?"

"Um, well," said Doctor Alpha, "I'd really prefer—" But Mr. Gill had cut him off.

The acoustical engineer did not appear the following day, however, and when Doctor Alpha tried to reach him by phone, he was informed by a secretary that Mr. Gill had made an emergency trip to the East Coast to deal with a defense crisis. Doctor Alpha frantically explained his predicament, and the woman assured him that Mr. Gill had taken care of the matter, and in fact that he had left full instructions which would be delivered in plenty of time.

Nevertheless, it was not until Sunday morning, barely half an hour before the services, that a messenger arrived at the church to deliver a small package to Doctor Alpha, who had not been able to muster the courage to inform the minister and the music director that there might very well be no organ music that day.

Doctor Alpha tore the package open. Inside was a stack of stiff cards, oddly perforated, and a brief handwritten note from Mr. Gill: "Insert in Slot A."

Doctor Alpha gathered up his robe and dashed from his office to the rear entrance. Already the congregation was filing in. The choir was all in place; the music director, cracking his knuckles, gave Doctor Alpha an annoyed glance. The processional must be started immediately.

Hastily, Doctor Alpha managed to locate Slot A, and without trying to puzzle out the precise function of the cards, chose one at random and thrust it into the opening.

The machine hummed and quivered. Doctor Alpha gasped in relief and stretched his hands eagerly over the keys. Before he was able to bring them down to begin the Bach prelude he intended to play, however, the organ itself burst out with the opening of Handel's *Messiah*.

Doctor Alpha sat transfixed, his hands poised in air above keys which moved by themselves. He was aware of the wonder of the music director, of the alert attention of the choir—and even more, of the glory of the music, which sounded and resounded throughout the church. It was magnificent beyond imagining, and yet Doctor Alpha thought it not quite right that the organ should have taken the initiative, when he, after all, was the organist. Besides, the *Messiah* was not appropriate for the occasion. He tried to assert his authority by beginning the Bach, thinking he could somehow manage a transition, but the keys he pressed refused to move, while those operated by the machine continued perversely to sink and rise again. There seemed to be no way of stopping the Handel.

Doctor Alpha glanced guiltily about. The music director was leaning raptly against the choir stall, his eyes closed; the members of the choir were as still as if carved from wood, and a quick glimpse of the congregation disclosed a similar state of immobility. Some stood in the aisles, as though impaled there by the beauty of the music, and it seemed that others had actually been arrested in the process of sitting in the pews, for they remained half-crouched, like figures in a frieze.

Doctor Alpha tried to take stock of his situation. The organ played marvelously, it was true, but on a basis that was not fully to his liking. He examined the perforated cards. Each was labeled with the title of a composition and the name of the composer. Of course! It was like a player piano, operating by cards instead of a roll; or rather, it was a musical computer, whose electronic memory had been stocked with organ compositions activated by the insertion of the cards. He was forced to admit that the engineers had done an excellent job. The Handel was faultless.

It finally ended; the *Messiah* card was neatly ejected through a slot marked "B" and into Doctor Alpha's lap. The music director emerged from his reverie and headed toward the organ. Doctor Alpha quickly slipped the stack of cards beneath his robe. The music director extended his hand; there were tears in the man's eyes, and as Doctor Alpha nervously accepted the handshake, he sensed an ecstatic flow of delight within the church. There was even that unheard-of phenomenon—a rush of spontaneous applause. The music director smilingly led Doctor Alpha out of his niche to acknowledge the response.

The organist bobbed his head, then hastened back to the machine. He had gotten the credit, for although his head was visible to others, his hands and feet were not. He thumbed anxiously through the cards—yes, the hymns were there, fortunately, and during the remainder of the service he inserted the proper card at the proper time, and sat dumbly at the machine listening to it produce music that was now delicate, now commanding, now inspiring, all with an artistry beyond his own powers.

It was wonderful—and also humiliating, particularly when he was forced to bow and smile at the end, accepting the enthusiastic approbation of congregation, choir and minister, all the while aware of the stack of computer cards he had thrust for safekeeping inside his shirt.

That night he telephoned Mr. Gill long distance.

"Excuse me," Doctor Alpha said, "but this organ—it plays by itself."

"Of course."

"But—I'm the organist."

"Who said you weren't?" asked Mr. Gill.

"But how am I supposed to play?"

"You aren't," said Mr. Gill cheerfully. "We engineered out the human factor."

"But I *want* to play."

"Look here, Alpha. You're taking a pretty old-fashioned approach to the question. Think of those boys of ours up in space— the astronauts. How would it be if they wanted to foot-pedal their way in orbit, eh? Do you think they'd be out there at all if we took your attitude about human factors—if we didn't have the whole business operating on systems, eh?"

"But I'm not an astronaut. I don't even think I'm a human factor. I'm an organist."

"That's your problem, not mine," returned Mr. Gill. "If you've got any complaints about the machine, get in touch with my office, but it's got a fifty-year guarantee on it, Alpha, so it occurs to me," he added consolingly, "that it will very likely outlast you."

"I see," said Doctor Alpha, and when the conversation was over, he replaced the receiver and sat down on his bed, staring at his hands.

The next few months were difficult for Doctor Alpha. Each Sunday, and on rehearsal days, he surreptitiously inserted the cards into Slot A and then pretended to play the music which the organ produced, for he never knew when someone might approach from behind, and it would not do to let the keys be seen moving by themselves. As his hands wandered uselessly over the boards, he often reflected that, whereas in the old days he had played the organ, now this new organ was playing him.

And yet he was forced to admit that the organ was a success. The church was packed as never before; the motorists, even, were coming inside to the pews, in order to obtain the fullest values of resonance emitted by the engineers' creation.

But Doctor Alpha was restless. He wished the machine would just once play a sour note, or fumble a phrase. At the same time he had a guilty horror of being found out. Suppose, for example, he had a fainting spell in the midst of a hymn and toppled backward off the stool while the organ played on? Suppose Mr. Gill happened to mention the automatic nature of the machine to the church authorities?

Doctor Alpha also wondered to what extent his artistic skills were being impaired by disuse. In another year, perhaps, he would be unfitted to play anywhere except in some humble little church where few went and no one cared. He became jealous of the organ. During its recitals the congregation sat with a dreamy, breathless stillness, enfolded by the music as it had never been when he had been the performer. This hurt his professional pride.

As time passed, he lost weight and sleep. He had nightmares in which he was the victim of the machine: it would vanish, leaving him playing on nothing; or its teethlike keyboards would bite off his hands. At length he decided that he must somehow assert himself or lose his reason.

He began to experiment. First, he snipped two cards in half and glued the odd halves together. Obediently, the organ played half of each composition, not missing a note in the abrupt transition. That was something, thought Doctor Alpha. But not nearly enough.

Next, he punched an extra hole in one of the choral variations. The result was a tremendous bass belch in the midst of a complex contrapuntal passage, which caused a thousand heads to jerk up—but only for a moment, as the organ proceeded to render the rest of the work in its usual impeccable style.

Doctor Alpha became possessed by the implications of that belch. If he could not perform, he might at least compose. He set to work fashioning blank cards identical to those supplied by Mr. Gill, and then perforated them here and there. He had, of course, no idea of the effects these random holes would produce, and so he went quietly into the church at night to find out. The results were remarkable. Some of his compositions, drawing liberally on the computer's memory, sounded like kaleidoscopic mélanges of all the organ music ever written: snatches of fugues, of chorales, of masses, leaping back and forth across centuries of styles and skills. Others caused the organ to execute absurdities. One card, for example, elicited an explosion of jazz so compelling that Doctor

Alpha found himself shuffling about in the shadowy nave, snapping his fingers and giggling with delight.

But, of course, he could not play anything like that in church. He continued to experiment, and although he failed to discover any rational method of composition by hole puncher, he did manage to come up with several cards that he felt Bach himself would not have disowned. These he puckishly labeled *Alpha, Opus I*, and so forth, and used from time to time as processionals or during collection interludes, without causing any particular notice.

The blow fell on a Saturday. The music director revised his program for the following day, including a Buxtehude choral fantasia which, as luck would have it, had been on one of the cards Doctor Alpha had snipped in half in his pioneer experiments and had ruined.

Doctor Alpha blanched. "I'm sorry. I—I can't play it."

"Of course you can play it. You've done it dozens of times."

"Isn't there something else? How about the Chaconne in C minor?"

The music director was a busy man and easily vexed. "Come now, Doctor Alpha. The fantasia is what I want," he grumbled, stalking off.

Doctor Alpha rushed to a telephone, hoping that Mr. Gill might have a second set of cards in stock, but the engineering office knew nothing about any spare cards. As for Mr. Gill, he was unavailable, being himself in orbit. "Don't you read the papers?" asked the secretary rather crossly.

Doctor Alpha did not sleep at all that night. When he failed to perform the Buxtehude, he would be severely cross-examined by the music director, most likely in the presence of the minister, and he knew he would be unable to stand it. He would break down. He would blurt out the truth. He would be dismissed, disgraced, humiliated, and then they would hire one of the choirboys to take care of the simple function of inserting cards into Slot A. The machine would play on just the same, while he would end his days in lowly circumstances.

The clock struck one. Doctor Alpha leaped from his bed. Very well, he thought. If the machine could not play Buxtehude, then it would play—Alpha. And it would play an Alpha the like of which had never been dreamed.

The organist set rapidly to work. He cut out a card and began punching holes in it. Then he decided that the conventional approach would not do for this crisis, and so he cast the card aside and fashioned another one. Instead of making it the usual six inches in length, he made it sixty, and in the process of perforating it, he not only used the puncher but also pricked it with pins and needles and stabbed it with an ice pick. Not yet satisfied, he slashed it with a knife, drove nails through it, and even took it into the basement, set it up on his dartboard and flung darts into it, and as a final gesture, took a big bite out of it with his teeth.

By morning, Doctor Alpha's giant computer card was so pierced and riddled that it lay limply in his hands, its ends trailing off on either side onto the floor (a fortunate flexibility, however, for it permitted him to wrap it about his waist like a cummerbund and thus sneak it into the church).

His loss of sleep, his worry over his future, and his furious attack on the huge card all combined to make Doctor Alpha unnaturally sensitive and alert. When he approached the organ, he thought that it shuddered, as if in anticipation of the ordeal awaiting it. He noticed, too, that the church had never been so crowded. People were standing in the back, for the lack of pews. Everything seemed to be possessed of a remarkable radiance. The black robes and white ruffs of the choir glistened as though freshly painted, and the stained-glass windows seemed to bulge with light.

The moment came. Doctor Alpha had uncoiled the card from his waist under cover of his robe, and when the music director gave him a curt little nod, he fed one end of it into Slot A. He had trouble inserting it; the machine seemed to be trying to spit it out at him, but he mercilessly forced it back in until he heard the hum of mechanical life begin. Then he sat back judiciously to see what would happen.

His opus began sedately enough. It was clearly not Buxtehude (and the music director scowled forbiddingly); still, it was proper church music, a gentle little fugue modestly working out its destiny in the middle registers. Soon, however, a different element was heard, a soft persistent bass that seemed to be climbing stealthily up toward the little fugue. The fugue, as if taking alarm, jumped an octave, became confused, began to ring a bell, and as its pursuer rose after it, took on a despairing tone.

Doctor Alpha was fascinated. He glanced at the music director, whose scowl had been succeeded by an expression of doubtful resolve, as though he were debating whether to walk over and command the organist to end his unseemly improvisation. The choir members also were regarding Doctor Alpha in a puzzled way, and the congregation was muttering. The bell now rang steadily. The music director clenched his fists and took a step in Doctor Alpha's direction.

Then the organ screamed. It was a prolonged scream of high intensity which instead of gradually dying away rose in pitch and power until it vanished, as if it had ascended to a frequency beyond human hearing. The scream was followed by a cannonade of explosive blasts, on top of which came a furious machine-gun staccato pierced by siren-like wails, swooping dizzily from the highest to the lowest registers.

Doctor Alpha involuntarily pushed back his stool. The music director, he saw, was on his knees, staring open-mouthed at the organ. The choir members cowered in their stall, the congregation sat shocked all in place, and the minister, as if fleeing from goblins, had scampered up into the pulpit.

The organist wondered if perhaps he had not gone too far. His head was throbbing with the din, and he had the impression that the organ was producing far more than could be heard, at terribly high frequencies, for the church itself seemed to be quivering, and the glass in his own spectacles had cracked.

The sounds of battle muted, and were succeeded by quick little melodies, jangling strangely together, some intense, others playful, and these in turn merged into a single theme which leaped and fell unpredictably before settling into a lush, ornate richness. Doctor Alpha removed his ruined glasses and squinted around the corner of the organ. No one was leaving. The minister remained in his pulpit; the music director was struggling again to his feet, but feebly, and the choir was huddled together.

That theme—it was growing in sensuousness. One could almost

feel its texture in the vibrating air. Its counterpoint began, and the conversation of the two elements moved from introduction to familiarity to intimacy, becoming more urgent the more they were entwined, until at length the theme was made explicit with great climactic gasps of passionate affirmation. Nor did it end then, but increased in strength.

Doctor Alpha was perspiring freely. He alone seemed able to move. The organ's shameless performance held everyone else immobile, and answering moans of emotion now were heard here and there in the church. The earlier battle noises crept back in, pianissimo, and as the moods of love and war built gradually up in volume, Doctor Alpha was perturbed to hear among them other sounds: the neighing of horses, it seemed, and the yelps of foxes and honking of geese. And there was laughter—the organ was laughing . . . and sobbing, too.

Doctor Alpha stood up, clutching his head. Something was happening in the church. There was movement. He saw the pulpit in elevation, slowly bearing the white-faced minister aloft. The chandeliers, too, were in motion, some rising, others descending, and the aisles had tilted down.

He must stop it somehow. The crescendo was howling up toward its climax, and he had the impression that when it arrived there, some barrier would be broken, and all the sounds would take on palpable shapes and forms, that demons and dwarfs and impossible animals would come tumbling out upon them all. He staggered over to the loft door and went inside to the ladder. The little metal boxes glowed red-hot above him, and their wires were spitting sparks. He climbed up a few rungs. A spark stung his cheek. He cried out and clambered down again.

The whole church now shook with sound. The organ was blaring away at a furious tempo, and everything was quickened. The pulpit was shooting up and down, with the minister clutching the lectern; the chandeliers were not only speeding up to the ceiling and down again, with icy metallic screams, but also were swinging from side to side; some had become entangled, their bulbs exploding. The aisles as well were in constant motion, and some of the worshipers who had left the pews—where the bucket seats were quaking—had lost their footing and were rolling and sliding to and fro.

And still the organ played. It was in eruption, belching out tortured rhythms, howls, roars, explosions, laughter and great whistling sighs.

Most of the congregation appeared to be in a frenzy. Indeed, many were tearing at their clothing; others were crowding into the aisles, not to escape, but in order to be swept back and forth amid the growing mass of tumbling bodies, while still others stood atop the rocking pew seats bellowing, flinging garments in the air, wrestling with one another. One elderly man had succeeded in leaping on a chandelier; as it swung him about, he shrieked with laughter.

Doctor Alpha rose to his feet. The choir was massed around the music director, pummeling him. There was a blast of light—the church windows were bursting, showering down flakes of colored glass.

He threw himself at the organ. From Slot B one end of the card protruded. He gripped it with both hands, braced his feet against the organ, and pulled with all of his might. The organ gave one last tremendous shout as the card was ripped from its workings. Doctor Alpha fell backward, his composition in his hands.

For several minutes he lay there, as the tumult in the church slowly subsided. Then he arose. Everything was silent. The minister was slumped on his pulpit. The man on the chandelier hung by his hands, then dropped to the motionless aisle.

Doctor Alpha advanced to the altar, trailing the shredded card from his hand. He gazed uncertainly at the people below.

"I'm—I'm sorry—" he began, and then broke off.

The congregation seemed to be too stunned to hear him. They were bruised, bleeding, disheveled. Bits of torn clothing were scattered all around among broken glass and splinters of wood.

"I'm really . . . terribly—" Doctor Alpha tried again, weakly.

Then the applause began. They were clapping their hands. They began to cheer him. Soon they were drumming their heels, banging on the pews, shouting, waving. They were calling for more.

Doctor Alpha stood quite still for a moment. Then he gave a little sigh. And, as was his habit, he made a modest bow.